Murder Has No Guilt

Phillip Strang

BOOKS BY PHILLIP STRANG

DCI Isaac Cook Series

MURDER IS A TRICKY BUSINESS
MURDER HOUSE
MURDER IS ONLY A NUMBER
MURDER IN LITTLE VENICE
MURDER IS THE ONLY OPTION
MURDER IN NOTTING HILL
MURDER IN ROOM 346
MURDER OF A SILENT MAN
MURDER HAS NO GUILT
MURDER WITHOUT REASON

DI Keith Tremayne Series

DEATH UNHOLY
DEATH AND THE ASSASSIN'S BLADE
DEATH AND THE LUCKY MAN
DEATH AT COOMBE FARM
DEATH BY A DEAD MAN'S HAND
DEATH IN THE VILLAGE

Steve Case Series

HOSTAGE OF ISLAM
THE HABERMAN VIRUS
PRELUDE TO WAR

Standalone Books

MALIKA'S REVENGE

Copyright Page

Dedication

For Elli and Tais who both had the perseverance to make me sit down and write.

Chapter 1

Giuseppe Briganti had come over from Italy fifteen years previously with a smattering of English and not much else. Life had been tough back home for Giuseppe, or Peppe as everyone called him, the third son of a farmer. Not that he had reason to complain, as his father was a good man, and he loved his mother dearly. It was just that Peppe was not cut out for farming. So much so that at the age of twenty he left for Milan.

He learnt his trade well, so well that within five years he was at the top of his profession, and constantly in demand in the hairdressing salon that was owned by a man who treated Peppe as if he was his own son.

Yet it was the salon's owner who had by his actions been responsible for Peppe's hasty departure for England; the reason Peppe was in his salon in London cutting the hair of Alphonso Abano, another immigrant to England, although Abano came from Sicily, mafioso country.

Back in Milan, Peppe had been in love, but she had preferred the salon owner, clearly apparent when

Peppe had walked in on the two, in flagrante delicto, in the back room of the salon.

Peppe knew that he should have hit her first, and then the old man second, but he did neither. Without saying a word, he moved back out through the salon, only stopping long enough to pick up his scissors and a couple of combs. Peppe was never a man for material possessions, and it took him just one hour to pack his suitcase, pay the outstanding rent, and catch the first train heading north. One day later, a train pulled into London, and Peppe stepped off. He had sufficient money not to worry for a few days, and he checked into a hotel.

On the fourth day, he answered an advert for a hairdresser at the salon where he now worked, and in time purchased the business from the man who had first employed him.

Life now consisted of enjoying his nights alone, his days in the salon catering to celebrities, the upwardly-mobile bankers and financiers, and, thankfully, only one gangster.

In Italy, Peppe had catered to both sexes, but in Kensington, on Kensington High Street, not far from the palace, it was strictly men only, although women came in with their men.

In one chair sat Guy Hendry, talk show host, a man about town, and a man who graced the front page of the celebrity-obsessed magazines on account of his film star looks, his perpetual suntan, and the women he took out. Peppe thought he was a Dorian Gray character, in as much as the man was ten years older than when he had first walked in the door of the salon, yet his women had become progressively younger, and the one he had now in tow, Gillian Dickenson, was five years younger than the previous one.

Peppe would have said she was vivacious, with a permanent smile, a bust that looked artificial, and a skirt that barely covered her underwear, and yet she looked as if she had just left school.

On another chair, having his hair cut, the vain and obnoxious Paul Waverton. The whizz kid they called him in the press for his ability to read the financial markets and to make the right call. His Bentley was parked outside, close enough to be admired by Waverton and the people on the street, illegally enough to get a ticket for parking where it shouldn't be. Not that it worried Waverton as he flaunted his money, even giving a fifty-pound tip to whoever worked on his hair. And work was the word, for Waverton, in spite of all his financial acumen, was an unattractive man with hair like steel wool, almost like a Brillo pad, and as hard to keep in shape.

Peppe focussed back on Abano. 'Not so busy today,' the little man said. Peppe would have happily refused his custom, but Abano was not a man to fall out with, the sort of man who had friends in low places who wouldn't have any issues about giving someone a savage beating.

'It will be later,' Peppe said as he combed Abano's hair back over the top of his scalp, the expensive treatments for premature balding not working, and certainly not willing to tell the gangster.

Abano liked to talk big and to show off, not that Peppe wanted to hear the stories, only to take the man's money and to shuffle him out of the salon. Time at Peppe's salon was by appointment only, and in another forty minutes an important customer was due, a friend of royalty. He was more the salon's type of customer, as were Hendry and Waverton.

It didn't happen often, but sometimes people without appointments came in, and as it was a Tuesday, typically the slowest day of the week, there was a spare chair and a spare hairdresser. But the person who came in was not a well-heeled man, nor a celebrity, not even a gangster. It was a celebrity seeker, a woman in her thirties, carrying more weight than she should, and definitely drunk.

'Mr Hendry, Guy,' she gushed as she made her way over to the man. Gillian Dickenson stood up to impede the woman's progress, but she was pushed to one side. One of the other hairdressers attempted to grab the woman's arm, but she wrenched herself free.

'I need your autograph and a photo,' she said to Hendry.

'Not now, later,' Hendry said in a friendly manner, in an attempt to maintain his on-screen persona.

'Now, it's got to be now. My friends will never believe that I met Guy Hendry.'

'Please, now is not convenient. Send an email to my publicity company, and I'll make sure you receive a promotional package and an invite to a recording of one of my programmes.'

'You're like all the rest of them,' the woman sneered. 'All smiles and teeth on the television, but total bastards in real life.'

'Please, will you leave,' Peppe said.

'Who are you to tell me to do anything?'

'I'm the owner, and this is private property.'

'I'll go once Guy Hendry gives me an autograph and a photo.'

'Very well,' Hendry said, raising himself from where he had been sitting, running his fingers through his hair.

'Hey, you can take the photo,' the celebrity-obsessed woman said to Hendry's girlfriend.

Nobody looked at the door to the salon, only at the commotion to the rear of the room. Peppe was nervously pacing around the room, Abano was on his phone calling for a couple of his men to wait outside the salon and to deal with the woman if she didn't leave.

Hendry, seriously annoyed and not in a good mood, smiled through gritted teeth, not even complaining when the woman put her arms around him and thrust her breasts forward.

'The real stuff, you don't know what you're missing,' she said.

'That's enough. Out of my establishment,' Peppe said.

A man who had come in unannounced stood just inside the door of the salon. He looked around him and at the people assembled. From inside the long coat that he wore, he withdrew a semi-automatic rifle. He released the safety and sprayed the salon, making sure that no one avoided the bullets. He then walked around to each of those lying or slouching or still groaning. He withdrew a pistol from his pocket and shot each person at close range in the head.

In all, a total of twenty-eight seconds from first shot to when he left the salon. Outside, he casually walked away down Kensington High Street. Once clear of the area, he deposited the rifle and the pistol in a rubbish bin.

Back at the salon, the screaming of the people on the street could still be heard, as could the sirens of the police cars and the ambulances. The man knew that they were too late and all they would find would be dead bodies. A most satisfying day, he thought.

Chapter 2

Kensington High Street, with the rush hour traffic building and multiple homicides, was not something that the local police were prepared for, although practice for terrorist attacks had helped. With no option, the busy thoroughfare had been closed, causing anger with those already stuck in traffic, and frustration with the other motorists as they were diverted around the area.

Outside the hairdressing salon, Detective Chief Inspector Isaac Cook, the English-born son of Jamaican immigrants who had come over in the sixties, stood. He cut a striking figure: tall, athletic and erect. Alongside him, Detective Inspector Larry Hill, Cook's second in command, and a man who struggled with his weight, self-induced as he was partial to overeating and drinking too many pints of beer, much to the consternation of his loyal wife.

'Not good,' Hill said, a typical understatement from the man, as he peered into the salon.

Isaac Cook looked as well. The crime scene investigators were already on site checking the bodies, conducting their examination of the scene. On the street, barriers were being erected to isolate the scene from the view of the curious onlookers who were aggressively taking photos on their smartphones, and talking amongst themselves and to others.

The two police inspectors donned coveralls and gloves, as well as overshoes, before entering, stepping to one side to clear the body of a young woman lying on her side, her heavily-bloodied face still visible.

'Gillian Dickenson,' Isaac Cook said.

'She's always on the television. Supposedly she was going around with Guy Hendry.'

'She was. He's over the other side.'

Larry Hill, a man who had seen death more than once, looked around and at the young and very dead woman. 'You never get used to it, not totally, do you?' he said.

Isaac Cook realised that he had, and that he felt inured to the scene. It had caused him concern on more than one occasion, and it had even ended one of his relationships when he had come home ambivalent about a murder scene. That time it had been a husband and wife who had been shot by a disturbed son. The girlfriend at the time, blonde and in love with the DCI, had seen the murders on the television. She was close to tears at the story of how the dead couple had adopted the son as a child, knowing of his mental difficulties, and then the person they had heaped love and care on had murdered them.

'It's so tragic,' she had said. Isaac's reaction had been to turn off the television. Two days later, she moved out.

Larry Hill's ever-loyal wife continued to pressure him to achieve more, to allow them to upgrade their house again for the third time in ten years. He knew that he had neither the motivation for study nor the inclination for promotion with its added responsibilities. He was a man who enjoyed being out on the street, meeting with the villains, solving the crimes, not sitting in an office. And whereas he had the greatest respect for the man who had brought him into Homicide at Challis Street Police Station, he had no wish to take Isaac Cook's position as the lead officer in the department once he had moved on.

'It looks like a terrorist attack,' Gordon Windsor, the crime scene examiner, said. He was a small man with thinning hair who Isaac Cook respected enormously.

'But it's not,' Isaac replied. The three of them were standing to one side of the salon.

'As you say. What we have are eight bodies, each with a bullet to the head.'

'It looks as if they were shot more than once.'

'We'll send the bodies to Pathology, so you'll have a more exact idea of what happened.'

'Your initial observations will suffice for now.'

'Okay. We believe that one person came in to the salon and used a semi-automatic rifle. We've no idea what make, although we've retrieved a bullet from the wall. It will help to narrow it down, but that's about all. After that the man…'

'Man?' Larry said.

'An assumption, and besides, we've got shoe prints. Typically, it's men who commit these sorts of crimes, that's all.'

'Assume it's a man,' Isaac said. 'What else do we have?'

'The killer then shot each person in the head, a precise shot.'

'Not all could have been the target, and this was not the act of a hot-headed idiot.'

'Hot-headed idiots don't eradicate the witnesses with such precision, and normally they have a death wish, end up shooting themselves. This was professional,' Windsor said.

'Not typical of London.'

'It is now. You've recognised some of the dead?'

'Gillian Dickenson and Guy Hendry.'

'There's one more you know.'

'Who's that?'

'He's not so easy to identify, not from here.'

'His name?'

'Alphonso Abano.'

'Minor villain, drug dealer?'

'That's the one.'

'He'd not be a target, not for a killing this elaborate,' Larry Hill said.

'Larry's right,' Isaac said. 'He's the sort to end up knifed in a back alley. These murders were orchestrated, which means whoever did it was paid well, and may not even be a local, not even English.'

'That's for you to figure out. We're not sure who the others are, except for Giuseppe Briganti. His photo's up on the wall.'

'We'll ID them later.'

With the traffic so heavy Isaac and Larry left their car and walked two hundred yards to where they could be picked up by Sergeant Wendy Gladstone, a woman in her fifties, with enforced retirement closing in on her due to her arthritis and her general low level of fitness.

'It's chaos out there,' she said.

'It'll be chaos for the next five to six hours. They're attempting to clear one lane on the road which should help, but the traffic will be backed up for miles,' Isaac said.

'The ghoulish hanging around?'

'As usual, not that they'll see much.'

'You'll need to make a statement. There's a camera crew at the police station already.'

'And at the crime scene, not that I intended to talk to them there,' Isaac said. 'And besides, the details are sketchy. What do you know about Guy Hendry?'

'He's one of my favourites. Is he…?'

'Dead. As well as Gillian Dickenson. Some of the others we've not identified yet, apart from that slimy weasel, Alphonso Abano.'

'Guy Hendry and Gillian Dickenson were an item. The latest in his long line of conquests,' Wendy said.

'She doesn't look so attractive now.'

'Professional?'

'That's what we reckon, but why? Whoever did this must know the pressure will be on us to solve it as soon as possible, no stone unturned.'

'No shortage of resources, either.'

Wendy Gladstone eased her car through the London traffic, difficult at the best of times, horrendous as she had to divert to make her way through, even flashing her badge a couple of times to ensure the police officer on traffic duty let them through.

***

Challis Street Police Station, an edifice that had been built sixty years previously, had been modernised over the years. The Homicide department on the second floor was not the best area in the station: that was reserved for Detective Chief Superintendent Richard Goddard up on the top floor. However, Homicide was clean and modern and suited those that worked there.

Bridget Halloran, a long-time friend of Wendy Gladstone, looked after the administrative side of the department. She and Wendy had pooled their resources and moved in together a couple of years earlier, when

Bridget, a woman in her late forties, had kicked her layabout lover out of her house, and Wendy's husband had died.

In Isaac's office, apart from the plant in the corner, a gift from Wendy and Bridget when one of his previous romances had ended, the furnishings consisted of a filing cabinet, a desk replete with laptop and monitor, a chair for the incumbent, and three more for the department's core team.

'We need to identify those at the scene,' Isaac said. He was leaning back on his chair, glad of the chance to rest. The night before the team had worked late wrapping up a murder investigation, the death of an old man. In that case, it had been the daughter desperate for the man's money who had been arrested, but now all she was going to get was a lengthy stay in prison. And besides, unbeknown to the woman, her father had changed his will six months previously, writing the daughter out.

'Who do we have a positive ID on?' Bridget asked.

'Guy Hendry and Gillian Dickenson. Also, Giuseppe Briganti, the owner of the salon.'

'Hairdresser to the Stars.'

'Is he?'

'Even to the Royals, so they say.'

'They?'

'The magazines that obsess about such matters.'

'Pure nonsense, just entertainment. But Briganti is well known and expensive.'

'Alphonso Abano was there as well. Two of the others appear to be employees of Briganti's, so they shouldn't be too difficult to identify. That leaves two others, a man in his thirties dressed in a suit. There was a car outside, appeared to be his. Follow up on the registration.'

'I have,' Bridget said. 'Paul Waverton, banker.'

'Who's taken responsibility for informing the next of kin?'

'It's your job, although they won't suppress Guy Hendry's identity for very long.'

'You've got the addresses?'

'I have.'

'Very well. Let's go. There was also another woman there. She didn't look to be an employee, and she was dressed cheaply. Not a customer, and not related to anyone else in the salon. Also, she was clutching a magazine, the type that you two like.'

'A fan of Hendry's?'

'It's probable. Let's deal with the next of kin first. Who's nearest?'

'Gillian Dickenson's mother lives five minutes from here.'

'Okay, we'll start with her. Wendy, it may be best if you come with me. Larry, return to the crime scene, follow through on the unknowns. And see if there's any more evidence that we can work with.'

'If it's professional, then it's unlikely.'

'Then find out who the target was. The others would have been dispatched to prevent witnesses.'

'It's very sad,' Bridget said.

'It's those who are left behind that suffer the most. And besides, we're here to do a job, not to get emotional,' Isaac said. 'One more thing, I knew Gillian Dickenson. Nothing in itself, but she was at a party I went to about six months ago.'

Chapter 3

'It's Gillian, isn't it?' Maureen Dickenson, an attractive woman in her late forties, said as she opened the front door to her house. She was dressed similarly to the way her daughter had been when she was killed. Wendy thought that on another woman it would have made the person look cheap, but not with her.

'Can we come in?' Isaac said.

Inside the house the woman sat on the edge of her seat.

'I'm sorry, but your daughter has been killed.'

There was no initial reaction for what seemed like an eternity.

'How?' Maureen Dickson eventually said.

'There's been a shooting. Your daughter was an unfortunate consequence,' Isaac said.

'Was she with Guy?'

'She was. He has died as well.'

'I knew no good would come of her associating with him.'

'You knew him?'

'I was younger than Gillian when I went out with him, but I saw through him soon enough, the same as she would have. But now, she'll not get a chance. Can I see her?'

'Later today, maybe tomorrow,' Wendy said. 'We'll need an identification. It's either you or her father.'

'Her father's dead, five years ago.'

'Can I ask how?' Isaac said.

'There's not much to say. He died in a car accident one night. It was late, not one block from here when a drunk ran a red light and slammed into Gerry's car. He was a good man, strong on discipline, and we brought up our daughter well. But you know the young, always looking for that extra bit of excitement, and Guy was that.'

'Is there anyone who can be with you?' Isaac said.

'My sister. Her number's in my phone.'

Wendy took the woman's phone and called the sister.

'Five minutes,' Wendy said after she had ended the call.

Isaac returned to talking with the dead woman's mother. 'Sorry about this, but I must ask some questions.'

'If you must.'

'We don't know who was targeted. We're assuming it wasn't your daughter, but what can you tell us about Guy Hendry?'

'I told you. I knew him when we were both young, and then, he's there with Gillian. I told her to be careful. The man's a charming rogue, or should I say he was. I was with him for a few months in my teens before he became the big celebrity. I fell for him in a big way, but I could see no future in it. Gillian would have enjoyed the lifestyle for a while, and then she would have left him and looked for someone more suitable.'

'She was part of that lifestyle. I've seen her on the television, the occasional game show,' Wendy said.

'Gillian always had a good moral compass, the legacy of her father and me, but she was ambitious, and you've seen her. The sort of woman who turned men's heads, as I did in my day.'

'You still would.'

'I try to look after myself, but now it doesn't seem so important, does it?'

'It does,' Isaac said.

'You're a charmer too. I can see that.'

In the nearly thirty minutes they'd been in the front room of the terrace house, Maureen Dickenson had not once shed a tear or expressed remorse at her daughter's death. Isaac thought it unusual but knew that different people react in different ways. He assumed that, behind the façade, the woman had experienced sadness and disappointment and heartache in her life, and one more blow, as severe as it was, was not going to cause her to break down and show her true feelings. He imagined that once they were gone, she would relent and let the emotions flood over her.

After twenty minutes, more than the five initially promised, a knock at the door.

'I'm Gillian's aunt, Maureen's sister. How is she?' a woman who looked older than her sister said.

'She's holding up.'

'Was Gillian with him?'

'She was.'

Inside the house, the two sisters embraced; Stephanie, in tears.

'You mentioned Guy Hendry when I opened the door,' Wendy said when the two women eventually sat down.

'I didn't like him, not like Maureen and Gillian,' Stephanie said.

'It goes back a long time,' Maureen said. 'He wanted Steph before me, but my sister you'll come to realise is more sensible than me. She rejected him at the first instance, and that's when he came on to me. No doubt Gillian was the same to him, a plaything on the rebound from another.'

'That's not something that a mother would be pleased to think of their daughter,' Wendy said.

'Gillian had her head screwed on, and if a middle-aged lecher wanted to fritter his money, and if she wanted to think it was love eternal, then no harm has been done. And besides, she wasn't the sort to come home pregnant.'

'Were you?'

'I suppose I was foolish back then, but don't try and read anything into it. Guy had been my lover, and now he's Gillian's.'

'Men such as Hendry make enemies: jealous husbands, disgruntled boyfriends, discarded women.'

'Hendry was a total bastard,' Stephanie said. 'Not that there weren't some who didn't hate him, but killing him and Gillian in cold blood, that makes no sense.'

Wendy looked over at Maureen and could see that the enormity of what had occurred was starting to sink in. 'Do you have a doctor we could call?' she said.

'I'm a qualified doctor,' Stephanie said. 'I'll stay here and make sure my sister is fine. It may be a good time for you both to leave.'

'If there are further questions, we'll come back. I'm sorry that we had to be the bearer of sad news,' Isaac said.

'You're only doing your job. Just make sure you get the bastard who did this.'

'We will.'

Outside the house, the two police officers stood for a while.

'How do you think it went?' Wendy asked.

'Better than most. The one part of the job I hate, telling parents that their child is not coming back home again.'

'She took it well.'

'I know,' Isaac said as the two of them walked to their car. Gillian Dickenson was the first, she wasn't the last visit for that day. Guy Hendry's family had to be told next, and then there were the others who had died in that salon that day; Larry Hill could deal with some of those.

As for the others, additional police officers would be charged with the responsibility of informing the nearest and dearest. The time to inform had to be that day, as it would not take long for the identities of those in the salon to become known, and Guy Hendry would be on the evening news – a television personality, a man about town, a lothario, was always good copy.

As Isaac and Wendy drove away from the area, Isaac glanced up at the Dickenson house. Wendy phoned for a uniform to be assigned to the house to keep away the media and the onlookers.

***

Kensington High Street, and four hours had passed since the shooting. The traffic was lighter on Isaac and Wendy's return to the crime scene. Gordon Windsor was standing nearby, a coffee in his hand.

'They've all been identified,' Windsor said. Isaac thought the man looked drained, more than usual. They had worked together on many cases before and had seen sights that no sane person should see: headless corpses, bodies decayed after years in shallow graves, throats cut.

'Worse than most?' Isaac said.

'The women are the hardest to take.'

'I had met Gillian Dickenson once before,' Isaac said, realising that he had not mentioned it to the woman's mother.

'We've all seen her on the television. Very attractive once, I suppose, but now it seems ghoulish to make comments about how pretty she had been. She'll not look so good after Pathology's checked her out.'

'They'll all be subject to a full autopsy. Any clues as to who was the primary target?'

'None. Alphonso Abano was a criminal, but hardly justifying an assassination.'

'That's what it was,' Isaac said. He was now holding a coffee courtesy of a uniform who had fetched it from a café across the road that was doing sterling business with the additional customers. One lane of the road had reopened to traffic and the barriers were being pulled further back to allow the regular transit of vehicles in both directions. The front window and door of the salon were being covered to block prying eyes.

'Any ideas?' Windsor asked.

'Not yet. The other woman?'

'Sal Maynard according to her driving licence. She's not from around here. There's an address.'

'What can you tell us about her?'

'There's a photo on her phone with her arms around Hendry. Not the sort of woman that Hendry would go for.'

'What do you mean?' Wendy said, taking umbrage at Windsor's comment.

'No offence, purely an observation. Sal Maynard came from Stockwell, a ten-storey tenement, low-rental.'

Wendy realised that Gordon Windsor was only profiling, a necessary part of a police investigation, but her socialist leanings were offended when a dead woman was degraded in comparison to another who, by her mother's admission, was sleeping with the man that she herself had slept with in the past. Again, Wendy could see that the wealthy and the famous were excused for their failings, but for the poor and unknown and unattractive, a different set of rules applied.

'She could have been a decoy, paid to distract the others while the killer entered the premises, measured up the situation,' Isaac said.

'But she was killed as well,' Wendy said.

'Collateral damage. Who knows what she had been told, and what her history is. It could be relevant. We'll check her out next.'

Chapter 4

Neither of the two police officers was impressed when they parked outside Sal Maynard's address, the urge to comment muted on account of the woman's violent death. Due to their delay in arriving at the ninth-floor flat in the drab concrete and poorly maintained building, the local police station had taken the responsibility of informing the next of kin.

A uniform was stationed outside the entrance to the flat. He sharpened up, stood to attention upon seeing the senior officers. 'Not much to say,' he said when quizzed by Isaac. 'They've been informed, that's all I can tell you.'

'They've? You know them?'

'Down at the station, the Maynards are well known. Fencing stolen goods, stealing cars and a quick respray, the occasional incident down at the pub when the eldest gets drunk and starts throwing his weight around.'

'Sal Maynard?' Wendy said. She was not impressed with the uniform's attitude. A family was grieving, yet he showed no compassion, only disdain for those inside.

'She didn't get into trouble, not too much anyway. A few too many drinks sometimes, and she was argumentative. A conviction for shoplifting when she was younger, but nothing recently. I can't say I liked her very much, a foul mouth, but that's about it. Sorry for talking bad about the woman, but I thought you'd like the truth. Inside, you'll no doubt receive the saccharine version.'

'No doubt we will,' Isaac said. 'The neighbours?'

'A few want to get in and offer their condolences. A few just want to be nosy. You know how it is.'

'Unfortunately, we do. High crime rate in this building?'

'Not as high as you would expect. There are a lot of recent arrivals in the building, the women covered up, the men trying to do their best. I can't say I understand them, but on the whole they cause little trouble. There are others here who'd steal anything, and sometimes the drunks will bait the immigrants. One day there'll be trouble, hopefully not today.'

'Not sure I appreciate his take on the Maynards and the locals,' Wendy said as she and Isaac waited for the door to the flat to open.

'Don't judge him too harshly. They've got a difficult job with the disparate society down here,' Isaac said.

The door opened, a heavily-tattooed and burly man stood on the other side.

'DCI Cook, DS Gladstone, Challis Street Homicide,' Isaac said.

'Come in,' the man said, exhaling cigarette smoke over the two officers.

Isaac and Wendy walked down the narrow hallway, brushing against the coats hanging on hooks to their right. A dog barked from behind a closed door. There was a distinct smell in the air of perspiration, stale smoke and alcohol. Isaac felt like taking his handkerchief and holding it over his nose.

'A saint, I'm telling you she was,' a female voice shouted from the room at the end of the hallway.

Isaac and Wendy passed through the doorway to find a group of people sitting around. On the table in the centre of the room, a half-empty bottle of whisky.

'DCI Cook…'

'Don't bother with your names. You're not welcome here, nor is he outside,' the woman who had shouted, said.

'You are?'

'Beverley Maynard, her mother. Have you found the bastard who killed my daughter?'

'We're still conducting enquiries.'

'Then why are you here? We didn't kill her.'

'We're assuming that your daughter wasn't the primary target,' Wendy said. 'We need to ascertain her movements, to check if she or you may have seen anything. What can you tell us about your daughter?'

'She was a good girl, not like the others.'

'The others?'

'My two eldest. Alex, you've met. He's always in trouble for this and that. The other layabout sitting sheepishly, that's Harry, a nasty piece of work, and to think I carried him for nine months.'

'Mum, you shouldn't say that, not to them. They're the police, even if they're not wearing a uniform,' Alex said. He was leaning against the wall, a cigarette hanging from his mouth, a glass of whisky in his hand.

'I'll say what I like. I'm the mother, and I'm sad, even if you're not. You two made Sal's life hell, even when she was younger, and now look at what's happened. Snatched away from me, the only one who cared, and who's going to look after me now?'

'Mrs Maynard, if we could come back to your daughter,' Isaac said. He could empathise with the uniform outside. This was clearly a fractious family who not only gave the police trouble but would not have been liked in the area. He was sure that if they enquired they would find few that would speak kindly of the family in flat 923.

'What do you want?'

'Your daughter's movements. She was in Kensington. Did she go there often?'

'Sal liked to look in the shop windows. She was obsessed with those who had money and fame. I don't know why as she wasn't much to look at. When I was her age, I was a looker, mark my words.'

'You're a liar,' Harry Maynard said. 'Our old man, before you nagged him to death, said you were selling yourself not far from here. That's where he met you, said you were cheap, and not too fancy even back then. At least Sal didn't do that, not that she did much else.'

'Sal helped out at the supermarket for two or three days a week. Casual, so they didn't have to pay her much,' Alex said. He was on his third whisky since Isaac and Wendy had arrived in the flat.

'We're certain that she was at the murder scene because Guy Hendry was there.'

'He'd not fancy her. Apart from working sometimes, she'd sit in front of that television and read those magazines. She was keen on Hendry, not that I could see much in him. And as for that Gillian Dickenson, skinny as a rake.'

'She died, as well,' Wendy said.

'It's been on the news. No mention of Sal, only that an unidentified female had also died. They mentioned Hendry and the tart he was with, but nothing about my Sal.'

'The names are not revealed until the next of kin are informed. You must know that,' Isaac said.

'Of course I do. But it's not right. My Sal was a good girl, and they report it as if she was a nobody, whereas the suntan and the teeth, and his fancy woman, get their pictures splashed across the television. And what about Sal, nothing, not even a mention of what she meant to me.'

'Mum, stop talking nonsense. You didn't care for her, any more than you do for us,' Alex said, his words slurring.

Isaac and Wendy were glad when they left the flat. On the face of it, there was no more to be gained at the Maynards', but Isaac knew that with the most inconsequential, the most unlikely piece of information, they could be back there. Sal Maynard may have been of little consequence, at least at the murder scene, but she could have seen something, heard something at another time, which could have required her death. Nothing and nobody could be regarded as trivial.

***

Larry Hill left the crime scene at Briganti's salon and headed into the area's criminal underbelly. He knew that Alphonso Abano's death would ensure that the criminal community was on edge and they would be closing ranks.

The first stop, the Wellington Arms in Bayswater. Inside, one of his informers, a man of moderate height and intellect, yet taciturn, and very careful in what he said.

'Seamus, a pint?' Larry said to the man, who was sitting to one side of the main bar.

'I thought you'd be in,' Seamus said.

'What's the mood on the street?'

'Just talk, nothing more. Abano's not a great loss, and no one believes they were after him.'

'Any names?'

'Not for the killing. Abano was not a major player, even if he fancied that he was,' Seamus said, his Irish accent still noticeable even though he had lived in London, on and off, for over twenty-five years. He was dressed casually: a pair of faded jeans, a white tee-shirt, his receding hair parted to one side, the grey starting to show in the shoulder-length hair.

Seamus Gaffney was not a criminal, although he skirted on the edge of legality. Apart from running errands for an illegal gambling syndicate, and the occasional favour for some of the criminals in the area, he was clean. He'd spent three months in prison as a youth in Ireland for passing false cheques; he had even managed to purchase a car with one of them, only to have it break down after fifty miles, and when he had returned to take umbrage with the man who had sold him the dud, he was up and gone.

Gaffney had put it down to one dud in exchange for another.

'I'd agree,' Larry said. 'Who could have been the target at Briganti's?'

'Nobody knows, and that's the truth. Maybe they're careful not to speak in case they end up dead, but on this one, Inspector Hill, you'll need to look further afield. It could be someone brought in from overseas for the one job, and then shipped out.'

'We've considered that possibility. Whoever it was, they dumped the rifle and pistol in a bin as they left.'

'No fingerprints?'

'Nothing. We've got Interpol onto it, but no details.'

'The villains don't like someone coming in here and causing trouble. It makes it more difficult for everyone.'

'A downturn in crime for a few days, some small benefit,' Larry said.

'Briganti was a decent man, kept to himself, and Hendry doesn't seem likely.'

'Did you know either?'

'Briganti in passing. He'd sometimes have a glass of wine of a Saturday in here. Hendry I know from a long time back, before he became the big star.'

'How?'

'Not much in itself, but he used to do some modelling. Back then, he was a good-looking man, no money, but he always seemed to be able to find himself a woman. Some reckoned that some of them were paying him for his time.'

'Prostitution?'

'Escorting, more like. If he was, good on him.'

'Not something either of us would have been paid for,' Larry joked.

'Not a chance,' Seamus agreed, his empty glass pushed across the table.

'Make that three,' a voice from behind.

Larry looked up to see the menacing figure of Nicolae Cojocaru, a man that the detective inspector kept his distance from. Cojocaru, wanted in his home country of Romania for extortion and murder, but claiming immunity from deportation due to his notoriety back there not affording him a fair trial, walked tall in London. Even the police gave the man a wide berth, knowing full well that he kept a team of henchmen on hand.

It was only the third time that Larry had spoken to the man. The first was when Cojocaru had told him to back off on prosecuting another man, not that it had done any good, and Larry had not complied. But the man, according to the word on the street, had some dirt on the Romanian crime boss, and if he was incarcerated, then he might talk. Not that it was relevant now, but his first day in prison the man had had an unfortunate accident and was now dead and buried. The second time had been in the pub they were in now. Cojocaru had seen Larry sitting in his regular seat, and had made a disparaging comment about the police in general, and Larry in particular. On that occasion, Larry had stayed seated, and the man had moved on, evicted someone else from their spot close to the bar.

Cojocaru was a charmless man who ruled by intimidation and overt violence. Larry did not feel comfortable with him sitting alongside him, two of the gangster's henchmen standing to their rear.

'It wasn't my people,' Cojocaru said, leaning in Larry's direction.

'Not your style?' Larry said sneeringly.

'Now look here, Mr Policeman, I've sat here in an act of conciliation. Whoever was responsible, they frighten us.'

'You're a known criminal and not someone with a good reputation. Too many people have died around you. Why should we be discussing this matter?'

'I keep my ears to the ground. I know that you're someone who can be trusted. You want to solve this crime. I want those responsible out of here.'

'There are some who would want you out as well.'

'No doubt they would. I'm an honest businessman, although I'm a tough bastard. Those who get on my wrong side end up regretting it. You don't want to be one, do you?'

'Are you threatening a police officer?'

'I don't threaten. I say it as it is.'

'Very well, Mr Cojocaru, what do you know about the shooting?'

'My contacts tell me it was someone who was brought in from overseas and then flown out.'

'But why? It makes no sense to be so visible.'

'It sends a warning that whoever it is can act with impunity.'

'Are you frightened?' Larry asked.

'Only a foolish man has no fear. Whoever it was could come back and finish the job.'

'Why? And who was the target? Alphonso Abano doesn't seem worth it.'

'He wasn't.'

'The others are clean.'

'Nobody's clean, you know that. Everyone's got skeletons, some criminal, some not, that they'd rather not be known.'

'What do you want from me? I'm not going to look away while you maim and kill and ship your drugs into this country,' Larry said.

'Let's just say that I'm an honest businessman who sees the neighbourhood going downhill.'

'You can say it, I can't. But I don't want any escalation in crime. Tell me what you know, and we'll agree to act civil to one another.'

Larry wasn't sure, and ideally, he would have called his DCI for advice, but time was of the essence. He knew that men such as Cojocaru did not offer help often, and if the killer was an import, the Romanian, a swarthy man in his fifties, could assist.

'Another time, you and I will not be having this conversation. Get in my way and you know what happens.'

'A display of the rough justice from where you come from.'

'Not much of a legal system either. It's men such as me who maintain control, and fear's a great motivator, a deterrent as well. Anyway, what we have is a Mafia-style killing. I've put the feelers out, and it's not someone from Romania.'

'You would have known in advance if it was?'

'I would have stopped it if I had.'

'Late at night, local tip?'

'Inspector, don't keep baiting me, or I'll let you deal with this.'

'Very well. Who was the target?'

'I've heard about Hendry and his woman, Briganti as well. He came over from Italy, check him out, although I suppose you are.'

'Complete dossiers are being prepared on all those who died. The question is, as you say, why kill them all? There's nothing to be gained.'

'There is. An overseas syndicate wanting to establish their mark in this country. The easiest way to frighten any who would get in their way is to show their dominance, their willingness to use violence.'

'A threat to you?'

'An honest businessman, as we've agreed.'

'I forgot.'

'Hypothetically, assuming I was what you think I am, that sort of person would be seriously worried.'

'A bastard thing to do, killing innocent people.'

'Nobody's innocent. You'd learn that in my country. You're either the one in control or you're the flotsam, and of no consequence.'

Larry realised that the gangster had no concept of right or wrong, only in ensuring that he remained the most vicious crook in the area, the man that everyone else was afraid of, a man who could have used the hairdressing salon as an example.

'Keep in touch, Hill. We need each other,' the parting words from Cojocaru as the men separated, a brief handshake. 'Remember, take care with me. I'm a good friend to those who understand me.'

And a savage and malignant bastard to those that don't, Larry thought.

Chapter 5

Guy Hendry had an ex-wife and two children, that much was known. Failing any others, they were the next of kin, although according to the tabloids, the relationship between Guy and the former Mrs Hendry was acrimonious.

'I've no issues with Guy,' Liz Hendry said after she had opened the door to her house in a leafy suburb near Richmond Park. 'The man can't help himself, but he's looked after us well.'

The two police officers found themselves sitting in two chairs in the main room of the house. It was well decorated, the sort of place that featured in magazines.

'Guy paid for all this, not that he couldn't afford it.'

'You seem very composed given the circumstances,' Wendy said.

'I reported from a few war zones earlier on in my career, saw things no person should ever see. Guy's death, as well as Gillian's, has come as a shock to my children and me.'

'Your children, where are they?'

'They've left home now. Two daughters, the oldest is twenty-two and married, the youngest is nineteen, and living with her boyfriend. They've been over to see me, and my sister's in the other room, so is Guy's.'

'You knew Gillian Dickenson?' Wendy asked, her initial concerns about the woman in part allayed by her pleasant manner.

'I knew of his conquests. I was one when I was younger. I liked Gillian, and some may have said she was with Guy for his money, but he was still great fun. I would have had him back in a flash, but that's not how he was wired. One of the reasons that he's been so successful. He knew of his appeal to women, and he knew how to turn on the charm.'

'Sergeant Gladstone's right,' Isaac said. 'You don't come across as the grieving widow.'

'I am. Ask me what you want, and then if you could, please leave me in peace. At least for a few days. I will take responsibility for the funeral arrangements, along with his sister.'

'We should interview her while we're here.'

'She's not bearing up as well as me.'

'The truth is that we don't know who the intended target was,' Isaac said. 'The shooting was well-executed. Apart from a local criminal, no one of interest was in the salon.'

'Loved by all, was Guy. Loved by too many, the occasional discarded boyfriend might have said. Sometimes, the women would come on to him, and one or two might have been married or in a relationship. The one fault, minor I suppose, is that sometimes he couldn't say no.

'Any incidents that you know of?'

'One or two. Guy would phone me up occasionally to let me know, and when the children were younger, we'd all go away on our annual holidays together. Some may have seen it as strange, but we didn't, the reason our daughters are so well-balanced.'

'He should have stayed with you,' Isaac said. He had to admit that he liked Liz Hendry, a person with a refreshing honesty about her.

'He tried, but then the fame and fortune came along. When we first met, he was struggling. The occasional photo shoot for a men's clothing line, an in-store magazine, and we had no money to spare. But then he got the first game show to host, and for a while he was impossible to live with. We used to live in a one-bedroom bedsit, and then we had a four-bedroom house.'

'We've only heard good reports about his affability, although there was an autograph hunter in the salon. The photos of her with Guy don't show him as being overly friendly with the woman.'

'You'll not hear a bad word from me about him, nor will our daughters say anything against him. Our youngest has taken it badly, and she'll come back later to be with me. The eldest is more stoic, more like me in many ways.'

'Jealous husbands and discarded boyfriends don't hire professional killers,' Isaac said.

'Guy wasn't the target, nor was Gillian. I liked her and she thought it was love, no doubt Guy did, but after about six to nine months, there's another temptation. Don't get me wrong, he was a good man, as good as you could hope for. Now, if you don't mind, I've spent enough time putting on a brave face.'

'That's understood,' Isaac said. 'If we could meet with Mr Hendry's sister.'

Liz Hendry shook Isaac's hand and then Wendy's. She then left the room, a handkerchief in her hand.

After a few minutes, Guy Hendry's sister came into the room. It was clear that she was older than her brother by more than a few years.

'Step-brother,' Pamela Vincent said. 'We were close as children. I was more like a mother to him than our father's third wife was. She was a bitch, the wicked step-mother, and our father was a charmer, the same as Guy, but he didn't have the inherent decency that my brother had. More my influence than his parents.'

'Your mother, Guy's mother?'

'They both took off, and we rarely saw either of them. We came from money, yet Guy didn't want any of it. That's why he was down in London with Liz and struggling to make ends meet. If it had stayed that way, then he'd still be alive.'

'We can't control our destinies,' Isaac said, knowing full well that if he could, he would be happily married to Jess, but she was long gone and now had two children with another man. He suddenly felt sad, reminiscing about the one woman that he had really wanted.

'I stayed with the money, inherited enough to live well, but Guy never touched any of it. He made his fortune through sweat and hard work.'

'Any enemies?'

'Our father was a ruthless businessman. He would have made enemies, but not Guy.'

'Where is he now?'

'Dead and buried. A lifetime of smoking cigars, drinking whisky and burning the midnight oil. A driven man, he had a coronary at the age of seventy-one. Guy never went to the funeral, there was that much hatred between the two.'

'Your brother was capable of anger and hate?'

'Not towards any of us. It was our father he hated, almost as much as he hated his mother for deserting him.'

'Is she still alive?'

'She is. She's old now and lives in the country. I'll give you her address. I'll let you form your opinion when you meet her.'

'Your opinion?'

'I've never formed a judgement against her, no more than I have against my own mother. She's dead, by the way. Guy's mother was a frail woman, even when she lived with our father. And with our father, you were either with him, or you were out, and totally.'

'Are you saying she may have had no choice but to leave Guy with his father?'

'I could understand the rationale at the time, but I was nine years older when she left that night. Guy was only eight, so he didn't see these things in the same light. Whatever the reason, I don't believe he has met his mother more than a few times in the years since. I wish my brother were still alive, but he isn't, and we'll have to deal with it. I just hope that you're able to solve this horrendous crime as soon as possible and to bring whoever did it to justice.'

'That's our intention,' Isaac said.

***

The unexpected visit of Nicolae Cojocaru to where Larry and Seamus Gaffney had been sitting in the pub had not been a pleasant encounter, and Larry, usually not a man to express his prejudices, could not act with indifference towards the man. Cojocaru, with his adroit manipulation, his money, and his henchmen had cut a swathe through the area. In the past, the villains had been English, then Irish, then from the Caribbean, Jamaicans mainly, and the last group had been vicious enough. But compared to the Romanian gangsters, they were as children.

'Tough bastard,' Seamus said.

'He frightens me,' Larry said. 'He could have done it.'

'Too close to home, he's not responsible.'

Larry knew that while Cojocaru was capable of ordering violence, he was not a man who carried a gun or committed the acts personally. He was a godfather figure in his community, and there were those from the old country who looked to him for assistance; people not in a position morally or financially to condemn the man's criminal activities.

That night, late as usual, Larry found his wife waiting for him when he arrived home, her typical stern look not apparent.

'Busy night,' she said with almost a touch of affection. Larry knew that she wished he'd leave the police and get a job that wasn't so dangerous and didn't come with the temptation of boozy nights. He knew she had been right on a previous case when the Homicide team were getting close to solving some murders, and he had ended up in hospital, severely beaten. If it hadn't been that the hoodlums who had gone at him with baseball bats were ineffectual, he would have been dead. As it was, he had escaped with no more than severe bruising, a couple of broken ribs and a dislocated shoulder blade.

'You've seen where I've been on the television,' Larry said.

'Guy Hendry. Why would anyone kill him?'

'They killed his girlfriend and six others, a bloodbath.'

'And you're mixing with those who did it?'

'Not this time. We don't think it's local-based, and Hendry was not the target. Never can be sure on that, though.'

'He always seemed a charming man, but then on the television, these celebrities let us see what they want of them.'

'DCI Cook and Wendy have met with his family, also Gillian Dickenson's. According to them, Guy Hendry was a decent man. Gillian Dickenson came from a good home, as well. They had to tell the mother that her daughter was dead.'

'Not you this time?'

'Not this time, thankfully. Just hope there are no more villains out there with semi-automatic rifles.'

'And you in the middle of it. You know I worry.'

'I wouldn't love you if you didn't. Someone's got to deal with this.'

'But why you?'

'Let's not go there again. You know I'm not leaving.'

'I know. Your dinner's in the oven if you're hungry.'

'I'm starving. Any chance of sleeping upstairs tonight?'

'Just make sure you brush your teeth and use some mouth freshener. I can't be angry tonight, although I should be. Any suspects?'

'I met Cojocaru.'

'He gets as much publicity as Guy Hendry,' Larry's wife said as she walked out of the door to the kitchen.

'Not good, though. He's a man who frightens me.'

'He frightens a lot of people. Don't go getting yourself killed.'

'I don't intend to,' Larry said.

'But Cojocaru. He's a killer.'

'I'll make sure to call him sir every time I meet him.'

'Not you. You're more than likely to have a beer with him.'

'Reluctantly,' Larry said, knowing that Cojocaru was a man who would know what was happening before anyone else, even the police.

Chapter 6

Giuseppe Briganti's mother, an elderly woman, her back bent from years of working outside tending to the cattle and the vegetables that they grew for sale, sat in the corner of the farmhouse. In another corner, a television was on. For the woman, it was her only connection to the son she had seen three weeks previously when he had been on one of his frequent visits. She remembered the joy that he had given her when he had told her how successful his business had become. He had told her about where he lived and how he preferred to be on his own. She regretted that he had not married and given her grandchildren, but she knew the anguish that had driven him to London.

'I'll not last for much longer,' she said, desperately sad at the loss, aware of her own mortality; the stroke last summer, and now the inability to walk more than a few paces. She was sixty-eight, but life had been tough, and Giuseppe had offered to take her to London and look after her and to make sure that she received the best medical care. Once, eleven years ago, she had visited him, the one time she had left her Italy, and she only remembered the cold and the rain, and the fact that she did not understand what everyone was saying. Not that they were unfriendly, on the contrary, but she was a village woman, as was her mother, and her mother before that.

Her husband had died five years previously, and Giuseppe had visited to organise the funeral and to say a few words praising his father and mother for giving him life, and for caring for him. He had said that he wanted to stay, but his mother knew that it was just words for her, and he had never been a farmer. He had been destined for more, and she had seen him achieve that.

Around her in the farmhouse, her brothers and sisters, the ones still alive, as well as half the village. It had been a good life, the woman had to admit. She raised herself from her chair to make sure that everyone had something to eat and drink. A sudden pain in her chest and she slumped back in the chair. Ten minutes later the village doctor pronounced her dead.

***

Early morning in the office, DCI Cook's mandatory practice: the six o'clock meeting during a murder investigation. The others in the team had no trouble agreeing, only with complying. Bridget Halloran had worked late the previous night dealing with the paperwork, and setting up the reporting structure that a bureaucratised police force demanded. Not that she complained, as she enjoyed her work immensely and had great respect for her DCI. It had been two in the morning when she had left the office, and a twenty-minute drive, less than three hours sleep, and then back to the office.

Isaac could see that Bridget was suffering, as were the others, as was he. He had only slept for one hour. He'd lain in his bed for longer, but the events had been churning over in his mind. Wendy Gladstone, the ever-loyal sergeant, yawned. Larry Hill was another person who had had a late night, but his had been tinged with alcohol and Nicolae Cojocaru.

'Thanks for making it,' Isaac said. 'I needn't tell you the seriousness of what we have here.'

'We understand, sir,' Wendy said. 'Why can't the villains let us have a good night's sleep?' she said by way of lightening the sombre tone of the room.

'We'll ask them sometime, but in the meantime, what do we have? Larry, you first.'

'The word is that it's someone from overseas aiming to muscle in.'

'Cojocaru?'

'I met with him yesterday, not that I intended to. Most times the man keeps out of the way, but he wanted to talk.'

'Update us on what he said.'

'His arrival in the area has changed the pecking order amongst the criminals.'

'What about the West Indian gangs? You were friendly with them before.'

'They're still there, but they're maintaining a lower profile. Cojocaru is the most savage we've come up against, and according to the man, someone else is out there that frightens him.'

'Keep in contact with him, find out what else he knows, and keep us updated as to where you are. That man kills, whether you're a police officer or a gang member.'

'I know that. With the West Indians, I felt safe enough, but with Cojocaru, I don't.'

'Wendy, what do you have?' Isaac said. He'd noticed that the woman's arthritis had been troubling her less in the last few weeks, a sign that the weather was improving, and early-morning frosts had not been seen for some time.

'I'm working through the others in the salon. You've met with the more significant people, so I've concentrated on the other two hairdressers, Baz, short for

Barry, Hepworth and Frank Boswell. Hepworth was Australian, and I've got the local police in Sydney dealing with informing his family and interviewing them. If there's any need, I'll set up a video link from here, but the man seems clean. His father was English, and Barry Hepworth had an English passport, no immigration issues. The man paid his taxes, and Briganti's books seem to be in order. Frank Boswell seems to be clean as well. He's English, born in Liverpool. From what we know so far, he came from a middle-class family, the father is an accountant, his mother teaches at a local school. Nothing on him other than drunken driving a few years ago, and he'd been apprehended once for buying cocaine off the street. He was probably still snorting it, and Forensics and Pathology will confirm if that's the case. I'll go up to Liverpool if we find any negatives against him. Sal Maynard is of more interest. Her family has had more than its fair share of run-ins with the law. One of her uncles had been in Maidstone prison for five years for theft, cars mainly.'

'Delve into the others with Bridget,' Isaac said. 'Anything untoward and we'll follow up.'

'Cojocaru could be leading us down the garden path.'

'What do you mean?' Isaac said.

'A diversionary tactic.'

'He's savage enough to have been responsible.'

'The man's not stupid. Antonescu and Becali, his two offsiders, are not too smart, and I reckon that Antonescu would have no compunction in shooting innocent people, nor would Becali, but this time I reckon that Cojocaru's levelling with us.'

***

'I don't care who the bastard is, I want him dead,' Cojocaru said as he stomped around the living room in his penthouse flat. Standing not far away, afraid to sit, were his two henchmen.

Crin Antonescu, the first of the two, a squat pug-faced man, a wrestler in his youth, enjoyed violence, although only if he was not on the receiving end. He still remembered the time when he had been, the result of not throwing a championship match on which a gambling syndicate had staked a fortune. Not only had they lost millions, but Antonescu had lost the full strength in his left arm after four men had gone to work on him for not following orders.

'You live to tell others who may think that they are smarter than us,' one of the four men had said, and now Antonescu sat in the room in Kensington listening to the man who had controlled that syndicate.

Antonescu hated Cojocaru, although the thought of betraying him brought the pug-faced man out in a cold sweat.

Cojocaru knew that fear brought with it respect and devotion, the same way a maltreated dog will continue to follow its master, even after it had been starved and beaten.

The second of the two men in Cojocaru's presence, a tall, slender man with wavy hair and a dark complexion, went by the name of Ion Becali. He did not fear Cojocaru, only loved the man for what he had done for his family when he had been desperate and struggling to make ends meet in Romania.

'He's not a local,' Becali said, referring to the shooting at Briganti's.

'Ion, I'm not a fool,' Cojocaru said.

'Abano wasn't much of a target,' Antonescu said.

'He may have fancied himself as an important man in the area, but he was just small time. What was he involved with?'

'We used him a few times to sell drugs for us. We paid him well enough, and he kept his mouth shut.'

'You two are my eyes on the street, but you're coming up with nothing.'

'Nobody knows, or else they're clamming up.'

'I don't care what you do, who you hurt, but I need to know. If it's someone from the old country we'd know by now. If it's someone from elsewhere with fewer scruples than us, then it's war. Are we ready?'

'If it's locals, then yes. We've got them under control, but if it's unknowns from overseas, no chance,' Antonescu said.

'What are you suggesting? That we bring in more people to help?'

'How many of the locals did we kill when we came to this country?'

'You tell me.'

'Over twenty, but most of them were Jamaicans, the rest Irish, some from Scotland, and a few English, but they weren't used to our kind of violence. Or at least the English weren't, lily-livered the lot of them.'

'The police, any issues?'

'A few uniforms can be paid to look the other way, or if they don't take money, they'll respond to threats.'

'What sort of country is this, where the police are honest, the villains are harmless?' Becali said.

'The sort of country that has made us rich and feared. The sort of country where we can hold our heads up high.'

Becali thought back to Romania and how he had scratched out an existence, stealing what he could, fencing what he couldn't. And now he was living in an upmarket flat in Bayswater, a couple of women on tap, a cabinet full of drink, and the best hashish that money could buy. It had been a good eight years in a country that respected his right to be there, even paying him government money in the first few months while he established himself, while he and Antonescu with Cojocaru's planning had methodically eliminated all opposition. If the authorities had known what atrocities they had committed, especially against those from the Caribbean, the police would have been more diligent.

Concern over gang warfare had been raised in parliament at the time, and in the media on occasions, but not much had come of it, just blustering and grandstanding by a few. Cojocaru knew, as he had back home in Romania, that society needs discipline, not vague rules and regulations. The area that he controlled was calmer than before; there was a lower level of street crime, and areas that had been no goes late at night were now safe to walk in by the law-abiding majority.

The master gangster looked out of the window of his penthouse flat and surveyed his domain. He knew that the move to England had been right, as back in the old country there was a new government that had been elected on a platform of law and order. They weren't achieving much of either, but they had become a nuisance.

In England, the presumption of innocence before guilt had served him well, and apart from a few attempts by the authorities to muscle him and his men out of the country in the early days, he had managed to stay. And those that had shown the possibility of securing his deportation were either in his pay now, or keeping out of the way, or dead. Of the three options, Cojocaru knew which he preferred.

'The Russians would be capable of hitting Briganti's,' Cojocaru said, a shiver running down his spine.

'But why? We take the heroin they ship out of Afghanistan, pay them plenty for it,' Antonescu said.

Chapter 7

Detective Chief Superintendent Richard Goddard was not a happy man, Isaac knew that. The two had worked together since one had been an inspector and the other a constable on the beat. The relationship, akin to friendship, had served the two men well, although as Isaac, now a detective chief inspector, was well aware, it did not obviate the need for his Homicide team to provide a result.

'Isaac, I've got my seniors breathing down my neck, the same as I am down yours. What's going on, and what are you doing to prevent a repeat?' Goddard asked in the sanctity of his office.

'We're struggling on this one,' Isaac admitted, knowing full well that his senior appreciated an honest answer, even if it was not the one he wanted to hear. 'Apart from a minor villain in the salon, we can't find any reason to kill the others in Briganti's. We're still conducting enquiries, interviewing the next of kin, checking on the street for what's being said, who's suspected.'

'And?' Goddard said from the comfort of his leather-backed chair. His DCI had to do with a wooden chair, and not very comfortable at that.

'It appears to be a warning to the crooks in the area. Larry Hill's been in conversation with Nicolae Cojocaru, and the man believes that's what it is.'

'We take the word of a gangster?'

'Not normally, but it's more his style,' Isaac said. 'Not that we can pin it on him.'

'Men like Cojocaru don't get their hands dirty, you know that,' Goddard said. Isaac could sense a tenseness in the man. He'd thought he'd be heading up Counter-Terrorism Command by now, but was still stuck in Challis Street Police Station, courtesy of a police commissioner by the name of Alwyn Davies, an acerbic political animal who neither Isaac nor his chief superintendent liked, having had more than a few run-ins with him.

Davies should have been out on his ear after a string of terrorist acts in London. And then there was his bringing in of his own people into senior positions, temporarily removing both Isaac and DCS Goddard on one occasion and bringing in an incompetent to take their places.

But now stability reigned at Challis Street, even if there was an unease about the place. Isaac, in his younger years, had featured in a promotional for the television-viewing public as the face of the modern and cosmopolitan London Metropolitan Police: urbane, black, degree-educated. There were some who saw him as a future commander, even commissioner, but now he'd been languishing for too long in Homicide. Not that it concerned him unduly, not in the last year anyway, as his team were efficient, and he had just managed to upgrade his flat in Willesden for one in Hammersmith.

Detective Chief Superintendent Goddard was a political animal, but not with the savagery of Alwyn Davies, the senior officer in the London Metropolitan Police.

Goddard had gone out of his way to protect his protégé, Isaac, on a couple of occasions, both woman-related. The first time, a more youthful and less-experienced Isaac had slept with a woman who had later turned out to be a murderer. The second time was in the north of the country, when he had been snapped in an embrace with a woman. It had happened at a party in the hotel where he was staying during the hunt for a woman who had killed several men. A group of three women, all inebriated, had grabbed him to take a photo of them all before one of them had taken a picture of just the two of them, smiling, arms around each other. Isaac had thought no more of it until later that night when the woman – the murderer – had loaded the photo onto social media. For a while, he had become a laughingstock, although in the end he had regained some creditability by arresting her, but not before she had stabbed him with a knife.

'How do men like Cojocaru manage to evade the law?' Isaac said. He knew that it was a rhetorical question.

'Have you met the man?' Goddard said, choosing not to answer his DCI's question.

'Larry Hill has, I haven't.'

'Any advantage if you do?'

'If the man is frightened, then there's no harm done.'

'If someone's muscling in on his action, either they are planning to strike a deal with the man or to eliminate him.'

'They could have done that instead of killing innocent people.'

'Innocent?'

'Alphonso Abano is no great loss, but the others didn't deserve to die purely because there's a war going on out there.'

'Cojocaru was bad enough in dealing with the local villains before, but now this has taken a turn for the worse.'

'It has been quieter for a few months, up until Briganti's, that is.'

'A temporary lapse. Meet with Cojocaru, see if he'll help us. We can deal with him another time.'

Isaac knew that it was a compromise, in that dealing with one villain at the expense of withholding access to another, more violent, more unpredictable, more unknown, was necessary. He left DCS Goddard's office with the intention of getting Larry Hill to set up a meeting.

***

An air of palpable tension pervaded the air as Larry, fishing for information, entered into his and most of the villains' favourite pub, the Wellington Arms.

In one corner, propping up the bar, Crin Antonescu. He cast a steely glance over at the police inspector, a brief nod of his head in acknowledgement. Larry responded in the same manner, not pleased to see him there, not disappointed either. Ion Becali, the other of the two men closest to Cojocaru, was sitting down at a table, a woman in her twenties close by, her arm around his shoulder. Larry knew her by sight and by name: Betty Acton, black, beautiful, although starting to show the effects of selling herself and the drug abuse she had subjected her body to. It wasn't often that she came into the pub, nor was it usual for Cojocaru's two men.

Larry strolled over to Becali, passing by Seamus Gaffney and giving him his pint. He wanted to speak, but Larry had a more pressing question for another.

'Where's your boss?' Larry said to Becali, who had pretended not to notice the police officer approaching him.

'Our night off,' Becali replied. Not a good enough answer for Larry. Betty grabbed hold of Becali's face and pulled it forward to hers before kissing him firmly on the mouth, a clear sign to Larry to leave them alone. Usually, he would have. Becali was a violent lover, known to be so because another Betty lookalike had ended up in the hospital badly beaten and bruised. She had wanted to bring a case against the man, supposedly a dispute over the final payment for her services. In the end, the woman had left the hospital and moved out of the area. Larry had made some low-level enquiries, but nothing had come of them. Either she had found herself face down in a ditch somewhere, or she was feeding the fish and the crabs at the bottom of the river, or she had changed her name and was standing on a street corner somewhere selling herself for whatever she could. Regardless, no one, not even a next of kin or a friend, had come forward after the woman vanished.

'It's the first time I've seen you and Antonescu in the pub together without your boss.'

'Nicolae Cojocaru's not a man for drinking.'

'He's game for anything else.'

'What does that mean?'

'The last time I saw you, it was in here with Cojocaru. He was worried then, so were you, and here you are with your fancy woman. No doubt you've got a night of pleasure planned. I hope we don't have to visit the hospital later tonight or tomorrow to find her in intensive care.'

'Ion treats me well,' Betty said, the needle marks visible on her skin.

'We need to meet with your boss,' Larry said. 'If he's in the country, that is. If he's not, where is he?'

'He's here. Others are looking out for him. And he's entertaining tonight, the same as I am. Antonescu's keeping himself comfortable with a few beers.'

'He's not a lover?'

'He is, but he likes a drink now and then. For myself, a couple of pints and a good woman.'

'Betty's the good woman? I thought you had a couple of classy whores in your stable.'

'How dare you insult me,' Betty said indignantly.

'Take no notice,' Becali said. 'Detective Inspector Hill's just leaving.'

'It's my night off, Hill,' the man said, turning his gaze to Larry. 'And If I fancy a bit of rough, then that's my right. It's a democratic country where a man can make his own decisions.'

Larry sat down and looked over at the young prostitute. 'Betty, you heard the man, you're the rough. Just make sure that you don't end up as the beaten or even the dead.'

'Cojocaru will see you tomorrow morning,' Becali said. Larry could see the redness in the man's face, the tightening of his grip on his glass, the look of an angry man.

'I'll be there with Detective Chief Inspector Cook. There's a gang war brewing, and we want to stop it before it gets out of hand.'

'So do we. Now if you'll excuse us, go away and talk to your informer friend. And tell him to be careful. We don't like people sticking their noses into our business.'

'I'll tell him, but I'll be keeping an eye out for what you're doing. We're not sure that you weren't involved in what happened at Briganti's.'

'Okay, Mr Policeman, you don't like us, and we don't like you. Mutual dislike and distrust, is that it?'

'It is, but I've got the law behind me, you haven't.'

'Idle threats. Mr Cojocaru doesn't take favourably to people who threaten him.'

'We know his solution, and you and Antonescu carry it out.'

Larry stood and walked away, observing the look between Becali and Antonescu. Betty sat to one side of Becali; she was not holding him as tight as before. Larry hoped that the woman would not regret selling herself to a vicious man for the night.

***

Seamus Gaffney, a man who appreciated a few pints of beer of a night after a hard day of not doing much, was waiting for Larry to come over to where he was sitting. That day he had organised the location for an illegal dogfight where bloodthirsty men would bet on the outcome of two half-starved dogs fighting each other, the victor being accorded the accolades, the other, either maimed or dead. Gaffney didn't appreciate the spectacle himself, but he had bills to pay, the same as everyone else.

There was a wife, a homely woman who preferred to stay back in Ireland, although he went over there every six weeks to see her. Not that he was idle back there, as there were six children and another on the way. He liked it there, and the cottage where his family lived was paid for. The only problem was that the community was honest and law-abiding, the sort of place where everyone went to church on a Sunday, and where he didn't fit in. In his childhood, he'd been hyperactive, and in his teens, he had been into graffiti and vandalism, painting the church door with his impression of art: bright orange and blue. And then as an adult, it was false cheques and a few months in prison. He had become a leper in Ireland, yet Sheila, the next-door neighbour's daughter, had always been there, even during his childhood and his adolescence, and then his time in prison. They had married on a Saturday, a small affair at the church where he had adorned the church door. Even Father O'Rourke, the village priest, had made a joke of it at the time of the wedding, although the day after the defacing of the Lord's house, he had turned up at the Gaffneys' home with a cane in his hand, and he had tanned the young Gaffney with it, putting him in bed for a week.

Seamus's mother had wanted O'Rourke to be prosecuted, but Seamus had pleaded with her not to do it as he would be ostracised from his friends, and Father O'Rourke was right in what he had done to him.

In time, life in the small community moved on, and Seamus never defaced the church again, even stopping every time he passed the place to enter and offer a prayer to be forgiven, and to apologise to the Almighty for what he had done.

England was the only place for Seamus Gaffney after he left prison, and although he had tried his hand at labouring, and then serving in a shop, he was a restless man. He was, however, reliable, and those in Notting Hill and the adjoining suburbs recognised that. He always had his ear to the ground, and he knew how to set up activities on the edge of illegality. Gambling on fighting dogs, bare-knuckle fighting, although there wasn't much of that in the last few years, and arranging a cheap car for someone: stolen, resprayed, the engine markings removed on more than a few occasions. He had spoken out of turn once and had inadvertently given a clue to the police; the outcome of that an arrest, and a man had spent two years in jail. On his release, he had grabbed Seamus by the collar, marched him up to the pub.

'You owe me a skinful of beer,' the released prisoner said.

'Why's that?'

'They never found out about the other crime. The money's safe from that one, and later tonight you're going to drive me to the airport. I've got plenty, and after two years that I spent inside courtesy of Her Majesty, I'm well ahead.'

Seamus had been relieved when the man had boarded the flight to Thailand, and a life of bargirls, cheap alcohol and drugs. The word came through six months later that for all his luck the man had been on the receiving end of a beating in a bar in Phuket and had died of his wounds.

'Seamus,' Larry said, having visited the bar in the Wellington Arms to order another pint of beer for the man, one for himself. 'What can you tell me?'

'You've been talking to Becali.'

'Why not? The man knows more than you do, or does he? He's a vicious bastard, so's Antonescu, but we need to find out who shot up Briganti's. Have you found out any more?'

Seamus took a drink, downing almost half the contents of the glass in one gulp. 'The rumour mill is working overtime. Everyone's got a theory. Most think it's the Romanians aiming to tighten their grip.'

'Their grip is already tight. Are there any dissenters?'

'Some of the gangs are in discussion.'

'To form an alliance against the threat?'

'If it's not the Romanians, then they need to be ready. There's talk of bringing in more weapons. It could get nasty.'

'That's why we need to meet with Cojocaru, the other criminal syndicates, the gangs.'

'*We!* Count me out. I'll talk to you here for a few pints and some of your money, but don't ask me to meet with any of them.'

'Seamus, you're letting your mind get away with you. It's the police who'll be talking with them. You can help with letting me know who's talking to who, or I can find out from them direct.'

'They'll not talk openly to you, not yet. Another incident and they may do.'

'Another incident planned?'

'That's the problem, just rumours. There are some that say the hit on Briganti's was aimed at the man himself, others say it was the hot-shot banker, others reckon it was Guy Hendry or the woman he was with, even the Maynard woman. Myself, I think they're all wrong.'

'What do you reckon?'

'I read that they shoot up places overseas.'

'It's not part of our culture.'

'You may be right,' Gaffney said. 'I've heard there is a shipment of weapons coming in.'

'A rumour?'

'It could be, but if it's correct, they'll be available to the highest bidder. You'd better be prepared.'

'We will be,' Larry said as he downed his last pint. He had kept it to four; he would not be sleeping on the sofa that night.

Chapter 8

Pathology had completed the autopsies of those who had died at Briganti's. Isaac read through the reports in his office. He had been joined by Bridget and Wendy; Larry was out on the street attempting to meet with the various gang members and villains, those that would talk to him.

'According to the reports,' Isaac said, 'Abano had been drinking, nothing excessive, and Briganti was clean, as were the other two hairdressers that died, although one of them, Baz Haywood, was found to have traces of cocaine.'

'Guy Hendry and Gillian Dickenson?' Wendy said.

'Nothing to report apart from Gillian Dickenson being two months pregnant. Paul Waverton, the banker, was heavily into cocaine. And as for Sal Maynard, her autopsy reveals that she was verging on obese, no sign of any other ailments. What do we have on her?'

'The family has some criminal history, hardly enough to warrant execution,' Wendy said. 'I'm following up in detail with Bridget on all those in Briganti's. We're not excluding that one of them was targeted and that Cojocaru is not responsible.'

'Correct,' Isaac said, knowing that he had trained his team well. 'We can't assume anything. Larry's out there trying to find out more details, and we're meeting with Cojocaru.'

'Be careful,' Bridget said.

'I've already run it past Detective Chief Superintendent Goddard. He's given the go-ahead, and we'll have armed backup not far away.'

'So will Cojocaru,' Wendy said.

'The fact that the man's worried indicates that it's a foreign syndicate attempting to take over.'

'But why Briganti's?'

'Depends on the reason. An arrogance on whoever's part that the English police are ineffective, a warning to the Romanians and the other criminals in the area.'

'Are we ineffective?'

'We go by the book. It's still more effective than the alternatives, and we're not dealing with terrorism here.'

'It's worse than that,' Bridget said.

'Terrorism is usually committed by low-intellect, religiously dogmatic and radicalised peoples. Organised crime overseas is not run by fools, but by people who are smart and know what they're doing,' Isaac said.

'As I said, it's worse.'

'The upsurge in weapons in the area?' Wendy said.

'There are enough already, but there could be more. We'll see what Larry's got to say, and what Cojocaru tells us.'

***

Four men sat in a room heavy with the smell of ganja, the Caribbean name for marijuana. Their collective criminal empires overlapped and included the area covered by Challis Street Police Station: from Paddington in the east, through Bayswater and Notting Hill and Holland Park to the West, up north as far as Ladbroke Grove and then south taking in Shepherd's Bush and Kensington.

The house where the men sat was not affluent Kensington or Holland Park, not even Bayswater, but Ladbroke Grove and a council property. The men, leaders of their various gangs, did not often meet, and then only on the street and mostly late at night when a dispute had to be settled that invariably resulted in violence.

Larry, who had smelt ganja many times before, had to admit to a feeling of light-headedness as he waited in an adjoining room. Across from him, two Rastafarians.

'They're not sure what to do with you, copper,' one of them said. Larry could see the glazed look in the man's eyes, the colourful and expensive clothes he wore. He could also see the knife in its sheath pushed down the front of his trousers. Larry knew him as Delroy Williams, a man who had spent time in jail for selling crack cocaine. He wasn't the only one in the house who had served time, but of the four leaders, only one had. He had been caught in an affray three years earlier, stating that a man had come at him with a knife and he had defended himself.

'Talk to me, that's what they'll do. They're scared,' Larry said. He had liked Rasta Joe, a former gang leader and part-time informer, when he had been alive, as big a villain as any of the four in the other room, but he had been charismatic too. Delroy Williams was not, and he had a surly manner about him and a hatred of the police.

'We're scared of no one,' Williams said, although Larry had the measure of the man. Williams was a coward, feeling brave on account of the four men in the other room, and the fact that he was spaced out on ganja. Larry chose not to indulge in any more conversation with him.

The other man in the room, a short, unattractive individual, was unknown to Larry. 'Your name?' he said.

'Liston Hayes.'

'After the boxer?' Larry said, assuming that he had been named after Sonny Liston, a former world heavyweight boxing champion.

'Never heard of him,' the man said.

'How long have you been here?'

'A couple of hours.'

'This country, I meant.'

'I was born here, up in Manchester.'

Larry looked intensely at the man, recognised the speech patterns, knew that the man had not been in England for more than six months to a year.

Liston Hayes was only small, but he had a look about him that Larry didn't like. As if he was a man who was more than he seemed, a possible murderer brought into the country in anticipation of the gang warfare which could explode at any time.

The door beyond opened, a man stood at the entrance beckoning Larry to enter. The smell from the room was stronger than where he had been sitting.

'Don't worry, Larry. We'll open the windows, put a fan on high for you. We don't want one of London's finest corrupted by us,' the man said sarcastically.

'Long time, no see,' Larry said. 'I thought you were doing five to ten in Pentonville.'

'I served three, out for good behaviour. I'm a model citizen now.'

'Not you, Marcus Hearne, you'll always be a villain.' Larry remembered the man from before his imprisonment: good-looking, polite and friendly, a dealer in drugs, a loyal friend to those he liked, ruthless to those he did not. In the end, he had served time for the drug dealing, not for the murders that had occurred on his orders. Personally, Larry liked the man; professionally, he did not. But he knew one thing: if Hearne was one of the four, then he would be safe. Outside on the street, two blocks away, an unmarked patrol car. Larry made a phone call. 'I'm fine. Don't stay where you are, leave,' he said.

Information was coming through from sources on the continent about Briganti's. Larry would use it if it helped with the discussion, keep it to himself if it would not. The information was dynamite, and the West Indians were touchy at the best of times; he didn't want them rushing to mobilise their people. He also did not want them arming themselves more than they already were.

***

'What did you find out?' Cojocaru, an even-tempered man most times, said. He was sitting in a leather chair in his penthouse. It was early in the afternoon, and the view out over the area was excellent, not that he could enjoy it, not that day.

'No one knows anything,' Becali said. He was standing up, as was Antonescu. To sit in the presence of their boss without his express permission would be a marked show of disrespect, almost a challenge to his leadership.

'It's the Russians,' Cojocaru said.

'None of our contacts have confirmed that,' Becali said.

'Your contacts are just the minnows, mine are the sharks.'

'What are you going to do?'

'I need to meet with them.'

'But why? If they don't like what you say, you don't return.'

'We need a neutral location where I'm safe.'

'In London?'

'Here's as good as anywhere.'

'But what do they want? We take whatever they send to us.'

'There's a bumper crop in Afghanistan of opium poppies. It'll drive down the price, and the Russians don't want to ship more to maintain their margin, they want to increase their profits.'

'But how?' Becali said.

'They'll go through England and Europe taking out whoever opposes them, drop the price of the drug, ensure more addicts, and then bring up the price. The strategy is good, the only problem is that they want to cut us out.'

'They've always hated us,' Antonescu said.

'They hate Romanians as much as we hate Russians. What's new? We can still do business with them.'

'How did you find out their plans?'

'Yuri Aliyev.'

'He's our primary contact with the Russian mafia?'

'Bratva if you want to use their Russian name. And yes, Aliyev has served us well, ensured that the shipments arrive on time and the quality is good.'

'Do you trust him?'

'Aliyev is one of them. He can't be trusted, but business is business. I need to convince those in their senior hierarchy that we are the best option.'

'Are we?'

'We have to be.'

'This meeting with the police, are we prepared?' Becali said. 'What will you tell them?'

'I will judge at the time how much they need to know and how much we confuse them. We weren't responsible for Briganti's, and I don't want them trying to pin that on us.'

'You don't intend to tell them it was the Russians who shot up the hairdresser's?'

'I may hint, I may not.'

'Are you sure it's the Russians?'

'Aliyev is the messenger. He could have lied. He may not even know the truth. A loyal lieutenant, no more, the same as you two. Now, what do we have to confuse the police and to give us time to negotiate with the Russians?'

Chapter 9

Isaac paced around Homicide; his team were letting him down, which meant that his leadership was not up to par, and he had seniors to answer to. Not only was DCS Goddard looking for results, so was Commissioner Alwyn Davies, and he was not a man to take no for an answer, let alone an 'I don't know'.

And that was precisely what the man had received from Goddard, although couched in police jargon, and now Goddard was in Isaac's office, and he wasn't looking happy.

Unable to avoid the confrontation, Isaac entered his office, a perfunctory shaking of hands before sitting down.

'Isaac, you're stuffing around on this one. A man can't just walk into a hairdresser's, shoot the place up, and then walk out of the door and down the street. Hell, he could have been sat across the road, a cappuccino in front of him, a cream bun in his mouth, having a laugh at you, at us.'

'We interviewed everyone in the vicinity. He wasn't there.'

'If this is someone from outside the country, then it's organised crime. Have you contacted Serious and Organised Crime Command?'

'I have. They're looking at that angle. Although, if it's the Russians, what happened is not their normal modus operandi in this country.'

'That's what's worrying everyone, even Davies. In the confines of this room, the man's a fool, but then we're both agreed on that. We answer to him, he answers to the politicians, the prime minister, the general public. If there's to be an upsurge in violent crime, he intends to stamp it out ASAP, with your help and mine, or without.'

'Has he threatened?'

'Not in as many words, but we know what happened last time. We've been out on our ears before, and it wasn't a pleasant experience. Returning me to Challis Street must have stuck in his throat when he issued the directive, and the man doesn't forget. And if you hadn't arrested the damn woman, being stabbed for your troubles, receiving a commendation for meritorious service, then you'd be out on the beat, back in uniform.'

'We brought the woman in,' Isaac said by way of defence. He realised that it was a lame response, but it was the only one he had. Goddard was right, Isaac knew that, but what could he say. Serious and Organised Crime Command was running with the information provided so far, including a detailed analysis of Nicolae Cojocaru and his organisation. Not that they had to do much as the man was well known to them.

And as for the others in Briganti's that fateful day, Guy Hendry's body had been released and buried, a moving ceremony according to the evening news on the television channel which had covered it, as well as a one-hour documentary on the life and times of the man.

Isaac had watched it at home with Jenny, his latest girlfriend, a willowy part-time model from a small town to the south of London, as white as he was black. One friend had commented that the two of them together was like a rerun of the Black and White Minstrel Show, popular in the sixties on television. Isaac had taken it in jest, Jenny had not, and the friend was now off the

Christmas card list, and not welcome at the flat that Isaac and Jenny shared.

The documentary on Hendry, the subject of a meeting in the office the following day, had emphasised the man's achievements, the charities he supported, loved by his colleagues. It had not dwelt on his female conquests, only to say that he was beloved by many, male and female. Gillian Dickenson had been one, and she had been buried in the family plot in her hometown, a smaller gathering than for Hendry, but Isaac had attended, noted that the man's first wife, the mother of his children, had been there and she had shed a tear for the dead woman.

The body of Baz Hepworth, one of Peppe Briganti's employees, had been sent back to Australia, and that of Fred Boswell, the other stylist, had also been released. Briganti's body still remained in the mortuary, as did the bodies of Paul Waverton, Alphonso Abano, and Sal Maynard.

Richard Goddard, normally agreeable, could be irritating on occasions, and now was being just that. Isaac could sympathise with the man, as he had to deal with seniors who were not always pleasant, and most of them were driven by ambition and internal politics. Goddard was a master of both disciplines, but his ambition was being thwarted, as was Isaac's, and neither wanted Alwyn Davies's stooge, the incompetent boot-licker Superintendent Caddick, back in Homicide.

'This Russian angle? Is it likely to hold up?' Goddard asked.

'Eighty–twenty,' Isaac said.

'Your estimate or that of Serious and Organised Crime?'

'Both. I'm meeting with one of them later in the week. No point before as they're in contact with their counterparts overseas.'

'In Russia?'

'They prefer to deal through Interpol: more efficient, less bureaucratised, more unlikely to have a mafia man on the inside.'

'A problem in Russia?'

'There's big money at stake.'

'It's not much to go with. I'll hold Davies at bay for as long as I can, but any more deaths or shootings, and you know what happens.'

'I know. Not something any of us want, and non-productive. If it's Caddick who comes through the door, then all bets are off. He'll only stuff it up.'

'If it happens, then make yourself scarce and keep working on it. Policing would be a lot simpler if everyone was competent.'

'A lot simpler if we didn't have criminals either, but that's life. Whatever happens, the team in Homicide won't let you down.'

'I know that, Isaac. While you and Serious and Organised Crime are working on the eighty, make sure your team continues with the twenty. It may still be homegrown.'

'We're still following through on four of the bodies. Everyone's got skeletons, and the four have histories of wrongdoing. Three of them are minor, and Abano was a criminal, but of little note. We should wrap up our investigations into them in the next couple of days and then we'll release their bodies.'

***

It was late in the day when the phone call came through. Bridget answered the phone, took the message, and called the others into Isaac's office. Larry had been dealing with paperwork, entering his day's activities into his laptop; Wendy was doing the same, although her typing was woeful, and her spelling was suspect. She was pleased that Bridget would fix it up for her afterwards, a ten-minute job for her, an infinity for her.

Isaac looked at the clock on the wall. It was nine-thirty in the evening, another hour for him in the office. He'd been running through the investigation so far, messaging his contact at Serious and Organised Crime.

'It's serious,' Bridget said as she took the seat in the far corner of the office. Wendy sat down alongside her, Larry remained standing and leaning against the door.

'What is it?' Isaac said.

'A phone call from the Irish police.'

'Why would they phone us?'

'Seamus Gaffney.'

'He visits every few weeks,' Larry said. 'A family man who commutes to Ireland on a regular basis. Devoted to his wife, and I asked the Garda, the Irish police, to keep tabs on him.'

'They found his rental car five kilometres from the airport, Gaffney inside.'

'Dead?' Larry said.

'Two bullets to the head.'

'Cojocaru?' Wendy said.

Larry looked ashen-faced. 'First Rasta Joe and now Gaffney,' he said.

'Occupational hazard,' Isaac said. 'He probably found out something he shouldn't have. Any contact with him, Larry?'

'Not since the last time I met with him. If he had found out something, he was either keeping it to himself, or he was aiming to see who'd pay the most.'

'Assume the latter. Larry, get yourself over to Ireland. There should be a flight tonight.'

'It'll be tight. Bridget, update me on the way. Contact, phone numbers, and book a hotel close to where I'm heading.'

'Get to Dublin, rent a car. I'll place an order on the rental company, should save you some time.'

Larry left the office; Isaac phoned DCS Goddard to update him. 'Forewarned, forearmed,' Goddard replied. 'His death is not likely to be major news, or is it?'

'It's unlikely, but whoever killed him and for whatever reason is worried.'

'So are we. Cojocaru?'

'Too obvious,' Isaac said. 'And the man knows we've been keeping a watch on him. Bridget will check out the flights to Ireland, see if Antonescu or Becali have been there, although the man has others who could have killed Gaffney.'

'Stay with it. I'll consider how to keep the commissioner off our backs. The man's death in Ireland is another complication we could do without.'

'It means that someone's frightened. The question is what did he find out.'

Isaac turned to the other two in his office. 'We've got some work to do. Five minutes, get a coffee, and let's see what we've got.'

It was going to be a long night, and the meeting with Cojocaru was scheduled for the next day at a pub outside London. It had been intended for Larry to go with him, but Isaac knew that wasn't possible, and he wasn't going to cancel the meeting.

Upon her return, with a cup for him as well, he spoke to Wendy. 'How do you feel about meeting a vicious thug tomorrow?'

'He won't be the first I've met.'

'He makes the West Indians look like Sunday School teachers.'

One in the morning, the three left the office. An itemised list of questions to ask the master gangster and a file opened for Gaffney, although the man had been killed in another country so strictly speaking it was their case. Isaac had worked with the Irish police before; he knew there would be full cooperation between the two police forces.

***

Larry arrived in Dublin late, the last flight. He picked up his car at the rental company, a woman handing him the keys. 'The local police have been on the phone, so has a Bridget Halloran. There's a purchase order, and your driver's licence has been forwarded. No more to do, just sign on the dotted line,' she said.

'Thanks,' Larry said. It had been a long day, an even longer night. He found the car quickly enough, a local police car waiting alongside.

'Detective Inspector Hill?' the patrol officer, a ruddy-faced man carrying more than a few extra pounds, said.

'Yes, that's correct.'

'Fine. We've been asked to show you the way, save you trying to find it.'

With the patrol car leading, a late model Ford with a broad yellow stripe bordered by a thick blue line on both sides of the vehicle, it took fifteen minutes to make it out to where Gaffney had died. A Nissan, the same as Larry had rented, although his was green, Gaffney's blue.

'Nasty business,' Detective Inspector Buckley said as he shook Larry's hand vigorously, a bear-like grip.

'Not the first you've seen,' Larry replied. He liked the look of the man. It was well after midnight and the DI, although obviously well-primed at the local pub and expecting a night off, was alert and interested, and above all, an asset.

'The same as you, I suppose. Not that I expected to see Seamus like this. Harmless he was, although an idiot as a child, not much better as an adolescent. But as I said, harmless. Not the sort of man to offend anyone. You knew him?'

'As an informer, but you're right. I liked him in some ways, but he was into villainy, one step ahead of the law, and free on the street as long as he gave us the occasional titbit as to what was going on in the area.'

'What was going on?' Buckley said. 'I heard about the shooting. Your neck of the woods?'

'It was, and Gaffney was sniffing around. I assume he found out more than he should.'

'It looks professional. We found where the shooter had been, and he must have known Gaffney was on the way.'

'Which means advance information.'

'Someone back in London had tipped off whoever it was that did this. The man was regular as clockwork visiting. Every six weeks he'd be here, usually a Friday and then back to London on Monday.'

'You knew him well?'

'I came from the same village. I was even the best man at his wedding. I liked Seamus, and his wife, Sheila, is a lovely woman. Happy as can be, those two were, although an unusual arrangement. But then, I see my wife every night, and happy is not a word I'd use. How about you?'

'We're close. Mostly argue over money and my drinking, but apart from that, we get on well.'

'Goes to show, doesn't it? I have one Guinness, and I'm in the doghouse, although you didn't come all this way to hear me griping, did you?'

'Later over a Guinness we can talk, but for now, what do we have? Any evidence?'

'I've got the men in the dust coats on the scene seeing what they can find.'

'You mean the crime scene examiners?' Larry appreciated the man's relaxed manner, although he wanted answers. He needed to phone back to his DCI, knowing that the man would be waiting for his call.

'Yes, them. A good bunch, and if there's anything to be found, they'll find it. What we've got so far is a shot from a distance as the man slowed at the intersection, and once he'd veered off the road and into the ditch, the second bullet to the head.'

'The same as what happened at Briganti's.'

'What do you mean?'

'The person who killed those in Briganti's hairdressing salon shot the people at random with a semi-automatic, and then went around them individually and shot them in the head.'

'The same person?'

'It's a possibility.'

'The most obvious is usually the most reliable. Any idea as to height, weight, dark or light hair?'

'Dark hair, we've got a sample. Although in a hairdresser's, it's not so easy to be sure. Forensics are not

72

willing to commit to it. If you've got anything here, they'll be interested. It's important to know whether we're dealing with the same shooter or someone else.'

'It sounds as though you've got a tough case over there,' Buckley said. 'Here, put on some protective gear, and we'll go over nearer to the car and where the first shot was taken.'

Larry phoned Isaac to update him, raised the possibility that the Briganti shooter was not on mainland Europe, but could still be in England, and as of six hours previously, in Ireland. Isaac phoned Bridget who issued an update to the points of entry into Ireland, the ferries and airlines, although the details were vague. The chance of apprehending a professional assassin by such an obvious tactic seemed remote. It was three in the morning. Isaac turned in his bed for another thirty minutes before deciding that sleep was going to elude him for that night. He got out of the bed, careful not to disturb Jenny who looked at him with one eye, said nothing, and went back to sleep. Isaac knew she'd not complain at his leaving the flat at such an hour.

Isaac arrived at Challis Street just before 4 a.m. to be greeted by Bridget. 'Work to do,' she said. He phoned Larry.

'Inspector Buckley, Ryan, is with me. He's done a great job. We're working with the crime scene team. We've got a hair sample, a shoe print, and a possible piece of clothing from where the shooter took the first shot. It could be the same man as at Briganti's, but we'll need Forensics to work overtime on this one,' Larry said.

'If there is the possibility of a gang war, then that's what they'll do. The murder belongs to the Irish police. Any issues?'

'Not here. We'll work together on this one. The inspector's a family friend of the Gaffneys. We're off to see the man's widow.'

'Do that, and then take a couple of hours to clean up and rest. Unless there's any reason to call earlier, we'll talk again at 10 a.m. We're meeting Cojocaru at 11.30 a.m. I'm taking Wendy.'

'I'll stay another day, follow through on the same shooter possibility. I'll aim to take the flight back to London late at night.'

'Time for a Guinness?' Isaac said.

'Buckley's fond of a drink. I'm sure we'll manage a couple.'

Chapter 10

It was early in the morning in Homicide and activity was at a high level, Larry having phoned from Ireland, although he had been instructed to get some rest and not contact them before ten that morning. Detective Chief Superintendent Goddard was in the office as well. The death of Gaffney in Ireland, the possible forensic evidence connecting the shootings at Briganti's and in Ireland, were at the forefront of the DCS's mind.

Commissioner Davies was watching closely to see how Goddard and his team were performing and whether he should bring in additional help. It wasn't his decision to make, but as Goddard said to Isaac, 'Don't wait for the man to follow procedures, and don't expect any civility from him. His skin's more important than those that died, and if there's to be warfare on the streets, he wants himself clean, he wants scapegoats.'

Isaac, a detective chief inspector, did not need the old and by now tiresome reiteration that the sword of Damocles hung over his head. Davies was a difficult man, but sometimes Isaac wondered if DCS Goddard wasn't using the man's name for effect, in an attempt to impose his authority and to sharpen up Homicide by using the name of another. Whatever the truth, Isaac was pleased when Goddard left the department and retreated back upstairs to his office.

It was still not eight, and Isaac and Wendy were on heightened alert, an adrenaline rush due to the impending meeting with the Romanian.

'We leave here at 10 a.m.' Isaac said. 'That'll give us plenty of time to get to the meeting point.'

'Where?' Wendy asked.

'Cloak and dagger on this one. Cojocaru's not given us the final destination. He's frightened that we'll get our people in there before and bug the place.'

'Would we?'

'I'll not jeopardise the meeting for the sake of incriminating evidence against the man. What's possibly brewing out there is more important than putting that man behind bars, or getting him deported back to Romania.'

'It's a golden opportunity. If the man's frightened of others, his guard is likely to be down. He could say something, not to us, but to others, that could give the courts enough to deal with him.'

'Serious and Organised Crime Command is interested in what's discussed, and they'll want a full report.'

'Are we wired? Or are our smartphones on record?'

'Not this time. We'll meet the man in the pub, but Antonescu and Becali will not be far away. They'll check us out first.'

'I thought it was just him.'

'It is. Larry met him in a pub full of patrons, but we have to go through this subterfuge.'

'Why?'

'It wouldn't pay for him to be seen talking to me, and we don't know who else is watching. The man's neurotic, we can't blame him for that. If others are coming in to threaten his empire, he'll be weighing up the pros and cons, making sure to tell us what we need to know, not the full truth. Larry says he's smart, so watch out for him manipulating the conversation. And above all, be agreeable with the man. We're there to solve nine deaths now, not to express an opinion about the malevolence of the man.'

'I'll not say anything,' Wendy said. She was not willing to admit that she was nervous. The man they were meeting had a bad reputation, and those in the area where he operated gave him a wide berth, some even crossing the street as he approached, others doffing their caps, standing to one side for him. She had not seen the man in the flesh, only checked him out through the police records. Nicolae Cojocaru, forty-six, formerly from Bucharest, Romania, although born about ten miles to the north. A list of convictions as a youth, and then, in his early twenties, the leadership of a group selling drugs. From there, a rapid rise in the criminal echelons until, at the age of thirty-two, he was one of the four major criminal leaders in the country. Suspected of widespread bribing of politicians, the police, and the judiciary, a dozen unsolved murder cases attributed to his name, but unproven. His move to England had occurred nine years previously on the election of a new government in Romania; the man who headed it was known to be honest, and he had campaigned on a platform of law and order.

Of the four most significant crime figures in Bucharest, two had been jailed, one had been killed in a police shootout, and the other, Cojocaru, was in England, and not intending to go back. Apart from two judges and three senior police officers, nobody else had been arrested in the purge against corruption in the country. The honest prime minister had lasted twenty-three months before a bomb under his car had ended his period in power. After that, the habits of the past returned, yet

Cojocaru, according to an Interpol report, was unlikely to go back to his home country. A new criminal elite had arisen in the intervening years, and Cojocaru would have had to start afresh, to forge new contacts, to acquire politicians, judges and police officers to protect him.

Wendy put down the report and focussed on the current day. Larry phoned again, spoke to Isaac. The conversation was brief, and Isaac made no comment when he came out of his office and left Challis Street with Wendy. On the drive south, she asked him what Larry had said.

'He's just curious, disappointed that he'll not be there when we meet with Cojocaru.'

Wendy questioned no more, not sure that there wasn't more to the conversation. The final destination had been messaged to Isaac who had entered it into his GPS.

'I don't trust Cojocaru, and he could end up feeding us nonsense,' Isaac said. 'Larry's not so sure now that Gaffney and Briganti's are related. There are some differences.'

'Is that what he was talking to you about?'

'Sorry. I was distracted before. Alwyn Davies is sticking his nose in, and then we've got Serious and Organised Crime Command to update.'

'Superintendent Caddick?'

'Davies will use any excuse to get his man back, and in truth, we could do with some help, not Caddick obviously.'

'Serious and Organised Crime Command will be able to offer backup, more their case if Briganti's is proven to be the result of organised crime.'

'Cojocaru probably knows by now, although we can't be sure he'll tell us the truth.'

Wendy looked out of the car window: at the people driving to work or to the shops, the school children in their uniforms, heavily-laden backpacks containing their books. Every other child she could see had a smartphone and was busy texting. In her day, there had been no smartphones, no internet, no ability to send a message to someone around the world, or ten yards down the road. She missed those times: calmer, safer, more agreeable. A time when a child rode a bike to school with no helmet, no fear of abduction, and where the mother would be at home on the child's return after school, as her mother had been. But now, for most of those at the schools they passed, there would be an empty house, a meal in the refrigerator for reheating in the microwave, a computer in the child's bedroom for skyping, or Facebook, or for watching pornography. And now, she and her DCI were off to meet a thug, a man who prospered from the misery of others, a man who should not be in the country.

Sometimes, on the days when her arthritis troubled her, she felt that her time for policing had passed. Those were the times when she missed her husband the most, difficult though he had been in his final years with dementia setting in and an increasingly narrow view of people other than Anglo-Saxon and white. She knew what he would have thought of a Romanian gangster. It was a good job he was not in the car with them as they pulled into the pub car park.

'The Black Rabbit,' Wendy said as she looked up at the sign outside the building. 'Hardly seems appropriate, does it?'

'It depends who's the rabbit, him or us.'

Across from their car, Antonescu and Becali.

'They'll want to check us for weapons, recording devices.'

'We've no protection,' Wendy said. 'I don't like the look of the shorter one.'

'Crin Antonescu, a former wrestler, violent, and apparently he enjoys it.'

'I've read their files. The other one, Becali, looks more agreeable.'

'Socially, maybe, but he's a murderer. We don't think they were in Ireland with Gaffney.'

'Any reason why not?'

'They were in London four hours before the man's death, and two hours after. We've got witnesses who'll attest to that.'

'Reliable?'

'One was an off-duty policeman, the other, the publican of the Wellington Arms.'

'We're clean,' Isaac shouted across to the two men.

'Where's Hill?' Becali said.

'In Ireland. I've brought Detective Sergeant Gladstone instead.'

'What's in Ireland?' Antonescu said. He was standing on the other side of the car to Becali, alongside Wendy. She looked up at him; he, down at her. Neither smiled. Wendy could see that his eyes were too close together and his muscles bulged under a jacket two sizes too small for him. He reminded her of a Smurf, a cartoon that was still popular, but without the blue skin, and definitely without the smile.

The two police officers got out of their car. Becali patted down Isaac. 'Police business. I've left the phone in the car.'

'And how about you?' Antonescu said to Wendy.

'Clean.'

The man shrugged his shoulders and moved away.

'He's inside. Don't trick us or he'll not be pleased,' Becali said as the four walked towards the pub's low door.

'Don't worry. No one's coming if that's what you're worried about, and no one's listening in,' Isaac said. 'Let's hope Mr Cojocaru is going to tell us something. It was a long drive for just a drink.'

'What he tells you is not our business. We only follow orders,' Antonescu said.

Inside, the pub was typical of so many: horseshoes on the walls, old newspaper articles and photos of the area stretching back a hundred years and even longer. One picture of the pub, horses and carts outside, the men with their stiff collars and hats, the women dressed in their Sunday best.

'I've bought three pints,' Cojocaru said as he shook Isaac's hand.

Not wishing to be impolite, although not wanting to return the gesture, Isaac smiled and offered the typical, 'Pleased to meet you.'

'I though Inspector Hill would have been here.'

'He's in Ireland. Seamus Gaffney was shot.'

'I heard about it, tragic. I believe he was a friend of Hill's.'

'Not so much a friend, but Gaffney had his ear to the ground.'

'Too close. No doubt he upset someone, spoke out of turn.'

'This is Sergeant Gladstone,' Isaac said.

'Pleased to meet you,' Cojocaru said as he shook Wendy's hand. She thought the man pleasant, dressed as he was in a navy suit with an open-necked white shirt. He smelt of aftershave, the same one as her husband had favoured. 'You'll not want a pint, I assume. Let me get you something else.'

'Beer is fine,' Wendy said.

'No one's going to disturb us,' Cojocaru said. 'I've paid the publican to keep anyone else out, at least for the next hour.'

'Why here?' Isaac asked.

'Neutral territory. I prefer wandering eyes not to see us or to speculate.'

'Here is hardly secret.'

'I agree, but it's better than nothing. And besides, what I know is not that secret anyway. I just wanted us to meet and talk, a mutual problem.'

'Mr Cojocaru, if you don't mind me saying,' Wendy said, 'we don't have anything in common.'

'Under normal circumstances, I might agree. But I thought that if I scratch your back, you'll scratch mine. An English saying, I believe.'

'It is,' Isaac said, 'but Sergeant Gladstone's right.'

'Let me finish. I've had feelers out overseas, back in Romania and elsewhere. There's a group in Russia who are eyeing England and other countries for a major expansion.'

'Drugs?'

'Yes. They want to expand, cut out the middlemen, drive up the price. They're ruthless, and nothing or nobody will dissuade them.'

'This is England,' Wendy said. 'We will.'

'Unfortunately, the typical English resilience won't help you. Of course, you can stop whoever, but you know how English law works, how people think in general. A slow intrusion here and there, the occasional act of violence, the increased level of drug activity on the streets and people adjust. How many people are talking about Briganti's now? Not as many as on the day and nobody stops outside the salon. They just walk by, their faces glued to the screens of their phones, or earpieces listening to music.'

'I'll agree with you there,' Isaac said. 'But why should we work with you on this one? You're hardly a saint.'

'An honest businessman, if you want our meeting to continue.'

'Honest men don't concern themselves with criminal activities,' Isaac said, aware that he was testing the man, pushing more than he should, less than he would have liked to. He wanted the man in jail or out of the country, but for the present he was a man to be friendly with.

'I'll ignore your comment, a lady present. DCI Cook, there's a problem bigger than either of us, bigger than the London Metropolitan Police, and that's the Bratva. You know who they are?'

'The Russian mafia, the brotherhood.'

'They're well-organised, structured along the lines of a large business: a CEO, board meetings, lieutenants, rank and file hoodlums. And they're vicious.'

'Proof, names?'

'Briganti's was the starter. A test to see how the police would respond, your weak spots, your strengths, not that there are many of those.'

'Insults won't get you far,' Isaac said. He lifted his glass of beer and took a drink. He was aware that he needed to hold his own with Cojocaru, aware that the man was educated, able to converse in good English.

'Not insults, facts. What have you done so far? Checked out those in Briganti's, found out nothing, other than Abano was a criminal, two of the others used cocaine, and Hendry had good taste in women. While I, a man with contacts around the world, know more about the truth than you do.'

'Seamus Gaffney, relevant?'

'Not here. The man was useful to some, but he was an informer. His killer will be found in due course. You are aware of the gangs, the Rastas, as well as some others who are arming up, ready for a battle royal?'

'We were told they were not arming against the Russians, and what about this shipment? Do you know when it's coming in and how?'

'Believe me, Cook, I don't want this to escalate any more than you do.'

Wendy was not sure what to make of the man. On the one hand, he was pleasant, he spoke well, and he seemed obliging and generous in what he was telling them. Yet she had read his record: the violence, the torturing, the killing of others at his command.

'What do you want, Mr Cojocaru?' Wendy said. 'An amnesty, that we'll leave you alone for the duration?'

'Not me. I've done nothing wrong.'

'We'll not go further with that discussion,' Isaac said. 'But the Russians are disturbing. How do we find out more, and where are they? Who shot up Briganti's?'

'The name of the man is not important. It is the person behind the man, not the man behind the weapon. You know that as well as I do. I will give you a name, and we will talk again in two days.'

'The Russians are not going to be satisfied with our part of London,' Isaac said as he emptied his glass. The conversation was coming to an end.

'They're using us as the litmus paper, the toe in the water to check if the water's warm or cold.'

'Why us?' Wendy said.

'You'll need to ask them,' Cojocaru said.

Isaac knew, but he chose not to mention it. It was because Cojocaru was the funnel through which the Russians had been working. They were testing him, ascertaining whether he was up to the task or not.

'The name that you are going to give us?'

'Stanislav Ivanov. Check him out.'

Cojocaru shook hands with Wendy and Isaac and walked out of the door. Outside, he got into the back seat of his black BMW, Becali in the driver's seat, Antonescu alongside.

'What do you reckon?' Isaac said after the man had left.

'Charming, yet vicious. I wouldn't want to be on the wrong side of him,' Wendy said.

'He could still have given the order for Gaffney's murder. We need to know if that's the case. When Larry's back, the two of you check on Gaffney's movements, see if he saw or heard anything and if he was trying to set up a deal.'

'It'll not be easy.'

'That's why I've got the best team in Homicide,' Isaac said.

Chapter 11

Sheila Gaffney said little, her eyes red from crying. Ryan Buckley sat beside her, his arm around her shoulder.

'I know he was a rogue, but I loved him, he loved me, and he always had time for the children,' the woman said eventually. She had a happy look about her, Larry decided. Apart from the fact that she was pregnant, she was a short, roundish woman with red hair, rosy cheeks and a freckled face.

The house where the three of them sat was small, with no more than three bedrooms judging by the size of it, but it had a loved look.

'Your children?' Larry asked.

'They're not far away. The eldest, she's the most sensible, the closest to her father, is next door with her best friend. She'll be back here soon enough. The others are in the garden or with the neighbours. Seamus loved it here, and he was looking to come back on a permanent basis. Not that I had any idea how he'd fit in. He upset a few when he was younger, and they've forgiven him. But my Seamus wasn't the sort to stay at home.'

'Is that what he was planning to do?'

'He said it was. Something about how our future was going to be better. Not that I wanted anything to change. He's away for a few weeks, then back here for a few days. It was like a honeymoon every time, and now he's not going to walk in the front door again, is he?'

'Sorry, Sheila, but no,' Buckley said. Larry could see the man's genuine affection for the woman.

'Do you know who? I know that people could get angry with him, but killing someone, that's different, isn't it?'

'It is,' Larry said. 'Any enemies that you know of?'

'Not Seamus. Was he involved with crime in London?'

'On the edge. He was crafty, managed to avoid too much trouble. We let him go a few times with a warning, a swift kick up the rear end.'

'Literally?'

'Metaphorically. I used to meet with him occasionally, talk about this and that.'

'He gave you information for money?'

'He did.'

'I told him that it would get him killed, but he kept telling me not to worry, and it was only general knowledge that he was passing on.'

'Sometimes it wasn't. Easy to upset people doing that,' Larry said.

'That's what got him killed, talking when he shouldn't. Mind you, he never wasted his money, and he looked after us well.'

'We believe it was something more serious than that. Have you seen anyone suspicious around the house lately?'

'I should get you a cup of tea. Forgetting my manners. Seamus wouldn't like me doing that.'

'It's not important,' Buckley said.

'I must,' the woman said as she got up from her seat and left the room.

'You'd better go with her,' Larry said. 'Delayed shock.'

Five minutes later the two returned, Buckley carrying a tray with three mugs and a bowl of sugar, a jug of milk.

'Mrs Gaffney,' Larry continued after all three had settled again, 'we believe this was not a local with a grudge. If anyone's been around the house that looked out of place, we need to know.'

'Well, there was this one man looking for directions, a foreign accent and I didn't understand what he was saying at first.'

'Could you describe him?'

'Apart from the accent, he was about average height. I noticed that he limped with his left leg.'

'How was he dressed?'

'Smart. He wore a suit which was unusual for around here, apart from a Sunday.'

'Sunday?'

'Church. We're all firm believers around here, even if Seamus wasn't too keen. When he was back here, he came with me, never failed. Not so sure if he did in London. Probably not, I suppose. And he did like a drink, and he was close to the children.'

Larry could see the woman drifting. The initial tears had dried up. They were soon to be replaced by inconsolable anguish. After that, there'd be no more questions for some time.

'Mrs Gaffney, would you recognise this man again?'

'I would.'

Larry took out his phone and scanned through the photos of people of interest that he had on it.

'No, it's not any of them, although he looks similar,' Sheila Gaffney said, pointing at a picture of Crin Antonescu.

Outside, their collars turned up against a cold wind, Buckley lit up a cigarette, gave one to Larry.

'Was it him?' Buckley said, referring to the picture of Antonescu.

'We can prove that he was in London, and he doesn't limp. The person that Sheila Gaffney met may just have been a tourist.'

'We'll keep checking, but this time of the year the place is full of them.'

***

Isaac dropped Wendy off at Challis Street. She had work to do after their conversation with Nicolae Cojocaru. He continued on to New Scotland Yard, parking his car on the street outside, a police-parking designated spot. He walked through the security at the entrance, showed his warrant card and received a badge to display inside the building, before proceeding through the first door to the main building and taking the lift to the fourth floor.

'Isaac Cook, long time,' Detective Chief Inspector Oscar Braxton said.

'It's not often I get an invite to such a hallowed place,' Isaac replied in jest to a man he'd known for some years.

The two men, one black, the other white, sat down at a desk and spoke about old times, out on the beat, training, and what life had brought them both. Braxton, married with three children; Isaac, still single and hoping for the patter of little feet one day. Isaac could see that the man, a similar age to him, looked older by at least five years, but then, Braxton was a smoker and a drinker, and Isaac was neither, apart from the occasional social drink or when he was meeting with villains, as he had that day.

'Nicolae Cojocaru, slippery bugger,' Braxton said. 'We've been watching him, but he plays the game well. Apart from the deaths that occurred in his name, none proven, he maintains a low profile. We suspect him of being a major player in importing illicit drugs into this country, but he uses middlemen. Men who don't know who the others are, except over a phone, and the points of entry into the country change. And if they're storing the goods for any length of time, a factory unit on a weekly or monthly hire. With no actual contact linking back to Cojocaru, we can't prove anything.'

'How about his bank accounts?'

'We managed to gain access to one in the UK, but the money was legit. If he's being paid, it's offshore. The money moving around can't be spent that quickly, anyway.'

'Any reason?'

'What can you buy with it? A castle in Scotland, a Greek Island, a fleet of Rolls Royces?'

'Cojocaru lives well,' Isaac said.

'He's got enough businesses and property in London to justify his lifestyle. The man even pays taxes.'

Isaac realised that Braxton was expressing a personal view on the distribution of wealth. He thought it a naïve outlook for a man working in Serious and Organised Crime. Men such as Cojocaru, Isaac knew only too well, were not satisfied with sufficient; they wanted all they could get, a way of keeping score.

'He can't be the only player in this country,' Isaac said.

'He's not, but he concerns us more than the others. And he's been dealing with the Russians, but you must know that,' Braxton said.

'We do, but we're Homicide, not Serious and Organised Crime. If someone's murdered we're there, but drug smuggling and whatever else goes on in our patch is of interest, but not our primary focus. Briganti's is murder. Otherwise, it's up to you, and you're telling me you can't pin the man down.'

Not entirely true,' Braxton said, irritated by the impertinence of someone from Challis Street, not the prestigious surroundings of New Scotland Yard.

'Sorry if I'm blunt, but I've just spent time with the man in question, and he gave us the runaround, gave us a name.'

'Everyone thinks we've got it easy,' Braxton said. 'They know who the criminals are, so they expect us to go out there and arrest them. But it doesn't work like that, you know that. Cojocaru can afford the best legal advice, and the prosecution, good men and women, are paid by you and me out of our taxes. This is not Romania or Russia or the Middle East where these ratbags come from. We can't just go and pick them up, put on a show trial, slam them in prison or make them disappear. We're accountable, and they know it. No doubt they have a good laugh at our ineffectiveness, but that's the way it is.'

'We have the same problem,' Isaac said. 'What about Stanislav Ivanov? Cojocaru gave me his name.'

'What do you know about the Russian mafia?' Braxton asked. An air of cordiality existed between the two men.

'Not a lot, other than they're organised and dangerous.'

'That's it. They are exceptionally well-organised, and they regard crime as a business, not as anything dishonest, and now, in Russia with so much corruption, they're thriving. Ivanov heads the Tverskoyskaya Bratva, one of the most influential of the crime gangs.'

'What does the name mean?'

'Tverskoy is a district in Moscow. Skaya translates as belonging to. The Tverskoyskaya Bratva was formed in Tverskoy. Most of the mafia gangs take the name of the place where they were formed or where they're based. Bratva, I assume you know what that means.'

'The Brotherhood, although not much brotherly love from what I've heard.'

'None at all, and if you're a member and in trouble, you're hauled before their executive. If found guilty punishment is swift. No chance of an appeal with them, no right of reply.'

'Tough justice,' Isaac said.

'Don't feel sorry for whoever's on the receiving end. They're bad news, and so far, we've kept them out, but now, if it's Stanislav Ivanov, we've got trouble.'

'Tell me about him?'

'He's well known in this country. Fifty-two, educated in Moscow at the Lomonosov University. A master's degree in economics, a bachelor's in English. The man speaks flawless English. No convictions against him and he has a dacha outside of Moscow, heavily fortified.'

'Protection?'

'Men such as Ivanov get neurotic about their own importance. He's only in charge as long as there are no pretenders to the throne in the wings.'

'Where does Cojocaru fit into all this?'

'We're not sure. He wouldn't be a pretender, and he's only a small cog in the wheel. But he's a weak point, and the Russians are making a move.'

'Any proof?'

'We have our sources in this country and overseas. Not that the locals know any more than we do, but overseas there is a power struggle between the various mafia gangs in Russia.'

'I'm interested in solving the murders. The possible incursion of the Russians only concerns me if it has some bearing, if it will precipitate more murders.'

'It will, you can be sure of that.'

'So what do we do?'

'Prayer might help. What we really need is for Cojocaru to open up. He does not intend to allow anyone to come in and usurp him. He'll be in contact with the Russians, but be warned, don't get too close, or you'll end up regretting it.'

'From Cojocaru?'

'He'll play it strategically. Have you seen any Russians?'

'We don't know who we're looking for.'

'Okay, I'll give you a rundown on who is who, as well as photos. We'll be monitoring the airports in case anyone comes in. But Ivanov is not a criminal in his own country, no one would risk saying anything to the contrary, and it's not likely to change. He's got those who could change his status in his pocket, and he visits England on a regular basis. He's got a house, more like a mansion, close to the River Thames in Richmond, a place in Bayswater. His wife comes for the shopping, he comes for Ascot and the football, but most of the time she's at one place, he's at the other indulging in what crime bosses do.'

'What's that?'

'High-quality women. Sometimes he brings them with him, sometimes he sources locally.'

'No crimes against him in England?'

'None, and if Cojocaru is right and Ivanov is planning something here, it's a frightening development.'

'Cojocaru only mentioned the name.'

'He must be scared if he's talking to you.'

'He's still dangerous.'

'He'll double-cross you or anyone else if it helps him,' Braxton said. 'Keep in contact, and be careful.'

'I will,' Isaac said. He needed to get back to Challis Street. Larry was back from Ireland, and he had to be debriefed, and the additional information disseminated amongst the team.

Chapter 12

Wendy continued with her investigations into the others that had been in the salon that day, placing emphasis on the four whose bodies still remained in the mortuary. She discounted Waverton, the banker, soon enough. The man had no criminal record, no known associates, and although he was financially sharp, there had never been any suggestion of anything untoward. With him out of the way, her focus turned to Sal Maynard, once again travelling out to where she had lived.

Time had moved on for the Maynards, not a close family, in that though it was only a few weeks since the daughter had been shot, there was a raucous party in full swing at the depressing flat in Stockwell. Wendy parked her car, careful not to leave anything inside that suggested it was a police issue, and walked up to the tenement, pushing past a group of youths attempting to look menacing, but looking stupid instead. Wendy took the lift to the ninth floor where it stopped with a shudder.

At the flat, Sal's heavily-tattooed older brother opened the door to Wendy's knock. 'Bad time? Wendy said.

'It depends, doesn't it?'

'On what?' Wendy took two steps back as she didn't want to get too close to the man, who was clearly drunk.

'Are you here to party or to cause trouble?'

'I'm here conducting further investigations into the death of your sister.'

'Not partying, a shame. I like older women, more experienced.'

Wendy retreated from the door and back to the relative safety of her car parked on the street below. A teenage boy riding a bicycle, his shirt hanging out and a cigarette in his mouth, approached her.

'Are you here about Sal?' he said.

'Yes. What do you know about her?'

'Knowing too much around here only causes you problems.'

'It'll cost, is that what you're saying?' Wendy said.

'A man has got to make a living somehow, and you look as though you've got plenty.'

'Man? You should be in school.'

'What's the point? All they want to do is to teach us about other places, and how to spell and write and to add up. What use is that to me?'

'It'll get you a job.'

'Not me. I make enough.'

Wendy's two sons were a credit to her, both married with children and holding down good jobs, but the individual in front of her, no more than sixteen, was unlikely to make thirty, she thought, if he continued the way he was. His future, she decided, was either drugs or prison or both. Regardless, she needed to know what he was referring to.

'How much?'

'A good feed first, McDonald's will do. And five hundred pounds.'

'For what? To tell me that Sal Maynard didn't do much and the Maynards are criminals. Is that it? Or are you going to tell me that they robbed the local newsagents? I'm investigating Sal's murder, not chasing petty criminals.'

'It's more than that.'

'Very well. Fifty pounds and another ten for McDonald's. You can go on your own afterwards.'

'It's a deal. There's a park not far from here, down the end of the road, the second turn on the right. I'll meet you there.'

'If this is a trick…'

'It's not. It's good, you can trust me, and Sal, she wasn't such a bad sort. A bit stupid, but she would always talk to me, sometimes buy me a drink.'

'You're underage.'

'The publican doesn't worry too much, and besides, I go around the back. Sal deals with him, you know what I mean?'

'I'm not sure that I do. What's your name?'

'Ralph, although everyone calls me Ralphie.'

'Okay, Ralphie, you need to earn your money. The park or down at the local police station.'

'No deal. They know me down there.'

'And what will they tell me when I check with them?'

'They'll tell you I'm a liar and can't be trusted. But what do they know, stuck in that station of theirs? It's tough, and the police don't like it up here, and they don't like the Maynards, and they don't like me.'

Wendy could understand why. 'What's your surname?'

'I don't want to give it,' the youth said.

'Don't be stupid. You've told me your name is Ralph, and that you prefer to be called Ralphie. You ride a bike, you know Sal and the local pub, and you've got two earrings and I can see a tattoo in the shape of a cross on your arm, or I assume that's what it's meant to be. Did it yourself, did you? I'm sure the police could tell me your full name, where you live, the crimes you've committed, even the days you failed to go to school. Fifty pounds and a Big Mac is dependent on you playing ball with me.'

'Okay, Ralph Ernest Begley. Satisfied?'

'For the moment. Five minutes, at the park.'

Wendy phoned Bridget, updated her as to her movements, before driving the short distance to the park. Ralphie was waiting on her arrival, his bike propped up against a bench where he sat.

'You'll be seen,' Wendy said.

'That's alright. The others know I'm here, and I'm taking them all to Maccas afterwards.'

The highlight for the local hoodlums, McDonald's, Wendy thought but did not comment to the young man, knowing full well that he probably came from a dysfunctional home, his parents in and out of work, drinkers, and the father possibly with a criminal record. Ralphie's problem was that his outlook on life was an inherited trait.

'What do you have?'

'The money first.'

'If you think you can be smart with me, then you've got another think coming,' Wendy said as she opened her handbag, withdrew a small purse and handed over the money.

Ralphie looked at the money, the most he had seen in a long time, before stuffing it into the left pocket of his jeans. 'I saw Sal on the television. They said she worked in a shop,' he said.

'She sometimes did.'

'That's not all.'

'What do you mean?'

'Sal and me, we were friends. Nothing like what you're thinking, but we used to talk.'

'Why you?'

'I don't know. Maybe she saw that my life was similar to hers. She had ambition, did Sal. Not that she expected anything to change.'

'Why?'

'You saw Sal?'

'I saw her dead body.'

'Sal wasn't attractive. Heavy-boned she used to say, and she could hold her drink. She tried to better herself, but her family are trash. You know that.'

'I do.'

'Anyway, Sal told me about this man. It seems he fancied her, don't know why. That's her words, not mine.'

'Is this man important?'

'If Harry Maynard finds out that I told you, he'll find me and give me a good belting.'

'Why?'

'Harry is possessive. He regarded Sal as his property, not that he ever touched her. But Harry, he's bad news. Alex, the younger brother, doesn't do much, and the mother is a tyrant. I don't like her either. Strange really, that from that flat came Sal. If she had been pretty and slim, she could have made something of herself. Always had her head in a magazine about celebrities and movies stars.'

'An unhappy woman?'

'She was, but with this man, he used to pay her money, she was fine.'

'Prostitution?'

'Sal didn't think it was, but I saw him once.'

'Describe him?'

'Tall, foreign looking. Sal said he was from Europe somewhere.'

'Romania?'

'Where's that?'

'If you went to school, you'd know it was a country.'

'I've heard of Romans,' Ralphie said.

Wendy did not intend to give a geography lesson to someone who wasn't interested, and besides, she hadn't known a lot about the country before Briganti's and Cojocaru. And now, something about the Maynard woman. A woman who five minutes previously had been a bit player in the murders.

'Did Sal sometimes sell herself?'

'Harry, if he ever finds out it was me, he'll go crazy.'

'I'll not tell him it was you, but it's important. You want us to find out who killed her, don't you?'

'I suppose I do.'

'What does that mean?'

'I'm frightened. If they killed her, they could kill me.'

'Why?'

'I don't know. But I watch those programmes on the television.'

'That's fiction, this is reality. Sal wasn't the target, we're sure of that. But this man, he's important. Once again, was she selling herself?'

'Her mother did when she was younger, I know that. But yes, Sal was. Not often, not that she minded much. She would have done anything to get out of here. And those actresses in Hollywood, they're doing it all the time.'

'Ralphie, you need to get your head out of your backside and look around. What they write in the magazines and put on the television isn't fact, it's pulp for the gullible.'

'Sal believed it all, but then that was the way she was. Simple in some ways, smart in others.'

'Smart?'

'This man was promising to find her a place where they could meet, upmarket, with a concierge and all. She was excited, and she thought that he loved her.'

'Did he?'

'Not him. I saw him with her, the look on his face as he drove away.'

'Did you tell her?'

'Once I tried to, but she wasn't listening. And besides, I know who he is. I saw him on the television, standing not far from where she died. He was in the crowd.'

'You'd recognise him again?'

'I would.'

Wendy scrolled through the photos on her smartphone. 'That's him, that's the man that Sal used to go around with,' Ralphie said.

After Ralphie had gone, she made a phone call. 'DCI Cook's office, thirty-five minutes.'

Bridget hung up her end of the phone line and arranged for everyone to be in the office. Wendy had not told her what it was about, but she had known the woman for many years. Whatever it was, it was important.

***

Larry had attempted to leave Ireland, even getting as far as the airport in Dublin and checking in, returning the rental car on the way. The same lady who had taken his keys was surprised to see him standing back at the counter twenty minutes later.

'I'll need to extend. If you can use the same purchase order, it would be appreciated,' Larry said. He needed to be home, one of the children was not well, and his wife was fretting, but events in Ireland had taken precedence.

'I rented him the car,' she said.

'Who?'

'Seamus Gaffney. He's a regular, every six weeks, and he never misses one of the children's birthdays or a school open day.'

'How do you know all this? Larry asked.

'As I said, he was a regular. Sometimes you get to talking with the customers, and after so many years, we got to know each other well.'

'Strictly business?'

'Oh yes. Seamus was a family man, devoted to his wife. Not that I ever met her, but a good woman from what he said.'

Larry was anxious to be on the road as time was of the essence, but the clerk behind the counter had possible information. He could spare her a few minutes, and then he'd be off, returning to conduct a formal interview with her at a later time.

'He picked up the car from me the day he died. He was in a good mood, but then he always was when he came back to Ireland. I can understand that. I spent two years in England, not that I liked it that much. Apologies if I insult your country.'

'No apology needed. What can you tell me? What is there that would be of interest? Something has come up, I've got to go,' Larry said. His wife was on the phone, and she wanted to know why he would not be home that night.

'It was strange, not that I thought much about it at the time.'

'What was?' Larry said, eyeing the clock, running the car keys through his hand.

'I could swear he was being followed.'

'Any idea who? Can you describe the person?'

'That's it. I can't, not really. You tend to get an eye for people in this job, those who are going to feed you a stolen credit card, forged driving licence, those who should pay extra for additional insurance. Too many of them, I'm afraid. They rent a cheap runabout and then think it's a supercar or a four-wheel drive. And then they're back here with the vehicle claiming it was in that condition when they rented it, not that they get anywhere as they had a chance to complain at pickup, and we have photos before they leave. The insurance saves us a few arguments, that's all.'

'If you're so perceptive, how come you didn't figure this person?'

'Average height, average look, average clothes. It's as if he was experienced at blending in.'

'Professional, you might say.'

'Anyway, Seamus is off, and this person is agitating for his vehicle quickly. But if he's not booked ahead, or he's not on the database, it takes time.'

'Did he get the car?'

'He had to take one of the more expensive vehicles. Literally ran out of here, took off with his foot to the floor. The car's back here now, and there was no damage, so I assume he was a competent driver.'

'What luggage was he carrying?'

'Nothing special. A small suitcase, the type you can take on the plane with you.'

'His name?'

'It's on file.'

'English?'

'It's hard to tell these days, but yes, I'd say he was. Good-looking, if he wasn't so shifty.'

'Was he? How would you know?'

'It was him, wasn't it?'

'What do you mean?'

'He must have killed Seamus, such a nice man.'

'A nice man who saw and said too much,' Larry said, not elaborating on what he meant. 'I'll need you at the police station. I'll phone for a vehicle to pick you up. Is that okay?'

'Not really, but if it's important.'

'It is.'

Larry made a phone call, a patrol car arrived within five minutes. Larry left the office and jumped into the rental car. Twenty-five minutes later, he arrived at his destination. The crime scene was crowded with police officers, an ambulance, the crime scene examiners, the obligatory onlookers, the media. He flashed his warrant card at a police constable and was waved through. He parked back from the crime scene at a distance of twenty yards.

'I need to get up there,' he said to another constable who wasn't letting him through. 'It's important.'

'Not unless you're kitted up, it isn't,' the constable replied. Larry knew he was right, but it was urgent. Over to one side he saw one of the officers who had met him at the airport the day before.

'Can you get onto the crime scene team, get me some overshoes, gloves?' Larry said.

The officer walked over and gave him what he needed. 'We always keep some in the vehicle. It's tense here.'

'That's understandable,' Larry said as he ducked under the crime scene barrier. To the left of the road, a couple of floodlights. To the right, Ryan Buckley's car.

'In his driveway as he was coming home. You could be the last person to have spoken to him,' Fergus Turnley, the crime scene examiner, said after Larry had introduced himself and explained that he had only left the man a couple of hours previously.

Larry looked in the vehicle. Ryan Buckley was leaning back, his face covered in blood. His mouth was open, his eyelids still slightly open. Not far away, at the front door of the semi-detached house, a woman in her dressing gown could be seen. She was being held firmly by someone Larry assumed to be a neighbour or a friend. Larry remembered that Buckley had said that it wasn't a happy home, but the woman, thought to be the wife, looked sad, or maybe it was shock, or perhaps she had killed him.

Larry put the last option to one side; he knew that speculation served no purpose. The only known certainty was that Inspector Ryan Buckley, a man he had shared a Guinness with, was dead in his car, the result of a shot to the head at close range. The similarities to the murder of Seamus Gaffney were all too obvious.

Larry phoned Isaac to update him. They both kept the conversation short.

'If Seamus Gaffney and Buckley have been killed by the same person, that means the murderer knows you by sight,' Isaac said.

'I know, and I don't mind admitting it, I'm not feeling very comfortable at this time.'

'Work with the local police, keep us updated.'

'We might have a witness to the murderer, the lady at the car rental company. We'll go through the usual:

photos of known criminals, the passengers coming into the airport, driving licence, address.'

'Get back here as soon as you can. The situation is becoming more difficult,' Isaac said.

'I'll need two days,' Larry said.

'No more. See if you can find out who it was, and why.'

Chapter 13

Ralph Ernest Begley, a distinguished name for such a worthless individual, Wendy thought, but it wasn't her call to make character evaluations. Her responsibility had been to follow up on Sal Maynard and to confirm if she had been tied into what had happened at Briganti's, even if that proof came from an individual who would quickly be discredited as a witness in a court of law. Wendy knew how a smart defence lawyer would work, the soft build-up, pretending to be the man's friend, lulling him into a sense of security. And then, the shift in tactics, the ability to convince the witness that it could have been another day, another time. And had the witness been drinking, or maybe taken drugs?

Wendy knew that Ralphie wouldn't stand a chance, and even if they questioned the man he had identified, it wouldn't hold up, certainly not enough for a prosecution, not even enough to hold the man for twenty-four hours.

Isaac, not so pessimistic as Wendy, saw it differently. It was the first definite link between the crime at Briganti's and one of the victims, and now the triangle had been completed, and one of Cojocaru's associates was involved.

Ion Becali at home, occupied as he liked to be on a day away from his boss with a bottle of whisky and a woman, didn't appreciate the knock at the door, the two police officers standing there, requesting his attendance at Challis Street.

'Give me two hours, and I'll be there,' Becali had replied.

Two hours later, Ion Becali walked through the door of Challis Street Police Station. He was dressed in a suit, a white shirt with a tie. Isaac looked at him, knowing full well that the man's sartorial elegance wasn't going to save him from stiff questioning.

As Larry was still in Ireland, Wendy was seconded to sit along with her DCI in the interview room. The time was 2.30 p.m. Becali's breath still smelt of alcohol, although he was sober, and his face wore a scowl. Alongside him, Jerry Zablozki, a lawyer known to Challis Street. The man was a Jew, third-generation English of Polish descent. Outside of the interview room, Isaac liked the man: affable, open to discussing the law, his family; but inside, representing his client, the man wouldn't let anything pass. Isaac knew he would need to be careful.

Anything prejudicial or an inappropriate accusation would be noted by Zablozki, and if Becali came to be charged and standing up in front of a judge and twelve good people, the jurors, on a charge of murder, then Isaac's or even Wendy's statements would be used in the man's defence.

Isaac completed the formalities, informed Becali of his rights, the procedure to be followed. The man nodded his head, said yes as appropriate, gave his full name and address.

'My client regards his attendance here today as an affront to his integrity. He is an honourable and upstanding member of his community,' Zablozki said.

Isaac wanted to say the vicious and violent Romanian gangster community, but he did not. He merely said, 'Mr Becali is helping us with our enquiries. No charges have been laid against him, and we appreciate him coming here of his free will.'

'And if I hadn't?' Becali said.

'There are still questions to be answered.'

Zablozki turned to his client. 'Let it go. If you hadn't come, they would have obtained a court order, and you would have been regarded as a hostile witness.'

'I'm here,' Becali said. 'Let's get on with it.'

'Very well,' Isaac said. He had leant forward on his chair to assert his authority and to emphasise what he was to say. 'We have proof that you, Mr Becali, were meeting with Sal Maynard on a social basis.'

'What makes you think that? And yes, I know who she is.'

'It is necessary for you to state who she is, and what she has to do with my client,' Zablozki said.

Isaac knew the man was deliberately being obtuse.

'Sal Maynard was a young woman who was brutally murdered with seven others at Briganti's hairdressing salon. Mr Becali was meeting with her. The question is why didn't he tell us this before.'

Becali shifted uneasily on his seat. 'I meet with a lot of women.'

'Maintaining your image?' Wendy said.

'What image is that, Sergeant Gladstone?' Zablozki said.

Isaac gave Wendy a poke under the table, a 'keep quiet, don't bait the man' nudge.

'A man about town,' Wendy murmured.

'My client's personal activities are of no concern to the police or to anyone else. If he wishes to entertain a woman that's his prerogative. I'm sure you and your DCI would agree.'

'We would,' Isaac said. 'But the fact remains that we have irrefutable proof that Mr Becali and Sal Maynard were involved. We believe that the arrangement was commercial, at least on Mr Becali's behalf, although the information that we've received indicates that Sal Maynard was enamoured of Mr Becali, and even saw it as love.'

'Even if this was true, and we strenuously deny this, what has the woman's death got to do with my client?'

'Mr Becali was in the crowd outside Briganti's on the day of the shooting.'

'I don't deny that. I had heard about it, so I went down to look. Not that I stayed long.'

'Why not?' Isaac asked.

'I've seen shootings before.'

'In England?'

'Not here, but back home they happened from time to time.'

'And when you realised that it was a woman that you had been seeing?'

'If it was someone I knew, then she wasn't using that name.'

'Can you supply us with a list of names?'

'Not all of them, and sometimes they don't give a name. I don't spend time with them for their conversation. I saw a picture of the woman afterwards, not my type.'

'Plain, frumpish?'

'That's it. I like to spend a bit more. If you know what I mean.'

Wendy didn't appreciate the man's dismissive attitude towards a woman who had not met his ideal of perfection. She remembered back to her teens when she

110

had been the plain Jane and she had hung around with the prettiest girl in the village, the beauty and her friend. Sure, it had made her feel better, and there was always the drunken throwaway who'd give her some of his time, even make love to her in the back seat of a car, or behind a hedge. But Wendy knew her history had been different, in so much as her parents had been good people who had loved her, and she had been good at school. And then she had joined the police force, met her husband and married, had children. But Sal Maynard had had none of that. She had been doomed from the start, and she had followed her mother down the path to despair, and she had died because of it.

'Our witness will state that you dropped her off at the block of flats where she lives,' Wendy said.

'I don't make a habit of dropping them anywhere, not the rentals.'

'Neither my client's behaviour nor his morality are of any concern to the police,' Zablozki said, conscious of Becali's derogatory view of women.

'We are not here as arbiters of his beliefs,' Isaac said. 'We are trying to establish that he had a relationship with Sal Maynard. That does not mean that he was involved in her death, although it is suspicious.'

'Assuming I knew this woman, why would I want her dead? I've nothing to hide, and believe me, she wouldn't have learnt much from me, or maybe the art of lovemaking,' Becali said.

Isaac could tell that the man was becoming obnoxious on purpose, a belief that he had the interview in his control. Isaac knew that was when people started to make mistakes and to relax their guard.

'Mr Becali, are you categorically denying any knowledge of Sal Maynard?' Wendy said.

'I deny nothing. If I had been with her, I can't remember, and as for dropping her off, where did she live?'

'Stockwell.'

'Not me. It's a dump up there, not my sort of place.'

'Your continuing denial does you no credit,' Isaac said. 'We will continue to check, and there are CCTV cameras across London. It may take some time, but if you were with Sal Maynard, here or in Stockwell, we will find proof. Your visit to this police station will not be so cordial the next time.'

'Is that it?' Becali said. 'I've got one on the boil. I'd like to get back to her if I may?'

'Plain and frumpish?' Wendy said. She couldn't resist another go at the man.

'Beautiful and expensive,' Becali replied.

Isaac wrapped up the interview. Becali left, a car waiting outside for him. Wendy retreated in disgust back to Homicide and her desk. Zablozki came up to Isaac as both men stood outside the police station. Isaac had needed the fresh air after an odious encounter with a man who was known to kill people, although Sal Maynard seemed unlikely. He had been disgusted by Becali's dismissive condemnation of and disinterest in the woman, even if she had been part of life's flotsam. Whatever she had been, she deserved better in death.

'DCI, you're wasting your time with Becali,' Zablozki said. A short man, he barely came up to Isaac's shoulders. On his head, a kippah, or what most people referred to as a skull cap.

'I hope they're paying you well. It's not over yet.'

'Maybe I shouldn't mention it, but the rumours on the street are talking about the Russians. Any truth in it?'

'It's part of our investigation. I assume you're not too fond of them.'

'They were ruthless in my homeland. The reason my grandfather came to England. He was penniless then, worked hard, a lot of prejudice back then, still is in certain areas.'

'You've done well.'

'I'm English through and through. I took advantage of all this country has to offer. If the Russian criminal class is coming, I'd not like to see it.'

'Nor would we. What do you know of the Bratva?'

'The Russian mafia. Not a lot, only that they're ruthless.'

'Cojocaru's frightened.'

'DCI, we're heading into areas we shouldn't discuss. I'll bid you goodbye.'

As Zablozki walked away, Isaac shouted to him. 'Your client?'

The man turned around and smiled.

Isaac knew that his position was easier than Zablozki's. He had no illusions about guilt, all he had to do was to prevent further deaths, and find the culprits of those that had already occurred.

Chapter 14

Nicolae Cojocaru knew the man sitting opposite him, not personally but by reputation – Stanislav Ivanov.

Cojocaru had wanted the meeting to occur in England, Ivanov had not. A villa in the South of France was not of the Romanian's choosing, but he had had no option. The command had been given, and he had obeyed. To have not met with the head of the Tverskoyskaya Bratva would have been an affront, and as had often been with others, a death sentence.

Cojocaru studied Ivanov, careful not to be too obvious, aiming to gain an understanding of a man who had a fearful reputation. Cojocaru was nervous in his presence, the intended effect of someone who had the earthy look of a man of the soil, but clothing of the finest cut.

Surrounding the villa, there were expansive gardens. At the perimeter of the property, a high wall protected it from the view of those outside. Every fifty yards along the wall there was a man dressed in a suit, a Kalashnikov held firmly across his chest. The villa was a fortress and he, Nicolae Cojocaru, was inside it.

So much for a neutral location to hold discussions, Cojocaru thought. He was cornered, as was Antonescu. The squat man sat resolutely outside the room where the two crime bosses met.

'You have handled our business successfully for the last six years, but now there's a need to change,' Ivanov said. The message was clear. Do what I say, and you will survive. If you don't, you will die.

'Why the need to change?'

'Nothing is static.'

'Why here? Why not in London as I suggested?'

'I decide what happens. You will do what I command, or you will not see London again. Do I make myself clear?'

'You do,' Cojocaru said, seething at the way the man was dismissing him as if he were no more than a cockroach to tread under foot. He wanted Antonescu to come in from the other room and to shoot the man in the chest, but he knew that was not possible. In London, a possibility, but not in France, knowing full well that Crin Antonescu was unarmed and in the company of two of Ivanov's men.

'There are some who say that we should just take over, but I do not agree.'

'Tell me what you want. We have handled the distribution for you up till now.'

'You're a businessman. It's a scale of economics. We, the Tverskoyskaya, can lower the costs, increase the price, maximise the margin. You, Nicolae Cojocaru, cannot.'

'We have suppressed the competition.'

'Only in your area, and what are they, a bunch of spaced-out junkies from the Caribbean, no more than a handful of brain cells between them.'

'We agree, then.'

'Not on what is important. You've killed a few, frightened the others, no more than sheep, but what about the police? Are they in your pocket?'

'Some are, but England is not the same. They still have their rules and regulations, and most are incorruptible.'

'Then get rid of them. If you don't, we will. And what about that dwarf outside?'

'Crin Antonescu. He was a wrestler, I'd trust him with my life.'

'That is all well and good, but does he kill for you?'

'He has and often.'

'We showed you what we are capable of. Would he have been capable of that?'

'Was it necessary?'

'A man with morals. You'll not go far. I don't think we can use you,' Ivanov said as he raised himself from his seat. 'It seems another example is needed.'

Ivanov called to the other room. A bloodied Antonescu was dragged in, unable to stand without assistance.

'Will you work with us or will you die here, Cojocaru?' Ivanov said, pointing at Antonescu.

Realising that he was cornered, Cojocaru meekly replied, 'We will work together.'

Ivanov pulled a gun from inside his jacket and handed it to the Romanian. 'A sign of your loyalty. This way, I will know that you mean what you say.'

'Not Crin. He's been loyal to me, almost a friend.'

'There are no friendships in the Tverskoyskaya Bratva, only blind loyalty. Are you loyal?'

'I am,' Cojocaru said. He raised the gun and walked over to Antonescu. 'Sorry, my friend, I must do this.'

The former wrestler, then gangster, and now a victim, said nothing. Cojocaru pointed the gun at the man's heart and pulled the trigger.

***

Larry met again with the lady from the car rental company. It was surprising how upset she was.

'I saw him, the man who killed Seamus and now Inspector Buckley. I could have prevented it if I had reported the man.'

'Reported what? Larry said. Alongside him was Inspector Annie O'Carroll.

'You were not to know,' Annie O'Carroll, a career police officer, fifteen years in the Garda, and highly experienced, said. After Buckley's death there was an agreement with Buckley's and O'Carroll's superintendent and DCS Goddard for the two police forces to work together, a joint sharing of the case, given that the two murders had occurred in Ireland, yet the initial investigation remained in England.

The consensus was that the two men had been killed by the same man, although that was still awaiting final confirmation from Forensics and the crime scene examiners.

Seamus had been shot twice, the first with a rifle from a distance, a skilled shot. Ryan Buckley's shot had not required a great deal of skill, just the knowledge of where the man would be and when, the nerve to approach his vehicle in a lighted area and to pull the trigger. Buckley's street had been residential, and no CCTV cameras were nearby, although a person out late at night walking his dog had seen a car driving away at speed at the time of the murder. The description hadn't been good, only that the vehicle was medium sized, white or yellow, and the driver wore a cap.

The Garda, like the London Metropolitan Police, regarded the death of one of their own as a crime of the highest seriousness, even more so than the death of

Gaffney. Larry could understand the sentiment, having seen one of his partners die at the hands of a crime syndicate, a hit and run as he had crossed the road outside the police station.

'It doesn't pay to dwell on what might have been,' Larry said to the distraught woman. 'I could have had another drink, and who knows, Ryan Buckley might still be alive. What is important is that we apprehend whoever did it. Now, let's go back over what you told me. You said that the man was in a hurry to follow Seamus.'

'I did.'

'Are you sure it was Seamus? It could have been that the man was late for an appointment.'

'No, it was Seamus, I'm sure of it.'

'Why?'

'He wrote down the registration number when I gave the car keys to Seamus.'

'Assuming you're right on this, let's go back over what he looked like. And what about the vehicle he borrowed.'

'He returned it soon after Seamus died. He only had it for five hours, paid the full day rate.'

'We've checked the licence he showed you. It was stolen two months ago. Did you check the photo on it with the man?'

'I think I did, but I may have just taken a note of the name, the date of issue, the date of expiry. That's what the insurance people want.'

'The picture on the licence and the man could have been different?'

'I would have taken a cursory glance, but every day there are a lot of people renting, returning, extending. His insistence for me to hurry up didn't help.'

Larry could see that the seemingly unflappable woman who stood behind the counter was actually a nervy woman. He wasn't sure how much credence could be given to her testimony; however, the stolen driving licence was of concern.

'Not conclusive,' Inspector O'Carroll said. A red-haired woman in her forties, Larry had to admit to being impressed by the way she handled herself. Ryan Buckley, a hearty, friendly man had not impressed him. Sure, he had been competent at Seamus's murder scene, even handled himself well with the man's widow, but he had not had the attention to detail, the enthusiasm Larry expected.

'He wasn't the easiest,' Mrs Buckley had said when Larry met her. 'Sometimes we didn't talk for a few weeks, not that I can blame him totally. We're both fiery, and Ryan would drink too much, and then there was the occasional smell about him.'

'What kind of smell?'

'Another woman.'

'Any idea who?'

'I never asked, never wanted to know.'

'An unusual reaction,' Larry had said.

'I can deal with ignorance. The truth would have eaten at me. Not that it mattered, not after the first few times, and he kept to his room, I kept to mine.'

'You weren't sleeping together?'

'Not for four years. I suppose he had to do something about it, but I would have preferred us to be closer.'

'Then why weren't you?'

'It just became a habit, him and me, and now someone's killed him.'

'Anyone you can think of?'

'It'd be better if you ask down at the police station. There are plenty in prison because of him.'

After Sheila Gaffney, Larry couldn't help but make the comparison. Sheila was soft and comforting, even in her distraught state; Buckley's wife was not the same. A similar age to the other woman, she had maintained her figure, and it was clear that her appearance mattered to her more than it did to the other woman. He could warm to Sheila, but not to Dervla Buckley, a woman who had a husband that strayed. Larry resolved not to think badly of Ryan Buckley and to assist Inspector Annie O'Carroll to the best of his abilities. But London was where he needed to be, and even if the murderer was still in Ireland, the Irish police were as competent as those at Challis Street.

It was after midnight when Larry arrived back at his home in London, his wife waiting for him, a hot cup of tea and a meal. Not that he needed either, he was just glad to be home. For now, he would forget all that had occurred and savour his wife, and in the morning, it would be him that drove the children to school. He realised that if his wife was sometimes demanding and difficult, she was still the woman for him. He gave her a kiss, had a shower, and went to bed, asleep within five minutes.

***

Cojocaru arrived back in England no more than two hours after Larry. For the gangster, there was no welcome home by a loving wife, a meal on the table. All that he could look forward to was his penthouse flat with its view of the River Thames. Suddenly it did not seem so important. He made a phone call.

'The police are fishing,' Becali said on answering.

'They've got nothing. My place, twenty minutes,' Cojocaru said.

Becali wanted to say he was busy, but the tone in Cojocaru's voice told him that the female company he had was less important than a direct request from the man who had saved him from a dismal life in Romania.

'Antonescu is dead,' Cojocaru said as Becali walked through the door at the penthouse.

'How?' Becali said as he instinctively headed to the drinks cabinet to pour himself a whisky, another for his boss.

'They killed him in front of me, an example of what will happen to us if we don't comply.'

Becali knew that he should feel sad for the dead man, a colleague and someone who could always be trusted when there was violence to commit or murder to carry out. It was a time to say a few kind words about him and to reflect on the good times, the benevolent and generous acts he had committed, his goodness, but Becali could not. He could only remember the negatives, the Jamaican Rasta they had held down while they forced the man to give the names of those who could threaten Cojocaru, their strengths, their weaknesses, who they loved, where they lived. The man had said plenty before Antonescu had taken a brick and smashed it against the man's head. Apart from that, nothing came to mind. No times of sheer jocularity with the man, when both had been at ease with the world, and now he was dead.

'But why? We could have helped them.'

'We can and we will. The situation is difficult, and now you, Ion Becali, must raise yourself up and work with me. We are no longer the masters of our destiny, and what happened to Antonescu could happen to us.'

'We are doomed, you know that.'

'Our only hope lies in preventing the Russians from taking control, but I don't know how.'

'You spoke to the police. They could help.'

'They cannot stop this. Set up a meeting with the West Indians, let them know that the situation has become more serious.'

'Briganti's, did Ivanov admit to it?'

'Yes. It was a warning to us and to others.'

'I was hauled into Challis Street,' Becali said.

'Why?'

'One of my women died.'

'Zablozki?'

'He was there. They couldn't hold me, although they were trying to make a case out of it because I was seen outside her place, and then in the street outside Briganti's.'

'What is so important about her?'

'She was in Briganti's when it was attacked.'

'Hendry's woman?'

'The other one.'

'Why? You can afford better.'

'Sometimes, I fancy them that way. Reminds me of the old country when my choice was limited.'

'Why eat peasant food when you can afford the best?'

'It may be better in the old country for me now,' Becali said. A wave of nostalgia flowed over him, even a tinge of remorse that Antonescu was dead. He could not help but feel that Nicolae Cojocaru was not telling him the full story; the man never had in the past, only issuing commands. But now he was talking to him almost as an equal. Regardless, he would set up a meeting with the

West Indians, knowing full well that they would be suspicious.

Chapter 15

Larry sat in a café on Portobello Road. It was early in the day and whereas he had often been there for breakfast, now it was for a meeting with Marcus Hearne, one of the four at the house where they had met with Larry, put forward their concerns, even their willingness to open up on what they knew, what was happening. They had been worried then, and now Hearne admitted that they worried more.

'It's like this,' Hearne said. 'We met with you that day, told you what was going down, and how Cojocaru had taken over.'

'Not enough to bring the man in for murder,' Larry said.

'You'd need witnesses, a body.'

'And neither of them is likely.'

'That's why we brought you to the house.'

'Almost poisoned me, though.'

'Medicinal,' Hearne said, a wry smile on his face, the only sign of ease in the man. Larry couldn't warm to him in the same way he had to Rasta Joe, the beer-drinking Rastafarian. Larry, out on the street and ferreting around, heard plenty, always without proof. He knew for instance that Marcus Hearne was a murderer and that he had killed a man eight years previously in a vicious gang fight on a vacant block of land not far from Regent's Canal. It had been a settling of grievances between two rival gangs as to who controlled which part of the area. Larry would have said the police, if asked, but the gangs considered themselves masters of the area, although that had been before Cojocaru.

'I didn't feel any better for it,' Larry said. He ordered a coffee for himself, as well as breakfast. The importance of the meeting with the gang leader had exempted him from Homicide's early-morning meeting.

'We're willing to work with you on this,' Hearne said.

'You told me that before, but I don't remember anyone coming forward with anything worthwhile.'

'There wasn't much to tell you. After Briganti's, it went quiet.'

'There's always something happening, and you know it.'

'I'm not an informer.'

Larry felt no need to comment. Hearne had served time in prison before; he would be back there again, and if he, Detective Inspector Hill, had to be the person to arrest him then so much the better.

'Cojocaru, is that why we're here?'

'You know it is. What happened to Antonescu?'

'We don't know,' Larry admitted, not mentioning that it was known that the missing man had left England with Cojocaru and not returned. The French police were helping, at the request of the Met, and Braxton at Serious and Organised Crime was interfacing with Homicide.

'He's dead.'

'How do you know?'

'We don't need proof.'

'Do you know why?'

'Don't go wasting your time on him. He's not worth it.'

'It's still murder.'

'According to you, and what about Cojocaru wanting to meet with us?'

'When?'

'One day's time, a location of his choosing.'

'And what do you want me to do? Come to the meeting?'

'Of course not. But if we don't return, we want you to know about it, who'll be there and where.'

'You suspect a trap?'

'We do. Cojocaru never consulted with us before. All he did when he took over was to start killing anyone who got in his way. The man has his back to the wall now, and he wants our help.'

'If you let us know where and when we'll keep a look out for you. But you've got to level with me, no playing me for a sucker.'

'Not this time. If Cojocaru is going to issue ultimatums, it's going to get nasty.'

'And you and the others will be at the meeting unarmed and without backup.'

'We have no option.'

'I need something from you.'

'Name it.'

'Ion Becali and Sal Maynard, one of the women who died at Briganti's. We know he was messing around with her, although he denies it.'

'What do you suspect?'

'It's possible that Becali was involved. Possibly used her as a decoy. The woman was susceptible to the man's charm, saw it as love. He could have spun her a story about robbing the place. We don't have proof of anything, and it may be nothing, but we need to know if there was any more to it.'

'Becali hedging his bets, playing both sides?'

'Find out what you can and let me know. I'll protect you the best I can, but once the threat's been removed, I'll be after you for the crimes you've committed.'

'I'm not admitting to any.'

***

Two in the morning, Inspector Oscar Braxton phoned. Isaac took the phone call. 'Not too late for you, is it?' Braxton said.

'That's fine. I've not heard from you for a while,' Isaac said as he got out of bed, not wanting to disturb his girlfriend, and went into the other room. Instinctively he put the kettle on to make himself a cup of tea, knowing full well that a phone call at such an hour meant only one thing – developments.

'I'll do it,' Jenny said as she came into the room. Isaac had had problems with other romances, when the hours he worked, the midnight phone calls, had been something they said they could deal with, but none had, not until Jenny. She understood and he was grateful.

Isaac looked out of the window of the flat, saw a few lights in the other flats in the building, a couple arm-in-arm on the street, a drunk slowly making his way home. It was remarkable, he thought, that one of the world's major cities could be so quiet.

'Are you still there?' Braxton said.

'Yes. Just waking up.'

'Easy life at Challis Street, nine to five.'

'I wish.'

'Don't worry. I won't tell anyone you've got a cushy number.'

Isaac remembered the light-hearted repartee of the man from when they had first met years before. He took Braxton's comments in the spirit they were given.

'We followed up on Cojocaru in France. Disturbing news.'

'Give me the details.'

'Stanislav Ivanov.'

'I gave you the name,' Isaac reminded him. 'Cojocaru gave it to us, told me that he'd contact me in a couple of days, but never did.'

'Cojocaru and Antonescu were picked up at the airport in Marseilles and transported to a villa along the coast.'

'How do you know this?'

'Our counterparts in France keep a watch out for anyone of concern.'

'Cojocaru?'

'Not him. Ivanov has a villa down there. Surveillance picked up one of his cars at the airport and took a photo of the two men getting into it. It didn't ring a bell at the time, not a big one anyway. After we contacted them, passed on the details, they checked further. The car entered through the gates of the villa twenty-five minutes after leaving the airport.'

'Ivanov inside the villa?'

'He was, and some of his men. The French know he's got weapons in there, not that they can do much about it.'

'Why?'

'Model resident. He doesn't break any laws down there, uses it as his primary residence. Too hot, not the climate, in Russia, and he's always under threat of assassination. Makes sense if you're Bratva to keep out of the country.'

'Listening devices?'

'Not in the villa, and the area's been swept by Ivanov's men. Anywhere that could have been used to eavesdrop has been removed, including a couple of houses where the residents were obliged to sell.'

'Or else?'

'That's it. Anyway, Cojocaru leaves the villa after fifteen hours. He's on his own, and the same car drops him off at the airport. That's all we know.'

'Antonescu?'

'He's not been seen since.'

'Larry Hill's been told that he's dead.'

'A reliable source?'

'Not one hundred per cent, and there's no way whoever told Larry would have been in that villa.'

'Unless Antonescu appears we'll assume that he is,' Braxton said. 'The ball's in your court. Find out what's going on. And one other thing, a shipment of weapons was intercepted in France.'

'Forwarding address?'

'Cojocaru, not that it was on the manifest documents, but we know of a few aliases and how they get the drugs in.'

'Which means there's another shipment that you've missed.'

'The quantities indicate something major. You'd better get extra people on the street.'

'We're working on it.'

'Okay. I'll let you get back to sleep,' Braxton said.

'Not much chance of that now.'

***

Inspector Annie O'Carroll continued with the investigation into the deaths of Seamus Gaffney and Inspector Ryan Buckley. Forensics had given a ninety per cent probability that the two men had not been murdered by the same person. No gun had been found at either location, even after dredging the local waterways and scouring through the usual places where they could have been dumped.

Feeling the effects of being a woman in a male enclave, the eyes of others on her performance, she phoned Larry in London.

'Any chance of you coming back here?' she said. 'Ryan Buckley's death is professional, and we've no leads. Seamus Gaffney's is probably local.'

'What about the car that followed Gaffney from the airport?'

'Kathleen Pearse from the rental company has proven to be an unreliable witness. We found the driver here. He had dropped the car back at the airport but didn't catch a flight. He's in custody for a burglary he committed four years ago. We had him on our radar, that's why the false driving licence, the bogus address.'

'The reason for him hurrying off?'

'His mother was on her deathbed. He got there five minutes too late. Still, once we caught up with him, we had to arrest him. No doubt he'll be allowed to attend the funeral.'

'Which means Seamus Gaffney is still unsolved, and no leads.'

'I'm not getting a lot of help from my colleagues with Gaffney, plenty with Ryan. And we can't assume that the man had an English accent, doesn't hold weight now.'

'Not really. If he were Romanian, it would help.'

'Not that I'd know Romanian from Bulgarian or Greek,' Annie O'Carroll said.

'No one would. If we could link it to Cojocaru and his men, it would be a bonus. Although one of them is not around now.'

'What happened?'

'Went on a trip to the south of France, never came back. Serious and Organised Crime is putting him down as missing in action, presumed dead.'

'Murdered?'

'Poetic justice if he is. There's an attempt to bring in a large shipment of weapons from the continent, and the gangs are nervous, even meeting with Cojocaru. And then we've got Stanislav Ivanov not far behind.'

Larry had to admit to enjoying his conversation with the Irish police officer, but unless the situation changed, he'd have to stay in London.

Wendy had spent more time with Ralphie; his family, not as dysfunctional as Sal's, although still uncaring, had not impressed Wendy when she had met them. His father lounged in a well worn chair, the television showing the horse races, his phone at his side to place the bets. Apart from that, the man did little other than complain about how they had laid him off at work, a menial cleaning job, on account of his bad back, and he was going for worker's compensation for the permanent injury that he had suffered. Not that Wendy had seen much of the injury when the man jumped out of his seat when his horse had won.

'See, I told you that I could pick them,' he said to his wife, Ralphie's mother.

'About time,' the only words to emanate from the woman. Even when Wendy had questioned her about Sal Maynard, her replies had been monosyllabic, just yes and no. Ralphie's father had been more forthcoming in saying that Sal's mother was just a tart and the daughter was no better, just a useless lump of lard. Wendy could only sympathise with Ralphie, and she vowed to help him if she could.

Outside the house, Ralphie had been apologetic, although his vocabulary was interspersed every few words with a four-letter expletive.

'Did Becali kill Sal?' Ralphie asked.

'We've no proof.'

'You don't need proof to know whether he did or not.'

'We don't think so. And whatever you do, keep well away, the man's violent. I don't want you getting involved.'

'It'd be more interesting than around here.'

'It probably would be, but Ralphie, mark my words. Becali is not a person to be trifled with and never approach him. You must promise me that,' Wendy said, speaking to him as she would have her own sons when they had been younger.

'I won't. Promise.'

Wendy left Ralphie, having gained no more information. She had only come back to the area after Becali's importance in the investigation had risen. With Antonescu out of the picture, the murder of Buckley could have been at Becali's hand. A window of opportunity had been discovered for the second murder in Ireland, long enough for the Romanian to have made the trip over, probably using a false name and identification. And no need to use a rental car, as local transport, especially the train from the airport to a station, no more than a five-minute walk from Buckley's house, ran at regular intervals.

Becali was front and centre, and at Challis Street, the team met again. This time in the presence of DCS Goddard. The man was not happy, not that anyone else was, and an air of inadequacy had settled over those present. A team honed through numerous murder investigations, sometimes challenging, sometimes procedural, but now the clues were too few and far between.

Larry was the first to speak, that is after Goddard had given his usual speech about working 'the hours required, I expect everyone to do their bit, the eyes of the commissioner are on us'. They had all heard it before, and it hadn't been necessary, but Isaac could see that the man was wearying of the battle to keep Commissioner Alwyn Davies out of Homicide, as well as his man, Superintendent Caddick.

'Inspector O'Carroll believes the hit on Ryan Buckley was professional. If it was, then Becali's a possibility, and what about him and Sal Maynard?'

'I feel sorry for the woman,' Wendy said. 'She had a dreadful home life, and then scum like Becali treat her like a piece of meat.'

'We're not here to discuss the injustices of the world,' Isaac reminded her. 'Only who's guilty and who's not. And what about Seamus Gaffney? Larry, you knew him, what do you reckon, the sort of man to make enemies?'

'Apart from informing, I'd say not. A likeable man, but he knew what was going on, and was willing to part with some of it for a price. But I reckon he kept quiet on some things, too dangerous otherwise.'

'Would he have known about Briganti's?'

'Who knows? We're assuming Cojocaru didn't. Otherwise, he wouldn't have met Ivanov in France.'

'According to Oscar Braxton, you don't debate whether to meet the man or not. A command is what you receive, and failure to attend is at your peril.'

'Becali didn't go to France,' Wendy said.

'No chance. He was here with us, and we were keeping a watch on him. And if he was in Ireland, then he was busy. Maybe he wasn't summoned to France.'

'Which means he could be working for the man.'

The name of Stanislav Ivanov had filtered through to Westminster, and politicians on both sides of the House were out trying to gain brownie points by accusing the other of inaction over terrorism in the past, and now organised crime.

The team in Homicide knew which of the two was the worst. Terrorism was ideological, organised crime was commercial, and money speaks, and Ivanov had an unlimited amount. Yet the man, with no criminal record, freely entered England on a regular basis, travelling in his personal jet, a retinue of staff with him, a Rolls Royce on arrival, a house in Bayswater. To those who would see him in the best restaurants and the best clubs, at the football or the races, he was an example of the new Russia. To those who had examined his history and that of Russian organised crime, he was the most malevolent and foul sore to blight that country.

'Larry, the venue for the meeting with Cojocaru and Marcus Hearne and his colleagues?' Goddard asked.

'Colleagues? A generous term.'

'Compared to what we've got now, they're almost gentlemen.'

'Hearne hasn't got the venue yet. He's on the way, diverting here and there. He reckons it's a farce, but then he's not a patient man.'

'What would Ivanov say if he knew about it?'

134

'The Russians hate the Romanians, and they'll not take commands from Cojocaru.'

'Bridget, follow up with Larry. Once he's got the venue, attempt to set up the best surveillance we can,' Isaac said.

'Isn't that a job for Serious and Organised Crime?'

'We're working together on this.'

'I'm meeting with Davies,' Goddard said. 'The man wants answers.'

'We've not given him much.'

'I'll keep him off our backs for now. Rome wasn't built in a day, and the team's handling the case well. Mind you, I'd rather meet with Cojocaru. At least the man wants to negotiate. With Commissioner Davies, it's a one-way decision-making process.'

'The best of luck,' Isaac said.

'Don't worry about me. The worst he can do is throw me out on my ear. You're messing with people who kill.'

'We'll be careful,' Wendy said.

Chapter 16

Marcus Hearne never made the expected phone call about where the meeting was to be held. Larry was at the crime scene within forty minutes of receiving the notification.

'It's a messy killing,' Gordon Windsor said. He was standing to one side of the ditch, looking down at two of his team in the water. The body was face down, although its wallet had floated to the surface, a driving licence providing identification. 'What do you know about him?'

'Marcus Hearne, gang leader, someone I used to meet with from time to time,' Larry said.

'You pick your friends well.'

'We needed Hearne,' Larry said.

'That's why he's dead.'

'It makes no sense.'

'Is this to do with Briganti's?'

'Yes.'

Larry could see no more to be gained at the murder scene. He drove back to Challis Street. He was not in a good mood.

The first person he saw on his arrival at the police station, the obnoxious and unwelcome Superintendent Caddick. 'Bad day,' the man said.

'Not the best. What are you doing here?'

'What are you doing here, sir,' Caddick replied. Larry could see that the man hadn't changed: overly impressed with his own importance, incompetent without equal. The man was a walking disaster, and he was in Challis Street.

'Are you coming back, *sir*?' Larry said, adding emphasis on the 'sir'. It was close to impertinence, but he didn't care, and if Caddick wanted to write a report about his attitude, then that was fine. Larry walked away and left Caddick standing where he was.

In Homicide, the welcome face of Isaac in his office.

'Caddick's downstairs,' Larry said.

'He's been in here. I gave him his marching orders. If the man wants to make something of it, that's up to him. Marcus Hearne?'

'Dead, one bullet.'

'No idea where Cojocaru is?'

'The general area, but it doesn't help us.'

'Stanislav Ivanov landed in his private jet ninety minutes ago,' Isaac said.

'To attend the meeting?'

'We don't think so. He's at his house in Bayswater. We've got people staking it out.'

'Is he on his own?'

'A couple of women, they looked expensive. And then there are some bodyguards.'

'Armed?'

'Not on arrival.'

'It's all coming to us,' Larry said. 'And Caddick?'

'He's just sticking his nose in. The man's come to gloat. He'll wait until we've got the case almost solved. Then he'll be back to take my seat or DCS Goddard's.'

'We'd better solve it sooner than later,' Larry said.

'Marcus Hearne, what did you expect him to tell you?'

'If Cojocaru had offered him a sweetener, he might have told me nothing.'

***

The revelation, coming later in the day, was a shock. So much so that Larry had taken the first flight to Ireland. Upon landing, Annie O'Carroll had been there to welcome him. To see her there, a half-smile on her face, lifted the dark mood that he had carried all day.

'You've cracked it?' Larry said.

'One of them. I've booked you into the same hotel as before.'

'Not sure if I can stay. The situation in London is fluid. Ivanov's in the country, and Cojocaru's missing, as are three of the West Indian gang bosses. There's a palpable tension on the streets. No one wants to be caught in the action if anything happens.'

'Is that likely?'

'People panic, especially when they are being fed rumours from opposing sides. But if Ivanov has had Cojocaru and the others killed, then who knows?'

The two police officers drove in silence; Larry took the opportunity to close his eyes for a few minutes.

Inside the house they had driven to Sheila Gaffney sat silently in one corner of the room. 'I'm sorry about this,' she said.

'Why didn't you tell us before?' Larry said.

'I was upset over Seamus's death. I did love him, but he was away for so long each time. I had hoped he would have come back to live with us, and when he said that he would, I told Ryan that it was over.'

'How long had you been having an affair with him?'

'Five years, on and off. Ryan couldn't accept what it was, just a casual fling. He saw it as love, and no doubt with Dervla being difficult, I seemed the ideal choice for him. He became angry when I told him.'

'When was this?'

'The same day as Seamus arrived, early in the morning. Long enough for, well, you know.'

'We know now.'

'Mrs Gaffney, you're pregnant,' Annie O'Carroll said.

'It's Seamus's, I know that. I wouldn't have done that to him.'

'The full story, in your own time,' Larry said.

Sheila Gaffney got up from where she had been sitting and walked around the room before sitting back in the same chair. She seemed to have visibly shrunk.

'It was after the third child. Before that, they came at regular intervals, and I was always busy looking after them. And then a spell where I failed to get pregnant. Seamus was still commuting, supporting us as he always did. I became lonely, maybe because I wasn't expecting, and from loneliness comes melancholy and then reflection, and finally the need to do something. It was on one of Ryan's visits. He was always dropping in to see how we were. Seamus, the rogue that he was, and Ryan, a police officer. It's hard to believe the friendship between the two men, but it never wavered.

'Ryan is here, and I knew that he always liked me, always commenting if only his wife could be more like me, and then it happened. I wanted to say no, but I couldn't. And afterwards, I thought I should feel guilty, but I didn't. I felt loved, and by two men. After that, he'd come over occasionally, but he started to become serious. He even spoke of my divorcing Seamus, he divorcing

Dervla, and for us to get married. I had wanted to end it for some time, always too afraid to do it, and then Seamus is on the phone saying that he's coming back for good.'

'Ryan Buckley's reaction?' Larry said.

'He stormed out of here, ever so angry. He said he was going to have me one way or the other.'

'Which you interpreted as meaning that he intended to murder your husband?'

'No. Ryan could be hot-headed but I could never have imagined that he would harm Seamus.'

'We've proof?' Larry asked Annie.

'We had never considered Ryan as the murderer. A fellow police officer, a loyal friend of the family.'

'And?'

'When Sheila told me, we re-examined the evidence, checked on Ryan's movements. His car was fitted with GPS monitoring. We backtracked where it had been driven and found a layby where he had pulled in. Our people went there and found the weapons. It's conclusive. Ryan murdered Seamus,' Annie said. She had her arm around Sheila Gaffney.

Larry realised there were no words that he could offer that would alter the anguish and the shame that Gaffney's widow felt. He left the house and returned to Annie's car. Five minutes later she came out of the house.

'It came as a shock, but we have our murderer,' Annie said.

'What about Buckley's killer?'

'That still remains unsolved.'

'I should get back to London. If you could drop me back at the airport, I'd be grateful,' Larry said. He had spent just under three hours in Ireland before he boarded the plane for the return journey; his despondent mood had returned.

***

'It sticks in your throat,' Oscar Braxton said. Isaac and Larry were at New Scotland Yard in Braxton's office. On the television, a football match, and in the owner's box, Stanislav Ivanov. 'That's the trouble, people just don't care. Look at them fawning over him, making him out to be something special instead of the grubby gangster that he is.'

Isaac could sympathise, knowing full well that there were more villains outside of the prisons than in, and with enough money anyone was innocent. He realised that it was a pessimistic view of the law, and any attempt at meeting with Ivanov, possibly bringing him into Challis Street, would be met with a barrage of Queen's Counsels, all of them at the pinnacle of their legal prowess.

The philanthropic businessman was how the football team saw him, the general public if they knew of him, but never as the head of a violent criminal gang, only separated from the hoodlums causing trouble of a Saturday evening after a few too many drinks by his wealth.

'We can't touch him, I suppose?' Isaac asked.

'He doesn't break any laws in this country, and back in Russia, he's protected. Friends in high places protecting his back, him protecting theirs. And now, the man is making a move in this country.'

Larry, glad to be back home with his wife and their children, having arrived the previous night, said little, although the events in Ireland had unsettled him. Sheila Gaffney, the dutiful wife, a person who caused no harm to anyone, now tainted as a scarlet woman in the press; the reputation of Ryan Buckley in shreds.

'Look at that,' Braxton said. On the television, Ivanov making a speech about how he was honoured to be the owner of such a prestigious club, and how he was looking forward to making England his home.

'He wants the place for himself,' Isaac said.

'He intends to run his criminal empire from here. And there's nothing we can do about it.'

'Any more on Crin Antonescu?'

'He never left Ivanov's villa. And now you have another death, Marcus Hearne. He'll not be missed, I assume.'

'Not by us,' Larry said. 'His family maybe.'

'Not really relevant, is it? What about the other so-called leaders of their communities? Any chance of finding out what was said at the meeting with Cojocaru? He must be quivering in his boots with Ivanov coming here on a permanent basis.'

'They're not talking at present. Since Hearne died, I've not heard from them.'

'Cojocaru has left the country,' Braxton said.

'Where to?'

'Romania. He knows he's the meat in the sandwich. It would help if we knew the story of what happened to Antonescu.'

'We may never find out,' Isaac said. 'Was there a reason for us coming up here?'

'We've had a lead on who may have killed Ryan Buckley.'

'Who and how?' Larry said.

'We checked with our counterparts in Russia, the ones we can trust.'

'Some you can't?'

'Corruption's endemic there. You're either part of the system, or you're dead. But there are one or two who

142

keep a low profile, take the backhanders, keep us informed. We checked on a couple of names we received from them, men who Ivanov uses outside of Russia.'

'Do you have photos on file, any other details?'

'We've checked on the movements of the two men. One of them is arrogant enough.'

'Has he been in England?'

'He's French, and he's been in Ireland, as well. We've checked with the police over there, and we've had our CCTV people looking for him. He came in through Belfast and then took a train to Dublin. From there, he disappeared for a couple of days, probably stole a car or hired one using false ID. From Dublin, he crossed to Wales on the ferry and disappeared. The French police have a lead on him. I'm going to France on Eurostar tonight. I assume you'll both come with me.'

'I will,' Isaac said. He had promised to take Jenny out that night to a restaurant, a celebration of six months together, but he knew she'd understand.

'I'll pass,' Larry said. 'I need to be back in Ireland. If he's been there, we'll need proof that he spoke to Sheila Gaffney.'

'Agreed, that's a plan,' Isaac said. He had a phone call to make at the conclusion of the meeting; he had to phone Richard Goddard. The wolves were closing in on the man again, and a fresh lead, a link between a murder and an organised crime leader, would give Goddard and the Homicide department a breather of a few days before further questions as to why the shooting at Briganti's was still without a murderer.

***

The three remaining gang leaders considered their position carefully. As had been agreed with Cojocaru, they were lying low for a few days, a house on the south coast, a supply of good food, good drink, and five women, recent arrivals in the country who did not speak English, other than a smattering. Of the five, two had been known to Becali in the old country. They were there to ensure the men did not leave the house until the all-clear had been given. The other three were there for entertainment.

'It's either Stanislav Ivanov or me,' Cojocaru had said. 'You're smart men, you'd not want the Russian mafia, and they'd not want you.'

At the end of four hours, during which Cojocaru had stated his case and told the three about the barbaric acts committed by Ivanov, and that the man had admitted to the attack at Briganti's, there was an agreement to give the Romanian three days. After that time, they'd decide as to whether the Romanians and the other gangs would combine against a common enemy.

The second day. 'We're in trouble here,' Devon Harris, a tall man from Barbados, said. Back in the West Indies, he had been hustling the tourists out of their hard-earned money, but with an English grandfather who had been white, and a brother who had permanent residency in England, he had managed to deal with the bureaucracy and to legally enter the country. His contribution to the country that had taken him in: two murders, another maimed for life. And what had it given to him? The opportunity to use his streetwise cunning to build up his gang until he was supplying Notting Hill up through Bayswater and Paddington with drugs. He would have said that he had done well for himself, but now he wasn't so sure.

144

'Cojocaru has given us his word that we are safe,' Jeremy Miller, the second of the gang leaders, said. Second generation, born in London, he was a softly-spoken man, his Jamaican accent the result of growing up in Trench Town, a wild and lawless suburb of Kingston, the Jamaican capital. The left side of his face had a scar from just below the eye down to his upper lip, the result of a knife fight when he was fifteen. He shouldn't have been in his parents' place of birth, but his father had died after he had cheated on another gang leader in London, and Miller's mother had quickly taken the three-year-old back to Jamaica. Not that the place was much safer, but the threat against her son was reduced by distance. At the age of eighteen, Miller had returned to London and had used his quiet yet authoritative manner to work his way up through his gang, using his innate intelligence and his ruthless ability to remove anyone in his way by whatever means seemed appropriate.

'Cojocaru's word meant little when he came to England. Do you believe him now?' Harris said.

'He can never be trusted, but what can we do?'

'If we are to throw in our lot with Cojocaru, what guarantees do we have that he will honour what has been agreed?'

'What has been agreed? And what of Marcus Hearne? And these women can't be trusted, junkies the lot of them, apart from those two over there.'

The third gang leader, Claude Bateman, older than the others, sat without saying a word. He looked over at one of the three women who had just walked in the door. 'While you two debate, I intend to keep myself occupied. He grabbed the woman – blonde, no more than nineteen or twenty – and led her away. The two other women in the room, supposedly not available, looked at Devon Harris and Jeremy Miller.

'I'd take the one on the left,' Harris said.

'They understand what we're saying, or she does. Did you see her reaction when you mentioned her? We used to control everything, and now we're here, no more than children waiting for the parent to decide what to do with us.'

'We may not leave here alive, have you considered that?'

'I have. What do you suggest?'

'For now, nothing. Bateman had the right idea. If we leave here, then we have the Russians to deal with. If we stay here, then it's Cojocaru. I trust neither, but we must wait and hope that the cards are in our favour.'

'You are an optimist when there is no reason for optimism. We're sitting ducks in here, targets out there.'

'Then I'm taking the one who pretends she doesn't understand English. You can choose amongst the others.'

The woman who had previously resisted any advances by the three men stood up and took hold of Harris's hand. The other gang leader sat in his chair, pensively weighing up the options.

Chapter 17

Emotions were running high at New Scotland Yard in Commissioner Alwyn Davies's office. The man could see from the reports that the investigation into the murders at Briganti's was far from resolved. Goddard had nothing to say, not in defence of his position, and for once the blustering, belligerent and political animal Davies was right.

'We've got a lead on who killed Inspector Buckley in Ireland,' Goddard said.

'What's Ireland got to do with this? It's London I'm concerned about, and especially your part of it. I put you back there against my better judgement, and this is how you repay me. You could have got rid of Cook. The man's a walking liability with his laid-back approach to policing.'

'I don't believe that's a fair assessment of the situation and of DCI Cook.'

'Fair! When did fair come into it? We've got hoodlums running around the streets, arming themselves from what I hear, and you talk about fair. Get real, man. You're a chief superintendent, not a welfare counsellor. You need to ride your men, be there every minute, following up on every aspect of the case. But what do you do? Leave it to them, and now this. This Cojocaru, how long's he been in the country?'

'Nine to ten years.'

'And he's a major distributor of illicit drugs?'

'He is.'

'Why? You've had long enough to get him under control.'

'Attempts are being made to get him deported.'

'You can't deal with men like him through the courts. More QCs than you and I have had hot dinners. You need to bait him, let him show his true colours, force him to commit a crime. Time's against you on this one, and Caddick's waiting for the say-so from me. Give me one good reason why I shouldn't dump your Cook and put Caddick in. He'll not mess around.'

'Sir, with all due respect,' Goddard said, 'Superintendent Caddick is the last person we need at Challis Street at this time.'

'Don't give me "with all due respect". You don't like Caddick, nor does Cook, but that's not the point. We need to show action on this matter, and you're telling me it's under control and we have a suspect. Frankly, it does very little to quell my nerves. A gang war is the last thing we want at this time.'

'That's what we're trying to prevent. Isaac Cook is in France with Serious and Organised Crime. Inspector Hill is in Ireland checking on the Frenchman, gathering evidence.'

'I read the report of Stanislav Ivanov. A nasty piece of work if Serious and Organised Crime is correct.'

'They invariably are. We can't touch the man, not legally, and he's well-protected.'

'Why do we let such scum into the country?'

'You'd better ask the government. Obscenely rich and you're welcomed in. Poor and desperate and the doors are bolted.'

'Yes, we know all that, but what are you going to do? And don't give me your usual platitudes. The situation is not under control. Are we going to have a repeat of what happened at the hairdressing salon?'

'It's unlikely.'

'And how do you know this? The reports indicate that Ivanov is probably involved, yet you can't make the connection. So how can you say it's unlikely?'

Davies paced around the room, did not speak for what seemed to be an eternity to Goddard, but was less than twenty seconds.

'One week,' Davies said.

'And then what, sir?' Goddard asked.

'To come up with some results. And if there are any mass murders in the interim, don't bother reporting, just send me your resignation, an email will be fine.'

Davies had broken every rule in the book by his dismissive and derogatory dressing down of a chief superintendent. Goddard knew he would be wasting his time taking the matter forward.

***

With Larry in Ireland and Isaac in France, Wendy Gladstone was in the office with Bridget Halloran. One variable remained outstanding: the presence in Briganti's of Sal Maynard.

'If she was there as a distraction,' Wendy said, 'she wasn't looking to get herself killed.'

'Her life wasn't that good. Was she stable, mentally?'

'According to Ralph Begley, she was.'

'You reckon that if the woman was in there, it was because of Ion Becali?'

'Yes. Which would mean that he was involved.'

'Becali's playing it both ways?' Bridget said.

'Men have died for less, but why? Becali's a disgusting man, but he's not stupid. If you cross Cojocaru, you end up dead. If you cross Ivanov, you end up dead. Not good odds whichever way you look at it.'

'If you're faced with two imponderables, you choose the path of least resistance, the winning side.'

'Who's the winner?'

'Us, hopefully. But if I had to stake money, I'd say Ivanov.'

With no more to discuss, Wendy went back to her desk. The office felt cold without the other two police officers. She sat and looked at the blank screen of her laptop, realising that a feeling of negativity had come over her, negativity she could not shake. Inaction and apathy, two conditions that she had always avoided, had surfaced with a bang. She stood up with a start, pushing her chair back with such force that it upended.

'What's the problem?' Bridget said, not used to seeing her friend in such a state.

'Impending doom. As though there's something in the air so tangible that you could cut it with a knife, yet we can't see it.'

'You were talking about Ion Becali before. Is that it?'

'I'm not sure. The injustice of it gets to me sometimes. Becali is out there larger than life, Cojocaru is enjoying the sweet life, and Stanislav Ivanov acts as though he owns the country. And there's Sal Maynard who did nothing wrong in her life, except wanting to better herself; and there she is, forgotten and not even missed by her own family.'

'She wasn't the only one in Briganti's,' Bridget said.

'I know that, but the others had been loved, even Alphonse Abano. But with Sal, nobody.'

'There's Ralphie.'

'It's not sufficient.'

'Welcome to the human condition. If she wasn't loved, there's not much you can do about it.'

'There is. I can give her justice.'

'How?'

'By making sure whoever talked her into going into that salon and draping herself around Hendry is brought in and charged with being an accessory to murder.'

***

Cojocaru sat in his suite at the Radisson Blu Hotel in Bucharest. Located on Calea Victoriei, it was not far from Revolution Square, the scene of a disastrous speech by another Nicolae, Nicolae Ceausescu, the former president, who had been deposed and shot after a show trial, the guilty verdict predetermined. The irony was not lost on Cojocaru. He reflected on what he had achieved on his return to the land of his birth. It had been good to visit his parents' grave, to see the house where he had grown up, even where he had shot his first man, but Bucharest had changed. No longer as easy as it had been, it was now full of shops and cars, and the government, if not totally incorruptible, was not as pliable as before.

He had contacted one of the crime syndicates, a group that he had dealt with before. Back then, the leader had been a man his age, but he was dead, and in his place, his son, a smart thirty-two-year-old. Cojocaru realised that he was a man whose time was past, a man who did not belong. He had made a few phone calls, only to receive impersonal replies, or on two occasions the clicking in his ear as the phone was hung up on him. The visit had been a disaster, and he knew that the surly confidence he had had in London had gone.

Cojocaru turned on the television, found nothing of interest, walked out of his room, and went and sat by the swimming pool. The evening climate was balmy, and he was dressed in shorts and a polo shirt. He felt some serenity as he leant back on a reclining chair.

'Stanislav Ivanov will not be pleased,' a man who came up to him said.

'Your boss has no need to worry. I am here visiting my parents' grave, that's all.'

'Do not lie. The best thing you can do is to return to London and to pray that Stanislav Ivanov has a forgiving nature.'

'Does he?'

The man looked Cojocaru directly in the eyes. 'Not that I've ever seen it.' He then walked away.

Panic seized the gangster, the realisation that he was no longer the hunter but the hunted, and that Romania was no longer his home, nor was London. The only hope lay with the West Indians, but he knew that was futile. They did not have the tenacity to deal with the situation. But did he? The situation was too difficult to comprehend, but nothing could be resolved from Romania, and now Ivanov had men following him, men who at a command could kill him. He went to his room, packed his suitcase, and took a taxi to the airport.

In London, Becali received a phone call from his boss at eight in the evening. 'Pick me up at the airport, 11 p.m. flight.'

'Any success?' Becali asked. His situation had become difficult as well. His link to Sal Maynard would be confirmed in time, and regardless of what he had said, he had enjoyed his time with her. It wasn't love, but it wasn't hate or indifference. With him, she had been genuine. With the women who cost a great deal more, the show of enjoying his company was fake, but that simple and uncomplicated woman who had lived in a depressing ten-storey tenement building had confessed her love for him, her willingness to trust her life to him, her blind obedience if that was what he wanted.

'None. Ivanov has people here, and the old contacts are gone. London is where we are, where we must do what is necessary.'

'Is there no alternative?'

'None. You, Ion Becali, are the one who must do this. There is no one else who I can trust.'

'We will succeed, you and I.'

Cojocaru did not answer as he did not know what to say. Becali had always been a loyal servant to him, but now the man was about to become more. Whatever the outcome, Cojocaru knew that the relationship between the two men would be inexorably altered.

***

Larry was tired of being away from home. One of the children had a cough, another had a 'parents meet the teachers' function in three days. He wanted to be home for both of them.

'Buckley's wife?' Annie said.

'Any suspicions there?'

'Not with her. It's not as if Buckley had much to show for his years in the police force.'

'Neither do I. It's the life we choose, isn't it?'

'It is. Although with my husband and myself working, we're not so badly off, and Ireland is a lot cheaper than London.'

'Is Dervla Buckley at home?'

'She will be. I've phoned to tell her we're coming.'

Larry could tell that Annie O'Carroll still had a lingering sorrow for Buckley.

Larry had no such sentiment; a crooked police officer had abrogated his right to sympathy and concern.

Dervla Buckley was not in a dressing gown on their second visit. This time, she was dressed in an ankle-length dress, her hair coiffured, her makeup immaculate. She was welcoming to the two police officers.

On a table in the sitting room, a spread of sandwiches, freshly-brewed coffee, and a pot of tea. 'I thought we'd make ourselves comfortable,' Mrs Buckley said.

'Thank you,' Annie said, 'but we've got a few questions. There are disturbing aspects to your husband's death.'

'I don't miss him if that's what you expect me to say. I know about Sheila Gaffney.'

'How?'

'She came over here to offer her condolences.'

'What did you do?'

'I was angry at first. Seamus had died, and although she had been sleeping with Ryan, it just doesn't seem that important to bear any malice against her.'

'Have you known her for long?' Larry asked.

'A long time, almost as long as I knew Ryan. A good woman, good mother, and before what she admitted to, a loyal wife. It goes to show, doesn't it? People assumed I'd be the one to stray, not that I did, and humble and sweet Sheila is there, flat on her back, my husband on top of her.'

'There's another issue,' Larry said. 'We've identified the man who probably shot your husband. We believe that Seamus had told Ryan something of value. And that was why Ryan killed Seamus, hoping to grab the money for himself.'

'I never considered him to be dishonest. He loved being a police officer. I can't believe that of him.'

'Inspector O'Carroll would prefer to believe the same, but the facts are indisputable. Your husband died as a result of an order from a foreign crime syndicate. We need to know why it's important. Is there anything he said to you that seems obscure?'

'Nothing. We were barely talking, only what was necessary.'

'I hope you're telling the truth. Two people have died in Ireland, I don't want you to be the third,' Larry said.

'I don't know anything, believe me. Ryan's life insurance is still valid, although I don't expect his police pension is. I have been left financially secure, at least I can thank Ryan for that.'

On the drive to the airport, Annie spoke. 'Did you believe her?'

'The money that Ryan's life insurance will pay is not going to last indefinitely, no matter what she said. However, I do believe her. Just hope that others are of that opinion,' Larry said.

Chapter 18

Claude Bateman, the most ruthless of the gang leaders who had enjoyed Nicolae Cojocaru's hospitality, was the first to leave the house where he and the two others had been wined, dined, bedded, and given the runaround.

He had been spotted in the Wellington Arms. Larry heard of the man's reappearance through a contact who phoned him from time to time, a fifty pound note, a few drinks given in return as payment.

Bateman was in a corner of the pub when Larry walked in. This time he had brought Wendy, a woman who was also partial to a drink, but the visit was business not social, although Larry ordered a pint of beer for each of them.

'Over here, Inspector,' Bateman shouted.

Larry and Wendy sat down at the man's table. Around him, four men, members of his gang: Tony Hammond, a young man, skinny as a rake. Good with a knife if the word on the street was accurate, six months in prison at twenty for theft. Victor Powell, short, in his thirties, an open-necked shirt with a large medallion proudly showing. Larry hadn't seen him before and assumed he had been brought in if there was to be violence. The third gang member, Marlon Morris, a surly-looking individual who didn't like the police under any circumstances, and he had elbowed Wendy when she sat down. She had made a mental note to check him out with Bridget. To her, he looked more than a rank and file hoodlum. The fourth man, good-looking, well-spoken, and polite had shaken the hands of the two police officers, as had Bateman. His name was Colin Ross. Wendy thought he was charming, Larry did not.

'Where are the other two?' Larry asked Bateman. A woman came over and put her arms around the man's shoulder; he pushed her away.

'One of your admirers?' Wendy said.

Bateman, not responding to the question, looked over at Larry. 'The bastards killed Marcus Hearne.'

'There have been others in the past. Why are you concerned and why are we talking in this pub?'

'Where else? Either I declare my position or I sit on the fence.'

'And you intend to work with the police on this?'

'I intend to survive.'

'Your men here, what do they reckon?'

'They'll do what I say.'

'Until you're deposed.'

'Others have tried.'

'And died. Isn't that how you decide who's in charge?'

'Inspector, let's focus on our common position. You don't want an escalation in violence in the area, nor more drugs coming into the country, correct?'

'We want no violence and no drugs.'

'You're living in cloud cuckoo land,' Bateman said. 'This is the real world, crime happens, people take drugs, people get drunk, even you in the past when Rasta Joe was alive.'

'My habits are not of concern. What do you want from me? What are you going to give in return?'

Bateman turned away from Larry and Wendy and focussed on the other four at the table. 'Leave us alone. I've got two police officers to protect me now,' he said.

The four gang members moved away, taking up a position close to the bar. Of the four, Morris kept his eyes firmly on Bateman, Larry and Wendy.

'I don't like the look of him,' Wendy said.

'Marlon? He's harmless, just likes to look big and strong,' Bateman replied. His tone was mocking. Wendy didn't believe the man.

'What do you have for us?' Larry asked. His glass was empty. He looked over at the barman and held up the empty glass, a nod from the barman in return. Bateman followed suit as did Wendy. Soon there were three more pints of beer on the table.

'Devon Harris and Jeremy Miller will be here soon enough.'

'Why not now?'

'Cojocaru has been trying to make a deal. He's frightened of the Russians, so are we.'

'They killed Crin Antonescu, almost certainly were responsible for Briganti's and one other murder in Ireland.'

'We can't trust the Romanians, no more than the Russians. What do you suggest we do?'

'Seamus Gaffney knew something. He told someone else what it was, and he's dead. Whatever it was, it was lethal. I need to know what the man knew,' Larry said.

'You want a lot. We know less than you, and that we're unsure what to do. If Gaffney had found out something, why didn't he tell you?'

'It had more value if he sold it on, or offered his silence if they paid enough.'

'Gaffney was always a fool, playing the margins, listening where he shouldn't. He was going to die one day on account of his big nose.'

'Maybe that's true. What else do you have? Hearne's dead, yet you stayed with Cojocaru.'

'He told us about Antonescu, not that we cared for the man. Marcus was talking to the police, and secrecy was vital.'

'You accepted that? He did no more than what you're doing now.'

'We didn't accept it, but we needed to know what Cojocaru had to say. Men die, men live, and Hearne led a violent life.'

'The same as you.'

'The same as me. One day, one of those at the bar will challenge me. You know this.'

'Cojocaru's been in Romania, although he's back now. Have you seen him?'

'Not since that day when Hearne died. Cojocaru told us about Ivanov and what he's capable of. Is it true what he said?'

'That Ivanov is a mafia boss, more violent than anyone else you've ever encountered, and that one of his men shot up Briganti's?'

'That's about it.'

'He didn't lie.'

'That's what we thought, not that we trust Cojocaru. But the man had a message, we had to listen to it.'

'Why were the three of you out of touch with your people?'

'We weren't, not totally. Hammond knew where I was, but he was keeping quiet. We agreed to give Cojocaru three days, but then he never came back. We enjoyed his hospitality, and Harris and Miller are still there.'

'It must be good hospitality,' Wendy said.

'It was,' Bateman said. 'The best.'

Wendy needed to know no more.

Larry looked over at the four gang members. He could see that two of them were drinking heavily, Victor Powell and Marlon Morris were not.

'You need to stop Ivanov,' Bateman said.

'With what? The man's got no criminal record, not even a parking ticket, whereas you do.'

'I'm not the problem, Ivanov is. We've learnt to live with Cojocaru, even do business with him, but this Ivanov may cut us out altogether.'

'He may just remove you, chop you into little pieces and feed you to the fish.'

'We'll fight.'

'On a street corner, knives and fists? Not a chance. The Russians will be armed with guns, and they'll know how to use them. If this is not stopped, it's you who'll lose. What was Cojocaru's plan?'

'I don't think he knew what to do. He just needed to know that we'd be with him and not the Russians.'

'Will you?'

'We represent our community, not his or Ivanov's.'

'If you had to choose?'

'Better the devil you know than the devil you don't.'

Wendy could see that Bateman, the same as Marcus Hearne, was looking for de facto support from the police for the criminals. She knew that would not happen, and that Bateman was not a man to be trusted.

Marlon Morris came over, a scowl on his face, a disparaging look at Larry and Wendy. He carried a half-full glass of beer. He drank it before speaking. 'Devon Harris is back,' he said to Bateman.

'Where?'

'Not here,' Morris replied. Larry knew that what he was saying was that he was wherever the police weren't.

Larry stood up, offered his hand to Bateman, which he shook. 'Keep in touch and don't get yourself killed. You're playing with the big boys now, and they won't have any scruples about killing you and your men.'

'According to Cojocaru, they kill the police as well.'

'None of us is safe, you'd better remember that. If you want to meet Harris without us being present, then so be it. But don't blame us if you end up on the pathologist's table, cut open from top to bottom.'

'I'll be in touch,' Bateman said as he leant over and shook Wendy's hand.

Larry wasn't sure if he would see the man again. The West Indians were playing a dangerous game, a game they were not prepared for.

***

At 10.02 a.m. Stanislav Ivanov walked down the four steps outside his Bayswater residence. On the street, three men stood close to a Rolls Royce. On the other side of the road, another man looked up and down, checking. All four men were bodyguards, as were the two on either side of the leader of the Tverskoyskaya Bratva.

Ivanov was in a good mood: the latest financial statements were all in the black, and the planned expansions throughout Europe and England were progressing well. The two men at either side of him were anxious to hurry him away from the house and into the car, but Ivanov wanted to look around, to look at the garden, even to say hello to a woman pushing a child down the street in a pushchair, to wave to a man walking his dog. Those protecting the man knew that it was out of character for their charge, and that in France he stayed concealed most of the time, and in Russia he travelled in a convoy of ten to twelve vehicles.

The bodyguards were disturbed with the change in the man, the result of his decision to stay in England on a permanent basis, his belief that England was safe.

On the pavement Ivanov stopped once again to talk to a group of schoolchildren, not that they knew who the man was, other than he was wealthy and influential. He asked them about their lessons, and what smartphones they used, and were they on Facebook. The guards attempted to hurry him along, careful not to touch his person.

From a window on the upper floor of a block of flats one street away, another man watched the scene. He opened the window, confident that with distance came protection. He took aim with the rifle set on a tripod, its telescopic sight tested many times for accuracy. He loaded one bullet into the rifle and pulled the trigger. He then left the room, the rifle still in position. He had no need of the weapon again, no need to gloat over his handiwork, only to feel a wave of relief surge over him.

The bullet's target lay motionless on the footpath, the schoolchildren screaming in horror, the bodyguards unable to comprehend the scene, conscious of their fate if the man died, and even if he didn't, they were guilty of negligence.

An ambulance arrived five minutes later, a medic stabilising Ivanov before putting him in the back of the vehicle and transporting him to the nearest hospital, the Rolls Royce following as well as two other cars.

The first that Homicide heard of the shooting was a phone call from Isaac. 'I'm with Oscar Braxton. Get over to St Mary's Hospital in Paddington. Ivanov's been shot.'

Both Wendy and Larry were familiar with the place, as it was on Praed Street, just up from Paddington Station.

'We're heading back on Eurostar. We'll come to the hospital on arrival. Expect a media circus there.'

'Buckley and Briganti's murderer?'

'That's still ongoing. Stanislav Ivanov is the key, and if he dies, there'll be no Russian incursion into England. But if he survives, you can imagine the consequences.'

'Revenge?'

'And lots of it. The man is not the "forgive and turn the other cheek" kind of person. Whoever shot him must have known this.'

'Who? Any suspicions?'

'Not yet. Find out where the shot was taken from. No stone unturned on this one. I'll phone DCS Goddard. He's bound to have Commissioner Davies onto him soon enough.'

'Caddick?'

'God help us if he appears,' Isaac said. 'Got to go, taxi to the station. See you in a few hours.'

***

Not far away, Devon Harris met with Claude Bateman; Jeremy Miller was on his way. Everyone, including Cojocaru, the West Indians, the police, knew that whatever happened, a day of reckoning was coming when the opposing forces would be lined up against each other, either to come to an agreement or to fight.

At St Mary's, the police were attempting to keep the media at bay, setting up an area across the road, and bringing in metal barriers. At the entrance to the hospital, two uniforms stood, backed up by a patrol car.

Larry waved his warrant card at the uniforms. They let him and Wendy through after a call from DCS Goddard to tell them that the man in the operating theatre was part of a homicide investigation. The uniforms, nervous due to the importance of the man inside, had only been doing their duty, Isaac knew that. A high-profile patient, and forged identification papers, easy enough to come by, could have been used by the media, or by the assassin if the man showed up to check on his work.

'I need an update,' Larry said to the lady at the desk outside the operating theatre.

'I can't do that,' she said. 'I'll get a doctor to see you.'

Across the room, an elegantly dressed woman.

'Mrs Ivanov, I'm Sergeant Wendy Gladstone, Challis Street Homicide. Could I take a few minutes of your time?'

'Why? What has my Stanislav done? We intended to come and live in England but after this? Such a good man.'

Wendy could have said because he was a thug who controlled the most powerful criminal gang in Russia, the Tverskoyskaya Bratva, a man who killed and tortured people without a care, a man who had a couple of high-class women at his place in Bayswater, while, she, the wife, lived in Richmond in a mansion. Wendy could see a hardness in the woman's face and realised that she

164

would not have cared about the negatives, only the positives – the man was rich and generous, and he left her alone.

'Have you received any updates on his condition?'

'They told me to prepare for the worst,' Elena Ivanov said. At her side sat another woman of a similar age, although not as well-dressed. She held the other's arm in a sign of friendship.

'We will need to question him.'

'Not Stanislav. He does not answer to anyone.'

'This is not Russia. Here in this country, the police have the right to question. With citizenship comes responsibility. It is important that we find out who shot your husband and to bring that person to justice.'

'He will talk to you if he can,' Ivanov's wife said. Wendy was sure it was only an answer to make her go away.

Wendy knew that whoever had pulled the trigger would receive punishment. The answer to who would administer it remained unknown. With the British legal system, the man would be afforded the benefit of a fair trial. With Ivanov's cohorts, the man would be condemned and killed with little formality.

Wendy left the woman and returned to Larry. 'She'll not tell us much,' she said.

'Ivanov's wife. She would regard us as no more than insects to squash underfoot.'

'Not if she wants to stay in this country. Ivanov wants to be here, so does she, but why? He doesn't need to be in London to run his organisation.'

'Ivanov doesn't feel as secure as he did before. He wants out, he wants England and a peaceful life.'

'Peaceful to men such as Ivanov is subjective,' Wendy said.

Chapter 19

Nicolae Cojocaru sat back in his chair; he was a contented man. On one side of him, a bottle of whisky; on the other, mounted on the wall, a flat-screen television tuned to a news channel. The breaking news, the shooting of Stanislav Ivanov, the latest report from the hospital stating that the man's chances were not good. A brief synopsis followed of the man's career. How, at the age of ten, he had been abandoned in the height of winter, surviving by sleeping in heated basements when he could find them, underneath stacks of cardboard when he couldn't. How he had been taken in by an orphanage and had educated himself, taking every opportunity to better himself, eventually leaving university with two degrees. After that the television report became sketchy. There was mention of the ending of communism with Gorbachev, the rise of the oligarchs, Ivanov being one of the most prominent. Cojocaru knew that most of the story of the man's past was not true, having been put out there by a loyal employee. Cojocaru wondered how long before the veneer started to crack and the truth was revealed.

Becali sat in another chair. 'A great day,' he said. He lifted his glass of whisky in the air, a salute that the worst was over.

'It will be when they take him out of there in his coffin.'

'There is no question of his death.'

'That is what you said before.'

'They'll not give up on him that easily, but it was a good shot, I'll vouch for it.'

'On this, Ion, I trust you. What of the three West Indians?'

'They have left the house.'

'Good. Give them a bellyful of food and drink, a few women, and it's as easy as leading a camel to water.'

'With Ivanov gone, they'll go back to what they were before. Will you honour your agreement with them?'

'What agreement?'

'To deal with them in a more consultative manner in the future; to fight the Russian threat together.'

'Ion, still so naïve. No wonder you were starving in Bucharest. I never made any agreement, only suggestions. Are we ready for what happens?'

'The weapons are here, and Ivanov's people are ready to start shipping the extra quantities of drugs. Are you sure about this?'

'I am sure. What Ivanov planned, we will implement.'

'The Russians have agreed?'

'Whoever killed Ivanov has done them a service. They are very grateful.'

'They must never know.'

'Not from me, they won't. What now for you, Ion?'

'Today, I intend to celebrate. Tomorrow, day one of what has been agreed. It has all worked out better than could have been expected.'

'As long as Ivanov stays dead.'

'His bodyguards?'

'Some have disappeared, the others have been told to not indulge in reprisals. And besides, they don't know who was responsible.'

'Does it matter to them?'

'No, but without Ivanov and the Tverskoyskaya Bratva giving them clear instructions, they'll hold back.'

'Let's hope the man's dead, for all our sakes,' Becali said.

'I can feel it in my bones,' Cojocaru said. 'He's dead, and for once, I will join you in your celebration.'

***

As fast as Eurostar was, it wasn't fast enough for Isaac. As the train was pulling into St Pancras Station, he was off and running; Oscar Braxton, not such a fit man, struggled to keep up with him. In the taxi, Isaac caught his breath; Braxton tried to look at ease, but his face was red, and he was gasping for breath.

At St Mary's Hospital, the two men soon found Larry and Wendy. Updates on Ivanov's condition were slow in coming. Braxton, his tie still undone after loosening it in the taxi, contacted his department. Serious and Organised Crime, New Scotland Yard, had more clout than Homicide, Challis Street. He spoke to his commander who phoned the hospital's director of communications.

'There'll be a power struggle in Russia, survival of the fittest,' Braxton said to Isaac.

'Deaths?'

'It's probable, but it'll be internal and in Russia. It's not our concern. What's happening here is, though.'

Ten minutes later, a surgeon came out from the operating theatre.

'I'm Brian Forsythe, you'll need an update on the patient,' the surgeon, a man in his fifties, greying at the temples and as tall as Isaac, said.

'You're aware of who the man is?' Isaac replied.

'Not that it matters, but yes.'

'He's still alive?' Larry asked. A blunt question, he knew, but he had spent enough times in hospital to know that the surgeon would feel the need to give a description of the effect of the bullet entering a man's skull, the prognosis, how long he may or may not live, the difficulties in stemming the internal bleeding, and so on.

'It's important,' Isaac said.

'The patient is still alive. There was internal bleeding in the brain, fracturing of the skull. His survival is still dependent on a number of factors. We've put him into a medically-induced coma.'

'How long for?' Isaac asked.

'It depends on how he progresses. Anywhere from a few hours up to two weeks.'

'Ivanov wore body armour under his jacket, that's why the shot was to the head.'

'I only know the man from the media reports,' Forsythe said. Isaac could see that he was anxious to get away.

'What you've read is only part of the story,' Oscar Braxton said. 'I'm from Serious and Organised Crime Command, DCI Cook is from Homicide. The man is not what he seems.'

'He's still a patient. But what I can tell you is that even if he regains consciousness, he may not remember anything that has happened. And there is a possibility that he may be in a vegetative state for a long time.'

'Are you able to quantify the possibility?'

'Not at this time. We will issue a bulletin that our patient is receiving the best medical care and his chance of survival is good.'

'Stanislav Ivanov, whether he lives or not, will be the signal for a power play in Russia, a call to arms for organised crime in this country.'

'That I cannot help you with. Now, if you will excuse me, it was a difficult operation, and I have others to see,' Forsythe said.

***

Apart from one, Ivanov's bodyguards had vanished, not unexpected as questions would be asked as to who they were and what they knew of the assassination attempt, as well as why they had been carrying weapons. The one remaining was at Challis Street, voluntarily.

Wendy returned to the police station to work with Bridget. Isaac, Larry and Braxton went to the crime scene.

'What can you tell us?' Isaac said to Gordon Windsor.

'Here, not a lot.'

'Why?'

'Where the shot came from is more important.'

Windsor stood from where he had been kneeling. 'Up there is a possibility,' he said, pointing to a towering nondescript block of sixties' architecture, one of several in the area that had been built for the working class, and rented out, although some of the flats had been purchased under the government's Right to Buy policy that was introduced in 1980. Isaac knew this, as he had contemplated the purchase of such a flat before buying in Willesden.

'Have we people up there?' Isaac asked.

'We do, although it's a slow job. Not everyone is keen to see the police marching through, and some of the flats are empty or bolted shut. It's got to be on the top floors, twentieth and above.'

'I need to meet with Claude Bateman,' Larry said.

Isaac and Braxton drove the short distance to the block of flats. Outside, on the street, the obligatory crowd of onlookers, some hostile about the excessive police presence.

'Never here when we need you, are you?' one of the crowd shouted.

'If you're rich, it's a different law for them,' another screamed.

'Take no notice,' Isaac said to Braxton. 'It's not the first time in this building for us, not the last.'

'A lot of crime?'

'No more than other parts of London. The building's occupied by disparate people, some good, some bad. It's just that they're hemmed in, unable to get out.'

'There are plenty of other places.'

'If you've got money. The gang members, not Cojocaru's, like these places. Easy to hide.'

'Why would someone shoot from here?'

'Why not? It's some distance, but Ivanov was hit in the head.'

'We need to know if it's the same person who killed Buckley and carried out the attack on Briganti's.'

'Sal Maynard is still involved somewhere in all of this.'

'We keep coming back to Becali, but it wasn't him.'

'Not at Briganti's, but who knows. No one had a clear view of the man. That's the problem, the man on the street is not trained to observe.'

'We'd better follow through on what they find here,' Braxton said.

The two men entered through the front door of the building, a uniform checking their warrant cards before letting them through.

'He's keen.'

'New in the station.'

On the twentieth floor, two officers from Challis Street were working their way methodically through, flat to flat. 'We're getting a warrant to open up the flats if no one's at home.'

'How long?'

'Bridget Halloran is working on it for us.'

'Not long,' Isaac said. 'No luck yet?'

'Not yet. We've got others on the floors above. Gordon Windsor reckoned the bullet was fired from up high.'

'I'll take his word,' Isaac said as another flat door opened, a woman hiding in one room, covered head to foot in black.

'You can't come in here,' a man with a full beard said. He was dressed in the traditional clothing of Pakistan.

'We believe someone has used one of the flats to shoot at someone down on the ground.'

'I'm just home from work, and my wife won't let anyone in when she's on her own.'

Isaac, sensitive to the situation, phoned for a female police officer to come up to the flat.

After five minutes, Constable Jill Albertson reported for duty. 'Pleased to help. The crowds down below are restless. Some want to get home, and we're not letting them.'

'We'll need to set up a mobile canteen, toilets.'

'There's a church hall nearby, and the locals are helping out. But it's not the same, is it?'

'No.'

'Constable Albertson will check your flat, is that acceptable?' Isaac said to the man, now identified as Fahad Shaikh, a recent arrival in the country with his wife and three children.

'We are a law-abiding family. And yes, the constable can come in. Thank you for your understanding.'

Jill Albertson entered the flat, checking each and every room, placing emphasis on the windows looking out and over to Ivanov's house. She returned, thanking the Pakistani for his assistance and wishing him well.

'The flat on the corner,' she said to the police officers.

'You saw something?'

'It juts out from the other flats. It must have an extra bedroom. There's a small window that I could see in. I didn't want to mention it to Mr Shaikh.'

'What did you see?'

'A rifle.'

Isaac phoned Gordon Windsor to update him. Two crime scene investigators arrived soon after, their boss with them.'

'Are you sure of this?' Windsor said.

'I'm sure,' Constable Albertson said.

'We have to hold back until Armed Response arrives. We don't know who's inside.'

'Nobody, you know that,' Windsor said.

'I don't want to have to write a report on how you or one of your team were shot,' Isaac said.

'Fair enough. We'll get ourselves organised. It would be best if they didn't have to smash the door in.'

'Armed Response won't care too much for what you want. If there's to be shooting, they'll not be too fussy.'

'Understood. Regrettable, though. We should clear the people out on this floor.'

'Constable Albertson, up to the task?'

'Yes, sir. Leave it to me.'

'And keep it quiet. Those closest to the flat, set up some sort of a barrier as you bring them out, in case there's some shooting.'

As anxious as Isaac was to enter the flat, it was another thirty-five minutes before the all-clear was given. Armed Response was in place, Sergeant Northam in charge.

A knock on the door, no answer, Northam keeping to one side, protected by body armour. Isaac and the others waited at ground level. The arrival of the police officers with their weapons had increased the number of onlookers, some even leaving the church hall and their food to watch and to offer comments, some congratulatory, some critical, and some racial about the occupants in the block of flats.

'One more time and we go in,' Northam said. He hit the door hard with a metal bar. 'Police, we're armed. Come out at once with your hands up in the air.'

A break of sixty seconds for a reply. None was forthcoming.

'Okay, break it down,' Northam issued the command to one of his men.

The battering ram, known as the enforcer, made short work of the door, one attempt all that was needed before the door opened. Inside, a clear view through to the front window.

Down below, Windsor winced at the amount of evidence that the men would disturb. A formerly pristine crime scene devalued by the tactics of a group of men whose function was to secure the flat, not to concern themselves with where they walked and what they disturbed.

On the twentieth floor, Northam gave another command. 'Stand back.'

He then called out once again. 'Police, we're coming in, and we're heavily armed. Resistance is not advised, and we will shoot to kill.'

No answer.

'It's empty,' one of the other armed officers said.

'Okay, maximum care, and keep your weapons ready to shoot.'

At the rear of the flat, the rifle was found on its tripod. No person was discovered. The flat was declared safe.

Chapter 20

A hastily-convened press conference at Challis Street Police Station, and Richard Goddard's one failing would become apparent. Numerous courses and plenty of practice had convinced him of one thing – he was a lousy public speaker, his monotone voice tiring on the ear, his need to pause, when no words emanated other than 'Arrgh' and 'you know'.

At the back of the room, three cameras were mounted on tripods; at the front, iPhones on record. Goddard rose to speak.

'Ladies and gentlemen, thank you for coming. The recent upsurge in violent crime is of concern to all of us. That is why we are meeting here today. Let me thank Detective Chief Inspector Cook from Homicide for being here, as well as Detective Chief Inspector Oscar Braxton from Serious and Organised Crime Command. They will both make a short speech, after which there will be time for questions. I would ask that you allow them to make their speeches first.'

'What about Stanislav Ivanov?' a man in the second row of the assembled media contingent asked.

'And you are?' Goddard said.

'Colin Bartlett, Fox News.'

Isaac cringed. Everyone knew who Bartlett was. The man was the bane of the police force, forever criticising it for its inability to control terrorism. He had been scathing two nights previously on the television about the progress on the Briganti shooting, and now the chief superintendent was trying to control the man by belittling him. It wasn't going to work, Isaac knew that, and the press conference was a shambles before it had started.

In Russia, a group of men sat around a table in a boardroom, watching a live feed streaming into a laptop and then onto a screen on the wall. At a penthouse in London, two men watched smugly, confident that whatever happened their future was secure. At the Wellington Arms in Bayswater, the television was tuned to the press conference, although it was only the rank and file hoodlums who watched. The three gang leaders that Cojocaru had attempted to bring onto his side were ensconced in the house where Larry had met them previously, but then there had been four; Marcus Hearne now dead and in the mortuary.

'We'll answer your questions after DCI Cook and DCI Braxton have spoken.'

Bartlett sat quietly. Isaac knew it would not be for long.

'Detective Chief Inspector, would you speak?' Goddard said, directing his request at Isaac.

Isaac, confident in what he wanted to say, approached the lectern. 'Ladies and gentlemen. The first matter of interest is the attack at the hairdressing salon of Giuseppe Briganti. We have eliminated all those inside of any involvement, and all the bodies have been released to their families.'

'Why did you hold on to the body of Sal Maynard?' Bartlett shouted.

Isaac could see that the man had no intention of being quiet.

'Some discrepancies needed to be resolved.'

'She was involved with a major crime figure, sleeping with him.'

It was clear that Bartlett had inside knowledge – knowledge that was confidential.

'I am unable to comment on specific details of the case,' Isaac said. 'We have proof that the crime at Briganti's was committed by a foreign national. We have identified one person, and we are working with overseas police forces to bring this man to justice. We also believe that he was in Ireland and that he killed another man there.'

'From what was reported, Inspector Buckley killed Seamus Gaffney, a known informer, a man in regular communication with Detective Inspector Larry Hill.'

A general air of unease was apparent in the room. Richard Goddard took hold of the microphone. 'I would suggest that any questions are held for later,' he said.

Isaac knew that the man was wasting his time. Barely ten minutes into what was slated as a twenty-five-minute presentation, and nothing of importance had been said.

'Let me come back to where we are,' Isaac said after reclaiming the microphone. 'An overseas crime syndicate has been attempting to enter this country and to take over a large part of the illegal drug trade. They intended to base themselves primarily in the local area and to fan out from there. This has caused tension in the wider community, and unfortunately some deaths.'

'Why Briganti's?' A voice from the back of the room.

'The evidence we have received is that it was a show of strength, a warning to deter others who may resist.'

'Has it?'

'At this time, we believe it has.'

'There's a power vacuum, isn't there?' Bartlett said.

'There are elements in the community, as there are in other areas of the city and throughout the country, who believe they are above the law.'

'Elaborate on that statement.'

'At this time, I cannot. We are attempting to defuse the situation and to prevent further violence. Outlining our plan at this time would be counter-productive.'

'Let Braxton speak,' Goddard whispered in Isaac's ear.

Isaac stood to one side; Braxton came to the microphone.

'Detective Chief Inspector Braxton, Serious and Organised Crime Command,' he said. 'We have been working together with DCS Goddard and his team. An attack on a hairdressing salon by an organised crime syndicate, where innocent people were killed, was a senseless and cowardly attack and must be condemned.'

'Wonderful words, but worthless,' a woman in the front row said. Isaac recognised her, Lisa Saunders. The woman was on the television every night, debating law and order with a panel of so-called experts. She had a soothing and mellow voice, the type that sucked you in before she spat you out.

Braxton ignored the woman and continued. 'Organised crime, as in any major city, is unfortunately present here. The efforts of the police and the community have kept it at controllable levels up till now. I have been in France with DCI Cook, consulting with the French police. An arrest is expected soon.'

'Then why did you come back to England after Stanislav Ivanov was shot?' Bartlett asked. 'Is it because he is a major crime figure? Is he, in fact, the head of a Russian mafia crime syndicate that calls itself the Tverskoyskaya Bratva? A group of people who will stop at nothing to ensure their aims.'

'There are no criminal cases against Mr Ivanov.'

'Not in this country, not in Russia, but you know all about him. Everyone is careful in what they say, the result of his influence and wealth, but behind closed doors, what's the truth, what do you say about him?'

'Mr Ivanov has been shot. His life hangs in the balance. Speculation will serve no useful purpose.'

Isaac could see Braxton being pushed into a corner. He had thought that the man's attendance had been ill-advised, but Goddard had been adamant, and now the conference was being railroaded by the media.

'We are here to discuss the murders and attempted murders, not to speculate,' Isaac said.

'We're here for the truth. Marcus Hearne, a local gang leader, has been murdered, another drinking friend of Inspector Hill.'

'Inspector Hill is above suspicion.'

Lisa Saunders decided it was her turn to speak. An attractive woman, Isaac had to admit, but with a viper's tongue and a wasp's sting. 'In recent years, there has been a disturbing rise in the number of criminal gangs from eastern Europe entering England. Is that correct?'

'That has been reported by us,' Braxton said.

Isaac could see the subtle drawing in by Lisa Saunders, making her target relax his guard.

'There were some deaths some years back when one major crime figure entered this country, true or false?'

'There has been an escalation at times of criminal activity. Criminal gangs operate throughout the city, that's true. But it would be wrong to lay the blame on one group of people based on their ethnicity or their religion.'

'Why? Because it's not politically correct?'

'Apportioning blame to one group or another serves no purpose.'

'Are you telling me that you sit in your office in Serious and Organised Crime Command, and don't mention where someone comes from, their background? Are you telling those assembled here, and those watching on the television, streaming it over the internet, that you don't make decisions based on these factors?'

'We are conscious of the differences, and yes, we do discuss such matters, converse with our counterparts overseas.'

'Then, Detective Chief Inspector Braxton, why the subterfuge? Do you think we're all fools?'

Touché, Isaac thought, *Braxton's been taken hook, line, and sinker.*

'It is our responsibility to not exacerbate the situation by making claims without proof.'

'Nonsense. We have one such criminal, a Romanian by the name of Nicolae Cojocaru, running a crime syndicate. Isn't that true?'

'There are no crimes recorded against Mr Cojocaru.'

'Yet you have a case file on him, and there have been several attempts to deport him, a man who has been labelled a criminal back in Romania.'

'Speculation,' Braxton said.

'Did Cojocaru arrange for Ivanov to be shot?'

'Mr Ivanov is a successful businessman, the owner of the football club that I support.'

Isaac winced at Braxton's attempt at levity. The woman asking the questions wasn't going to be distracted by such a tactic.

Richard Goddard took hold of the microphone. 'Ladies and gentlemen, this press conference was scheduled for twenty-five minutes. We've run over time, and as you can appreciate we are busy.'

A flurry of hands from the other reporters in the room; a retreat by the three police officers.

'Disaster,' Isaac said. 'Was Commissioner Davies watching?'

'He would be,' Goddard said.

'Then you either drop your phone out of the window or you and he will be having a conversation soon. Oscar, you shouldn't have been there. You've connected Ivanov with organised crime, made it obvious that the man is of interest.'

'I'd disagree. Cojocaru was mentioned as well. Both of them will be very nervous now.'

'One will be. We should meet with him,' Isaac said.

****

'A Steyr SSG 69 PIV, Austrian, bolt-action, .308 cartridge,' Gordon Windsor said. 'It's been fired.'

'You've looked down the scope?' Braxton asked. He and Isaac were back at the flat where the shot had been taken to kill Ivanov.

'Kahles ZF84 10x magnification scope. More than accurate for the distance. It was focussed on where Ivanov had been standing.'

'A bulky item to bring up here. Someone may have seen whoever brought it in.'

'Too bulky to take out afterwards if you're aiming to get away, and if Ivanov's men had figured out where the shot had come from. There's not much to see in the flat. It's empty, and apart from the toilet being used, nothing to tell you.'

'The person who fired the shot?'

'He would have used his right shoulder against the butt.'

'Conclusive?'

'Yes.'

'How long do you reckon the person was here?'

'We're assuming anywhere from thirty minutes to three hours. It's cold at night, and there was no heater, no electricity either.'

'If it was thirty minutes, the shooter must have known of Ivanov's movements.'

'That's for you to find out,' Windsor said. 'If it were only thirty minutes, then the rifle would have had to be set up in advance, possibly another target to zero in the scope.'

'Needle in a haystack looking for another shot. Any help on that?'

'None. Some noise when fired, but it did have a silencer.'

'Around here, not too many people would have been asking questions even if they heard a shot.'

Wendy took responsibility for the door-to-door interviews in the building. The rifle had been removed and was with Forensics for further testing, not necessary according to Gordon Windsor, but required nevertheless as it was vital evidence.

As expected, no one had heard anything, except for the wife of Fahad Shaikh, but as she had explained to Constable Jill Albertson and Wendy, she had not seen anyone. In the two women's presence, she had removed the cover from her face. The two were astonished by her beauty. She looked no more than nineteen or twenty; it was found out on checking that she was twenty-two, her husband older than her at thirty-eight.

Bridget had checked out the shooter's flat and found out that it had been sold two years previously, and up until three months before the shooting it had been rented to a family of four. Apart from that, a dead end.

'Someone must have known that the place was empty,' Isaac said at his early-morning meeting in the office. 'And whoever it was may well be the breakthrough we need.'

'It was sold to a company, they've purchased a few in the building and throughout the area,' Bridget said.

'The principals of the company?' Larry asked.

'I'm checking, but it seems that efforts have been made to conceal their identities.'

'Suspicious?'

'It could be part of a complex tax-reduction strategy, not necessarily illegal, or it could be an overseas company hiding dirty money.'

'Criminal?'

'It doesn't mean they're the murderers.'

'We need the names of whoever they are,' Isaac said. 'Dirty money could mean drug money, and we've a few names there.'

'I'll keep checking,' Bridget said. 'It may take some time.'

'Time is what we don't have. And no one's going to come forward with a description of this man.'

'The same person as in Ireland?'

'Whoever it was, he was capable of it, but it wasn't a difficult shot, not if the person was trained and

184

the scope was lined up. According to Windsor, two shots had been fired before taking the shot at Ivanov,' Larry said. 'Even if we found the target for zeroing, it'll not tell us much. CCTV cameras?'

'We're checking, but if the man were organised, he'd only have to change his clothes. Some of the women in the building are covered, some of the men wear traditional dress.'

'An abaya?'

'It's always possible, although it seems bizarre.'

'I'll check,' Bridget said.

Chapter 21

Wendy Gladstone had thought that her time in Stockwell was at an end. She had conducted interviews with Sal Maynard's family, not that they had revealed much, in as much as the family were neither articulate nor still interested in a dead family member more than a few weeks after her death. It had saddened the police sergeant on the times she had visited the house, the drunken and foul-mouthed mother, the tattooed and violent elder brother of the dead woman, the drugged younger brother vacantly staring into space.

And now, a phone call from Ralphie.

Wendy and the young man met at McDonald's, which according to Ralph Ernest Begley was the best food that money could buy. Not that Ralphie was paying. Wendy ordered a Big Mac and extra fries for each of them, as well as a milkshake.

'What's this all about, Ralphie? I'm not out here on a wild goose chase, am I?'

Ralphie spoke between mouthfuls. Someone else was paying, and he was going back for seconds. 'It was something Sal said once. I didn't remember it before, and I suppose I wasn't listening.'

'Did you do that often?'

'What?'

'Not remember or listen.'

'Both. Sal could talk, and sometimes I just switched off. Not that she realised. I liked her, but you know that already. But she could talk rubbish sometimes, especially about celebrities and their perfect lives.'

'They have their problems the same as everyone else.'

'They don't have to live around here.'

Wendy realised that Ralphie wanted better, but as he sat eating it was clear that his time to change was limited. He was generationally unemployed and uneducated, his parents leading by example. The only hope for him was to leave the area, find himself a good family, re-engage with his education. She had already passed his details on to the local church and welfare services, but she knew they were inundated with worthier persons. And besides, she had three grandchildren, the eldest approaching school age, and she wanted to spend time with them, not to be a nursemaid to someone else's child, knowing full well that at the end of the day he would return to the negative influence of his family and friends. And even if Ralphie married, it would be the repeating cycle in that he would become the uncaring parent, possibly someone who would take a belt to the child.

'Do you want another Big Mac?' Wendy asked.

'My friends reckon I'm foolish talking to you.'

'Do you?'

'Not if you feed me and give me some money.'

Wendy left the table and went and ordered another Big Mac, bringing it back after a few minutes. 'Now, what have you got to tell me?'

'And the money?'

'Tell me what you know first.'

'Sal, it was the week she died. She was in a good mood, talking about this man and how he was going to take her away from here, put her on a pedestal.'

'Do you know what a pedestal is?'

'Not really, but Sal thought it was special.'

'It is, but who was this man, and why?'

'That's it. The one I saw was tall and slim, but that's not how she described him to me.'

'What do you mean?'

'She said he was the same height as her. And she didn't say he was slim.'

'But she was sleeping with Becali, the man you saw.'

'I'm certain of that, but I told you before that Sal made extra money.'

'You told me that Sal was keen on Becali?'

'I did, but I also told you about the face he pulled when he let her off that one time.'

'Can you be certain that it was Becali she was keen on?'

'Maybe I didn't hear right, and sometimes I'd tell her to slow down, but if she'd seen a celebrity, she'd not stop going on and on. I belong around here, so did she. It's okay to dream, but that's all it is.'

Wendy knew that she could have told him that life was what you made of it, but she did not, she had more pressing issues to deal with. If Sal Maynard did have another man, then who was he and where was he?

Yet again, the young woman had been thrust front and centre into the investigation. Not that she was guilty of any crime, but whatever she was, she was dead because of it.

Ralphie, his meal eaten, cycled away, fifty pounds in his back pocket. She had no intention of contacting him again unless it was vital. She sat at McDonald's for another ten minutes going through what he had said, wondering about the truth of it, and how to find Sal Maynard's mysterious admirer. She realised that it was not going to be easy.

***

Nicolae Cojocaru did not regard the presence of the two police officers as anything more than an inconvenience. In the past, back in Romania, if an officer of the law had not succumbed to gentle persuasion, either financial or with a gift, a car, a woman, then that officer had been sidelined or removed from circulation permanently. In the old country, when he had been a man of note, the bribes had been extortionate, and there was always a senior officer who would deal with a recalcitrant lower rank. In some ways, the gangster missed the old days where everyone and everything had a price or a solution. His recent trip to Romania had shown him that he was no longer a significant player and that a young class of villains had taken over. Even if he had wanted to go back, he couldn't, not without committing himself to violence and a large capital outlay to secure allegiances, to re-establish himself.

And now, back in England, two men who were incorruptible, two men he could not remove.

'Stanislav Ivanov is still in a medically-induced coma,' Isaac said.

'What has that to do with me?'

'You visited him in the south of France,' Oscar Braxton said.

'Did I?'

'Are we going to go around in circles on this?' Isaac said. The three men were meeting in a restaurant in Notting Hill, at Cojocaru's suggestion.

'I'm not sure what you mean,' Cojocaru said. He leant back in his chair, stifling a yawn.

'Are we keeping you up?'

'Busy night.'

'Celebrating that Ivanov is in the hospital?'

'How many times do I have to tell you that the man does not interest me?'

'We know the truth, even if you continue to deny it. We know that you were picked up in a car belonging to Ivanov at Marseilles Airport and that you entered the man's villa. Antonescu never left there. We believe he is dead.'

'You're living in a fantasy world,' Cojocaru said. He looked away and beckoned the waiter.

'A whisky for me,' he said. 'How about you two, or are you on duty?'

'I'll take a beer,' Braxton said.

'Likewise,' Isaac said. He didn't want to drink, and certainly not with the man opposite, but they needed to find out what he knew or what he was willing to tell.

'Crin Antonescu travelled with you to France, we can prove that,' Braxton said.

'And if he did, then so what? Travelling out of the country is not a crime. Maybe he's taking a holiday,' Cojocaru said, a tenseness in his voice.

'We're suspicious that you would meet with the head of the Tverskoyskaya Bratva after you had given us his name.'

'You cannot ignore people purely because you dislike them.'

'Let us be honest, Nicolae Cojocaru. You are the head of a crime syndicate in England,' Isaac said. 'We can't prove it, not sufficiently to arrest you and to send you back to the hovel you came from, but there is a more pressing matter, the shooting at Briganti's.'

'I thought you were going to say Ivanov.'

'He is another grubby individual who hides behind a veneer of respectability.'

'No doubt you don't say that to his face.'

'There are no investigations into his activities in this country, although we believe he was behind the shooting at Briganti's, also the death of a police officer in Ireland.'

'Then you'd better talk to him.'

'We will when he regains consciousness. And when he does, we'll tell him that you ordered his assassination. How do you think he'll respond?'

'I did not organise it.'

'Then who did?'

'I don't know.'

The two police officers could see that Cojocaru was not going to respond. Not that they had expected him to, but if he was unnerved and frightened then maybe he would act irrationally.

'We can't prove it yet, but it has to be you,' Isaac said. He looked over at Cojocaru, hoping to see the tell-tale signs of a man who was lying: the eyes looking away, the twitching hand, the beads of sweat on his forehead.

'We are trying to find out who owned the flat where the shot was fired from,' Braxton said. 'We will make the connection to you, and then it will not matter whether Ivanov lives or not. We don't even have to bother arresting you. All we need to do is to let Ivanov's Bratva know that it was you. Or maybe they've figured that out already. We're told there are a few after Ivanov's position. Whoever takes his position won't be coming over to England to thank you. He'll be looking to carry on Ivanov's work, and maybe he'll use you for a while, or maybe he'll just have you killed. One way or the other, you, Nicolae Cojocaru, are a dead man.'

'Time will tell,' Cojocaru said.

'And this drug shipment that's in the country. Do you intend to distribute it?' Isaac asked. He took a drink of his beer, realising that in the company of evil it did not taste the same. He put it to one side, not intending to drink any more.

'I am an honest businessman.'

'You are a malignant parasite on society. If Ivanov doesn't get you, we will. In fact, your best chance is to level with us, turn Queen's evidence.'

'Detective Chief Inspector Cook, Detective Chief Inspector Braxton, I'll bid you both farewell. I do not find your company agreeable,' Cojocaru said as he stood up from his seat. He then walked out of the front door of the restaurant and got into the back seat of a black BMW, Ion Becali in the driver's seat.

'We made him feel uncomfortable,' Braxton said.

'We did, but what next? He could still strike a deal with the Russians. Cojocaru has residency in this country, they may not.'

'We still don't know what's going on, do we?'

'If Ivanov regains consciousness, he'll be looking to reassert himself. We should follow through on that angle,' Isaac said. 'But this investigation has deviated from what it was. Challis Street was looking for whoever shot up Briganti's, but now we're working with you on organised crime. The focus has been lost.'

'The focus hasn't, but how do you find out what happened? If, as we believe, Ivanov was responsible for Briganti's, and that Cojocaru was behind shooting Ivanov, then the person who took the shot in that flat is important. Get one, you get them all.'

'No one's come forward, and the gun on the twentieth floor wasn't registered, and there were no prints.'

'I'll get back to Serious and Organised Crime, find out what information is coming in from overseas,' Braxton said.

'I've got to get back to Challis Street. Sergeant Gladstone has an update, one of her people. Keep in touch,' Isaac said.

The two men shook hands, one heading down the road to his car, the other heading up.

Chapter 22

One of Stanislav Ivanov's bodyguards remained at Challis Street, not because he provided protection to the Russian businessman but because in a drain close to the assassination scene a gun had been found, the obvious deduction being that one of them had dumped it there.

Isaac looked across at the man in the interview room. 'Your name?' he said.

'Gennady Peskov,' the heavyset man replied. His English was acceptable although guttural. A translator was offered, but declined, as was legal aid. In the man's passport, a visa entitling him to carry out business in England, although no mention of his protection activities.

'How long have you been here?'

'Eight weeks.'

Larry sat to one side of Isaac. 'Why did you stay at the crime scene?' he asked.

'It was my job.'

'You provide personal protection for Stanislav Ivanov, is that correct?'

'I do.'

'And you carry a gun?'

'In Russia I would, but not in England.'

'Yet we found a gun near where Mr Ivanov was gunned down. Was it yours?'

'Not mine, but some of the others may have carried them.'

'Even if it is illegal?'

'Even if it was. Not that Ivanov would have approved. He's an honest man, but men such as him are always under threat.'

'What sort of man? A criminal, the head of the Tverskoyskaya Bratva?'

'One of the wealthiest men in Russia. People such as him make enemies.'

'You've been schooled well,' Isaac said. 'We've checked you out. In Russia, you spent time in prison for violence, almost killed a man once.'

'When I was younger, and the law is not always honest as it is here in England.'

The two police officers realised that Peskov, a gun for hire even if he denied the fact, was not a stupid man and that he had the innate street sense to say the right words and to not exacerbate the situation.

'Stanislav Ivanov is in the hospital.'

'I will stay by his side. The other bodyguards were not concerned about him, I am.'

'Why?'

'We grew up in the same village. To me, it is more than my job. To me, it is an honour.'

'Your visa is in dispute. You are not here to be employed, only to conduct business meetings.'

'I do attend the meetings, and I am not paid in this country. I don't think that you will deport me.'

Isaac knew they wouldn't. Even if Peskov had been carrying a weapon, he was a witness to a crime.

'Let us come back to the crime scene,' Isaac said. 'You are there with Ivanov, yet he gets shot. Why?'

'He enjoys the freedom in England. He wants to act as if he's English. Sometimes he gives us concern by his actions.'

'At the crime scene?'

'He wanted to talk to the people in the street, to look at his garden. We were hurrying him from the house to the car. He was not allowing us to do our job.'

'Are you saying it was his fault?'

'Not entirely. And it's not ours, not mine, that he was shot.'

'And what will Ivanov's reaction be, assuming he regains consciousness?'

'He will be angry and he will blame others.'

'Who?'

'Those who did not stay at his side, those who were responsible.'

'Do you know who it was that shot him?'

'No. Once I am free of here, I will be at Stanislav Ivanov's side.'

'There are no charges against you, Gennady Peskov. Where will we find those that ran from the crime scene?'

'I've no idea. If they could, they would have left the country by now.'

'Back to Russia?'

'Yes.'

'Thank you, Mr Peskov. You're free to go,' Isaac said.

Gennady Peskov walked out of Challis Street and hailed a taxi. 'St Mary's Hospital,' he said.

***

Nicolae Cojocaru's initial optimism was starting to wane. His nemesis, Stanislav Ivanov, had now been in intensive care at the hospital for nine days, and each bulletin from the hospital always said the same – the patient's condition is still critical, although there are signs of recovery.

Cojocaru could see the implications if the man made a full recovery, the consequences even if he did not. So far, the Tverskoyskaya Bratva's approaches to him had been low-key, no mention of how and why and who had shot their leader, only concern about how to maintain business, how to increase the distribution of the drugs out of Afghanistan.

The Romanian was under no illusion, and his denial if they asked about his involvement in the man's shooting would mean little to them.

Ivanov alive was a threat, dead he was also a threat, but in the half-world that the man occupied, he was an enigma; he made everyone nervous.

Cojocaru turned to Ion Becali. Both were in Cojocaru's penthouse.

'While Ivanov is in the hospital, we are safe,' Cojocaru said.

'We have taken control of the latest shipment, and we are setting up more distribution outlets for the Russians.'

'At the reduced price?'

'That is what Ivanov planned, and we have complied.'

'What about the gangs in the area? Any trouble?'

'We've taken them on to help with the distribution, although there are some complaints about the lower payments.'

'We're still maintaining their percentage at the old rate. They've no reason to complain.'

'Even so, it's more work for them, more chances of being caught.'

'They know the alternative,' Cojocaru said as he looked away from Becali. The man had gone from loyal employee to friend, even a junior partner, but now with

Ivanov hanging on, Cojocaru could only see a man who had failed him; a man who had said his marksmanship was without equal. And yet he had been unable to kill Ivanov.

Cojocaru picked up his coat and headed out of the penthouse. 'You're driving,' he said to Becali.

'Where to?'

'St Mary's Hospital. I want the truth.'

'Is there any concern that what they are reporting is not correct?'

'It is always a risk. If he's dead, we will last longer, maybe even long enough to plot our return to the old country.'

'But we are not wanted back there.'

'I must maximise the profits in the short term. Back in Romania, I will buy myself a house in the country and grow vegetables.'

'Nicolae Cojocaru, you are not a man of the soil.'

'Becali, it is better to plant the vegetables than to be the fertiliser that makes them grow.'

'I don't want to go back to my old life,' Becali said as he grabbed the car keys. 'I want to stay here. I will deal with the problem on my own.'

In the basement of the building was Cojocaru's Mercedes. Becali eased it out of its parking spot and left the building, heading east in the direction of the hospital.

***

Serious and Organised Crime Command was watching the unfolding events with concern. The Russian mafia had, so far, had minimal impact in England, although they had made inroads into the former Soviet satellite states, but now their influence was starting to increase in

London. A mansion in Kensington had been bought by Alexei Koch, a colleague of Ivanov's.

Reports indicated that whereas Ivanov was a man with some charisma and education, Koch could not be tagged with the same attributes.

According to Oscar Braxton, the man who had bought into one of the best streets in London was known for his savagery, a man who had personally murdered and tortured back in Russia, a man who had ascended up through the hierarchy of the Tverskoyskaya Bratva, a man who frightened many.

In Isaac's office at Challis Street, the team assembled, as well as Braxton.

'Ivanov's condition has improved,' Isaac said.

'Any signs of retribution for his shooting?' Braxton asked.

'Not yet. He's in for a long period of convalescence, whatever happens.'

'And in the meantime, we wait,' Larry said.

'Any better ideas?' Isaac said.

'Bateman's worried. The Russians are becoming too visible.'

'We're keeping a watch on them,' Braxton said.

'And doing what?'

'As long as they don't break the law, and they've no crimes against them back in Russia, it's difficult to refuse them a visa.'

'And with enough money, no one's looking too hard.'

'Can't we pre-empt the situation?' Isaac said.

'What do you mean?'

'Ivanov's the key. No one is going to act decisively while the man's life hangs in the balance. What if we issue a bogus report on his condition, and then watch what happens.'

'Are you suggesting that you're willing to allow an upturn in violence while the Bratva fight it out amongst themselves in Russia, and Cojocaru and Becali attempt to quell the local villains?'

'Can we control it?'

'It would require senior management to buy into it. If it goes wrong, it's on our heads.'

'And the lives of a few villains, and possibly a few innocent bystanders.'

'You've been on the streets, what about the cut-price heroin out there? Neatly packaged and brought in from Afghanistan, a stamp of quality marked on the outside.' Larry said. 'Do we have an option?'

Isaac made a phone call; Detective Chief Superintendent Goddard appeared within three minutes.

'Davies suggested something similar. You'll never get permission,' Goddard said.

'What are the options?' Isaac said. 'The streets are being flooded with low-cost heroin, and the police are only making a dent in it. We'll not win on this one, and everyone knows it. We could handle the West Indian gangsters, barely contain the Romanians, but the Russians have the muscle and the money to ride over us.'

'DCI Braxton, put it to your boss, and then I'll want a joint report from both our departments as to what is proposed, the risks, the rewards, the collateral damage.'

'And then?' Isaac asked.

'I'll take it to Commissioner Davies, get his input.'

'What are the chances?'

'It depends on your report. Davies doesn't want the street flowing with Russian gangsters and cheap heroin. What will happen after they've flooded the market, increased the number of drug addicts?'

'The price goes up, and so does the crime rate.'

'Get me the report, and we'll see. In the meantime, what are you doing?'

'Continuing with the investigations into the murders of Marcus Hearne and Ryan Buckley and the deaths at Briganti's.'

'Buckley's death is a matter for the Irish Garda,' Goddard said.

'His murderer could still be in England.'

'Very well. Just keep busy and arrest someone. I don't like what you're suggesting. Too many variables, too many opportunities for a mistake.'

Chapter 23

Wendy Gladstone had confronted death many times, and the sight of a body hanging from a beam, or with a bullet in it, did not bring her to tears. But the body lying on the ground did. A cord was tied around its neck, the bike that the man had been riding was off to one side, propped up against a tree. It was a bike that she knew; it was the bike of Ralph Ernest Begley, or Ralphie as he preferred to be called.

In the times she had spent with the young man, she had seen a decent soul wanting to make a difference, unable to break the cycle that condemned him. And now he was dead, and Gordon Windsor was with the body.

'You knew him?' Windsor said.

'Ralph Ernest Begley,' Wendy said.

'Who found the body?'

'I received a phone call from him ninety minutes ago. I came out here to meet him.'

'Here?'

'We used to meet nearby, and then I'd pay for a feed at McDonald's for him. It was how he liked it.'

'And when you got here, he was dead?'

'He said it was important.'

'You're not sure if it was?'

'With Ralphie, you could never be certain. He may have just wanted a feed and some money.'

'He was killed for a reason,' Windsor said as he stood up. 'The others in my team can complete the investigation.'

'Strangulation?'

'A neat job, no signs of resistance from Begley.'

'Which means that whoever killed him, knew him, or they were in conversation.'

'A local?'

'Not from around here,' Wendy said. 'The area is full of minor villains and layabouts, but not murderers. What else can you tell me about the death?'

'Whoever did it was strong.'

'Anything more?'

'Not at this time. The investigators will go over the area. You'll have an updated report later in the day. Next of kin?'

'The local police have informed them. I'll talk to them after here, but I don't expect much from them.'

'Someone that's killed before, I'd say.'

Wendy left Windsor and headed for the Begleys'. *No time like the present*, she thought.

The front door was opened on the second knock by a young woman. 'What do you want?' she said.

Wendy looked at the woman; assessed her to be in her teens. She was wearing a tee shirt two sizes too small, a pair of faded jeans and her feet were bare. On both arms, tattoos were visible, and she had a ring in her right nostril. Apart from the affectation of disreputability, Wendy could see an attractive young woman already destroyed by the environment and the system, the same that had condemned Ralphie.

'Sergeant Wendy Gladstone, Challis Street Police Station,' Wendy said.

'A bit late, isn't it? He's dead.' It was the reply of someone who didn't care or was incapable, stupefied by the effects of one or another recreational drug.

'I came to offer my condolences.'

'Suit yourself. They're in the other room.' The young woman left and went back to the front room of the house, music blaring loudly. Inside the room, Wendy briefly saw an older man. Wendy held her handkerchief to her face, not to stifle the tears, but to lessen the smell of sweat mixed with marijuana and tobacco. In the back room of the house, a group of people sat or stood. Leaning with his back against the kitchen bench, the elder and violent brother of Sal Maynard.

'You still here?' the man said on seeing Wendy.

Wendy felt the urge to rebuke him and to tell him what she thought of him and his family, as well as what she thought of the Begleys, but did not. Ralphie and Sal Maynard had become friends out of a need to better themselves. Sal had become obsessed with celebrity to find her way out of her malaise. Ralphie had seen McDonald's and its hamburgers as his salvation. Neither had stood a chance, and here in this kitchen, was all that Wendy despised. She wanted to turn around and leave, but there were questions to be asked; answers, if there were any, to be drawn from people who did not trust the police.

'Mrs Begley,' Wendy said. She could see Sal Maynard's mother with her arm around a small woman, the tears rolling down her cheeks.' I'm sorry for your loss.'

'What are you doing here, tormenting this poor woman?' Mrs Maynard said.

'I liked Ralphie. He was a decent young man.'

'He said you were alright,' Ralphie's mother said.

'With some help, he may have achieved something.'

'We'll never know now, will we?'

Ralphie's father leant against the far wall. In his right hand, he held a bottle of beer.

Wendy could see some worth in the mother, none in the father. The other drug-consumed brother of Sal Maynard was not present. The blaring music from the front room continued to impede the conversation.

'Could that music be turned down?' Wendy said.

'No one dare interfere when she's entertaining,' Mrs Begley said.

'Why?'

'She does what she wants.'

'How old is your daughter?'

'Fifteen.'

'And you, Mr Begley, allow your daughter to prostitute herself in your house?'

'She's not mine.'

'We were separated for some years. Ralphie was ours, Rosy is mine,' Ralphie's mother said.

'I came here to offer my condolences and to ask you a few questions.'

'I'm not sure we can help.'

'Very well. Could the Maynards leave us for half an hour?'

Sal Maynard's brother opened the fridge door, took a can of beer and left soon enough. After a few more hugs and kind words from Mrs Maynard, she left as well.

Three remained in the back room, Wendy and the parents of Ralphie Begley. Fred Begley took another beer for himself, gave one to his wife. No sign of affection between the two was shown. In the other room, the music continued to blare, together with the sound of the daughter and the man she was with. To Wendy, the noises were not of an innocent fifteen-year-old female who should have been at school.

'Excuse me,' Wendy said. She left one room and walked down the narrow hallway and opened the door of the other; she did not knock. 'Get your clothes on, and get him out of here. Your brother has just died, and you're screwing around.'

'It's my house,' Rosy said.

'What business is it of yours?' the man said.

'Your name?'

'I've done nothing wrong.'

'A female of fifteen, under the age of consent, and truant from school. There's a police car outside, a couple of officers. They'll have a few questions for you on the way out.'

'She told me she was seventeen.'

'Ignorance is no excuse.'

'I'm not a tart, and Billy, he looks after me.'

'And Billy is over thirty, and if he's giving you clothes and money, taking you to fancy hotels and restaurants, that's prostitution. You, young lady, need discipline, but I suppose there's not much in this house.'

'You're not my mother.'

'If I were, you'd feel the weight of my hand on your backside. Now get Billy out of here, and I'll be pressing charges against him. You, Miss Begley, will come into the other room with your parents now.'

Wendy opened the front door of the house and beckoned one of the officers over. 'Check out Billy here. Book him for having sexual relations with a minor, and then take him down to Challis Street, get him checked out. I want the book thrown at him.'

'We know Billy Jepson,' the officer said. 'Smarmy individual, sells drugs around the back of the pub of a Saturday to minors. We'll make something stick.'

'This is police brutality,' Jepson said.

'It's justice,' Wendy said.

Wendy returned to the back room, Rosy with her.

Mrs Begley sat quietly sobbing, her husband stood, his back resting against a wall. Rosy crouched on the floor. Not one of the three spoke to the other.

'Rosy, let me start with you,' Wendy said.

'Why me?'

'Because I've not spoken to you yet. You were too busy with Billy Jepson before, but now I need to ask you a few questions.'

'If you must.'

Wendy saw another lost soul, but she couldn't feel the warmth for the young woman that she had for her brother. 'What was your relationship like with Ralphie?'

'We'd talk, that's all.'

'Is that it?'

'He was alright, but we didn't have anything in common.'

'I don't think anyone has in this house, do you? Rosy, you don't seem to be upset that your brother has died.'

'Why, should I be?'

It was clear to Wendy that the young woman was hostile, although she wasn't sure if it was a result of her abrupt removal from her lover, or whether it was the woman's natural state. Regardless, she needed to talk.

'Rosy, let me be plain here. If you've been selling yourself to Billy and others, I'll have you remanded and placed in care. Do I make myself understood?'

'You can't talk to Rosy like that,' the mother said.

'I can and I must. You seem to be upset over Ralphie's death, although your husband and Rosy don't.'

'Has your father ever laid a finger on you?' Wendy asked Rosy.

'I've never touched her,' the father said.

'I'll be reporting Rosy and her behaviour once I'm back at Challis Street. You, Mr Begley, if it is found that you have touched your daughter, then charges will be laid. Now, Rosy, has your father ever made any inappropriate actions against you?'

Rosy sat mute, her eyes looking down.

'No need to answer,' Wendy said. She knew the truth; others would deal with the father in due course.

'Ralphie was worried, I know that,' Rosy said.

'What do you mean?'

'He liked Sal, not me, but she was fat and plain.'

'Ralphie told me that he identified with Sal. Both of them wanted something better out of life, so do you. But giving yourself to Billy Jepson and others is not the way to achieve it. Sal Maynard thought that associating with celebrities would be her way out, Ralphie had no idea of how to get out and had resigned himself to his fate. But you, Rosy Begley, believe that giving yourself to older men is the way. You're still a child, even if you have the body of a woman.'

'It's better than what they do,' Rosy said, lifting her head, glancing over at her mother and father.

'It's not the solution. I'll ensure that you receive counselling if that's what you want.'

'Ralphie said you were a good person.'

'Not that good. I was wild at your age, but I had good parents.'

'Mum's fine, even if she's unable to control us.'

'Rosy, what did Ralphie tell you?'

'It was earlier today. He told me he was going to phone you, but he was frightened.'

'Of what?'

'He knew who the second man was.'

'That Sal Maynard mentioned?'

'Yes. He'd seen him somewhere, and the man frightened him. Ralphie was thinking of disappearing, and he wasn't sure of what to do.'

'Did you advise him?'

'I told him to vanish, and now he's dead.'

'Did he give you a name?'

'I can't remember what he said.'

'Why?'

'I wasn't listening.'

'Or maybe you were spaced out on drugs.'

'I might remember later.'

'And if you do, what will you do? Phone me or try to make some money for yourself?'

'I'll phone you.'

'Ralphie was probably killed because of this name. If you try to make a deal, he will kill you. Do you understand?'

'Yes.'

'Unfortunately, Rosy Begley, you don't. One of the men that Sal Maynard was involved with was a Romanian gangster, not a Stockwell villain, not a Billy Jepson. These men kill without conscience. If they or he suspect you know, then your life will be forfeit, as will your parents' lives. Does everyone in this room understand?'

Wendy looked at the other two, both nodding in acknowledgement. She knew they did not.

Chapter 24

In St Mary's Hospital Stanislav Ivanov opened his eyes for the first time since he had been shot. The time had come to see whether the football club owner, entrepreneur, and Bratva Godfather was to be a vegetable for his remaining days, or whether he was to make a full recovery.

Detective Chief Inspectors Isaac Cook and Oscar Braxton stood back from the bed.

Ivanov slowly moved his head, looked at his wife and smiled. She came closer and kissed him on his forehead. A nurse checked the patient's pulse, a doctor felt proud that the medical care that had been provided appeared to have been successful.

'What happened?' Ivanov said to his wife.

'There was an assassination attempt,' she replied.

'Who?'

'The police don't know.'

'They are unimportant. Where is Gennady Peskov?'

'He is here, but you must rest.'

'I need Peskov.'

'Your wife is correct,' the doctor said. 'We need to ascertain your intellectual acuity, conduct further tests. You are still under mild sedation, and will be drowsy for the next few days.'

Ivanov moved his head towards his wife and spoke, his voice still slurred. 'Peskov knows what to do,' he said. His wife nodded but did not speak.

Isaac Cook and Oscar Braxton heard the words but did not understand; a police sergeant, the child of Russian immigrants, stood next to them.

Outside Ivanov's room, the police sergeant reported all that she had heard spoken in Russian.

'Peskov's the key,' Isaac said.

'The key to what?' Braxton replied.

'We're none the wiser, but Ivanov seemed coherent.'

Gennady Peskov came out from Ivanov's room, as did Ivanov's wife. Isaac walked down the corridor with the woman, Braxton stayed with Peskov.

'Mrs Ivanov, you must be pleased that your husband will recover,' Isaac said.

The woman did not miss a step and kept walking. 'Yes,' she said.

'There will be violence. We cannot allow it to happen in England.'

'I am the wife of Stanislav Ivanov. What he does or does not do is not my concern.'

'It is your concern. So far, he has not committed a criminal offence in England. If that changes, it could jeopardise your welcome in this country.'

'Inspector Cook, I am powerless in such matters, the same as you.'

The automatic doors at the exit to the building opened and Mrs Ivanov stepped into the back seat of a black Mercedes, the chauffeur opening the door for her. The vehicle sped away, leaving Isaac standing by the side of the road. He returned to where Gennady Peskov was standing with Oscar Braxton.

'Peskov tells me that there is nothing of concern,' Braxton said as Isaac arrived.

'Mr Ivanov has placed his trust in you. You must know what he wanted you to do,' Isaac said.

'It is for me to let others know that Stanislav Ivanov lives and that it is business as usual.'

'Business – commercial or criminal?'

'With Ivanov, commercial. I need to bring in my own security,' Peskov said.

'There has always been a police officer outside Mr Ivanov's room,' Braxton said.

'But Mr Ivanov is awake.'

'Do you expect another assassination attempt?'

'Your police officers will be no match for someone determined.'

'Are you suggesting that the Tverskoyskaya Bratva will attempt to kill him, or will it be closer to home?'

'I am not suggesting anything. Stanislav Ivanov needs more security, that's all I'm saying.'

'We are wasting our time with Mr Peskov,' Isaac said to Braxton, ensuring that the Russian heard the disdain in his voice.

'If anything happens to anybody in this country, then you, Gennady Peskov, will be our primary suspect. Is that clear?'

'That is clear,' Peskov said as he walked away.

'There's going to be trouble. What about Cojocaru? If he was behind the assassination attempt, then he must be worried,' Braxton said.

*****

Larry met with Claude Bateman who had taken the role of lead police communicator for the West Indian gangs in the area. Bateman was affable, more so than on the previous occasion.

The Wellington Arms in Bayswater, the venue for their meeting, was full, mostly with locals enjoying a quiet drink, a few tourists winding their way through the area, a few West Indians, some gang members, some not, sitting quietly or propping up the bar. Larry sat towards the back of the pub; on his left, Bateman, and on his right, one of Bateman's men.

'What will happen?' Bateman asked. He had a cigar in his mouth, he offered one to Larry. The two men took a puff on their cigars before expelling the smoke; neither spoke for a minute.

'What will you do? Are you clean?' Larry said.

'Becali took the shot at Ivanov.'

'Did he take the shot, the truth?'

'He had been in that building before.'

'Why didn't you tell us before?'

'Tell you what? If you knew that he had been seen there, what would you have done? Nothing, other than to confront Becali and Cojocaru. You wouldn't have arrested them. And then what?'

'You'd be exposed.'

'Discretion is the better part of valour. If you arrest Becali for attempted murder, cast-iron evidence, then the person who saw him in that building will testify. Until then, nobody will say anything.'

'You're telling me now.'

'The situation has changed. Ivanov will live, others will die.'

'Becali entered the building, took the shot from the flat and left. Did your person see this?'

'Not the flat, but the man entering and leaving the building, yes.'

'It's still circumstantial.'

'That's why you've not been told. You can't prove it, nor can we, but Ivanov does not need proof.'

'You've not told the Russians?'

'If we told one of his men, could they be trusted? Would they believe us? They hate us more than they hate Cojocaru.'

'Have you had any more contact with the man?'

'He's keeping a low profile, and with Ivanov recovering he must be worried.'

'And worried people do stupid things.'

'We will not become involved. The Russians are smarter than Cojocaru, more violent, and better resourced. We'd not stand a chance.'

'Neither would the police. What can you do to help us?'

'What do you want?'

'Keep us informed at all times, no matter how insignificant. Any strange faces on the street?'

'Russians?'

'Or Romanians.'

'How do you tell the difference?'

'I'm not sure, apart from the language. Have you seen Ion Becali?'

'He was in here a couple of days ago, drank a couple of beers and left.'

'Did he speak to you?'

'He wasn't in a talkative mood. He met up with a woman, left with her.'

'Is she important?'

'She's known in the area, but no, she'd know nothing.'

Larry felt that his time was wasted with Claude Bateman and that the West Indians were bit players in the unfolding drama. A phone call from Isaac, an excuse to leave the pub.

Outside, Larry got into his car, acknowledged one of Bateman's men who had been keeping a watch on it for him. Graffiti, a nuisance in the area, had been on the rise, and a police car was a prime target for a quick spray, the words artistically applied, yet derogatory. No one would dare touch Bateman's car, but a police vehicle was fair game, and for those who indulged in such behaviour, a badge of honour.

At St Mary's Hospital, Ivanov was sitting up and enjoying a good meal. No hospital food for him, it had been brought in from a Michelin-starred restaurant.

'This would not have happened in Russia,' he said.

Larry had arrived at the same time as Isaac, and both had entered the man's room together. To one side of Ivanov's bed, Gennady Peskov. There was no sign of Ivanov's wife.

'We've tightened security,' Isaac said by way of an apology, which he knew was an inadequate response. 'We'll ensure that it doesn't happen again.'

'No doubt, but it doesn't help.'

In Ivanov's previous room at the hospital, one floor up, Gordon Windsor and his crime scene investigators were commencing their investigation, the bullet hole in the window clearly visible.

'We believe it was the same person that shot you before,' Isaac said. Larry said nothing, disturbed that with the security they had provided for the Russian gangster, no one had thought to check the possibility of another shot being taken from outside the building, the same as when the man had stood on the street outside his house.

'I thought the English police were the best, but it appears they are not. I may have to re-evaluate my time in your country. It may be that Russia is a safer place for me.'

Isaac knew this was rhetoric on Ivanov's part and that this incident would be breaking news in the media: a prominent and respected Russian businessman, the intended victim of a brazen assassination attempt, the second since the man had returned to England, the first since the football team he owned had won the FA Cup.

'Our investigation has been thwarted by a wall of silence. Mr Ivanov, who took these shots?'

'I am a powerful man, and in Russia, powerful men have powerful enemies.'

'Are you saying that the attempts are orchestrated from Russia?'

'I have said no such thing. Do not try to trick me with your English language. I am suitably fluent not to fall for such tricks. In Russia, business is sometimes conducted with a gun, but here in England, I thought it was not.'

'It is not an Englishman who shot you, and you know this. It was either a Romanian or a Russian. We are aware of your connections in Russia, of the Tverskoyskaya Bratva.'

'I am a legitimate businessman who abides by the law and the ethics of the country that I operate in.'

'Are you saying that the Bratva is legitimate?'

'It is you that mention the Bratva, not I. And may I remind you that I am an influential man, and any aspersions that I am in some way guilty of any crime are slanderous, and I will ensure that your superiors are informed of what you are saying.'

Isaac knew that once the words 'influential', and 'I have friends in high places' were mentioned, then the person saying the words was rattled, and they were guilty.

'If you'll excuse me, I will go and check on your previous room,' Isaac said. 'What will you do about this second assassination attempt?'

'I will rely on the British police to apprehend who is responsible and to bring them to justice.'

Both Isaac and Larry knew that the man would not.

Upstairs, in the room previously occupied by Ivanov, Gordon Windsor was busy, as were three of his colleagues. Outside, along the corridor, some of the other patients in the adjoining rooms were being moved. It was a crime scene, and it was neither as quiet as it should be nor as hygienic. A middle-aged woman from the hospital administration made herself known to Isaac, expressed her concern at what had happened, and asked how long it would be before the police were finished and that it was a hospital for the ill, and not there for a police training exercise.

Isaac soothed the woman, ensured her that all efforts would be made to keep the disruption to a minimum, but a man had almost been shot in the hospital, and that had to take precedence. After ten minutes of his best diplomacy, the woman left.

Isaac and Larry kitted up in coveralls, gloves, overshoes, and entered Ivanov's previous room.

'Not a good record,' Windsor said. He was looking out of the window at a building across the road.

'The police or the assassin?'

'Both. You'll be hauled over the coals on this one. The man was in our protective custody this time.'

Isaac did not respond. He knew that Windsor was correct. Stanislav Ivanov had been provided police protection. It was not so much an oversight, more a realisation that it was the first time that a bullet had been fired into a hospital, and this time, the point of the bullet's departure could be clearly seen, an open window no more than fifty yards distance.

'We've got people over there?' Larry asked. 'It was only luck that Ivanov moved to one side in his bed at the right time.'

'The shooter's been sloppy this time. We found some prints.'

'Larry, get over there,' Isaac said. 'Find out what you can and make an arrest. If you don't, we're in for a rough time.'

***

Two days after the second attempt on Ivanov's life, the man checked himself out of St Mary's Hospital and returned to his home in Bayswater. However, this time Gennady Peskov ensured that the security provided was the best possible, no more low-grade thugs from Russia, other than a core group of four personally chosen by Peskov. A private English security company were to patrol outside the house; they were not armed, not even with pepper spray or tasers, a result of stringent English laws restricting the carrying and use of weapons, and although Peskov thought it foolish, Ivanov could not agree. With the money being paid, and the incorruptibility of the men employed, he knew that he was safer with men who regarded security as a profession, not just a chance to carry a gun and act important.

Peskov and his chosen four, fellow villagers back in Russia, had an arsenal of weapons in the house, although when they left the building they ensured that only two of them would discreetly carry guns. In the event of a gun being used, that person would be whisked out of England before the authorities could question him.

Ivanov sat in his favourite chair, his wife nearby.

'I want to stay in England,' the wife said. She was holding her husband's hand, but not with the attendant affection that would be assumed, but then, Ivanov knew that didn't exist. They had married young and had had three children. One of them, the only daughter, was a doctor in Moscow, and she used her mother's maiden name, and never mentioned that she was the child of Stanislav Ivanov. The two sons, one was killed in a shootout in St Petersburg, the other, a lieutenant in the Tverskoyskaya Bratva. Of the three children, Stanislav and his wife were fond of their daughter, not the remaining son. Each year the three of them would meet at a dacha near to a Black Sea resort. For ten days, they would be a family and no mention would be made of where the wealth had come from.

'I intend to stay as well,' Ivanov said. 'You can stay at the country house, I will stay here. And let us not pretend with each other.'

'I was worried.'

'So was I, but we maintain the pretence. You are the face of respectability, but I have no need of you,' Ivanov said.

'And I have no need of you,' the wife said. 'I will return to my home with your permission.'

'It is granted. I have work to do.'

'Be careful, the police are not fools. They will be watching.'

'It must be done. I have upgraded your security, just in case.'

'Thank you, my husband. I will check on you from time to time, and if you need me at your side, then call.'

As soon as Ivanov's wife had left, Gennady Peskov entered the room.

'Is all ready?' Ivanov said.

'It is ready. When?'

'Five days. I want everyone to be lulled into a sense of complacency. I want everyone to believe that my return does not upset the equilibrium. Cojocaru?'

'He is outside.'

Ivanov raised himself from his chair, Peskov assisting. 'Let him in,' Ivanov said.

Nicolae Cojocaru entered the room, the sweat beads on his forehead clearly visible. It was what Ivanov had hoped to see. The last time they had met, the Russian had forced the Romanian to shoot Crin Antonescu, one of Cojocaru's henchmen, one of the very few that the man could trust. And now the Romanian was back in the lair of the Russian godfather, a lair where he, Nicolae Cojocaru, was a mere pawn.

'I am pleased to see that you are well,' Cojocaru said.

'I thank you for your kindness. As you can see, I am fully recovered,' Ivanov said, struggling to maintain an upright posture. 'Please sit down. We have matters to discuss.'

Cojocaru sat down, bolt upright; Ivanov slumped back onto his chair, hopeful that it looked as though it was planned, and not as the need to take the weight off his feet as soon as possible.

'The distribution goes well, up nine per cent on last week,' Cojocaru said, his voice quavering.

'That is not why you are here.'

'I don't understand.'

Peskov stood to one side of Cojocaru, his right hand inside his jacket pocket.

'I want you to kill Ion Becali and to bring his head to me,' Ivanov said calmly.

'Why?'

'I need a sign of loyalty that I can trust you. You killed Antonescu, but you did not learn that my benevolence is limited, my wrath infinite. You have attempted to kill me on two separate occasions, and you have failed on both. I should be dead, yet I live. You, Nicolae Cojocaru, live because I have need of you. Either you comply with my request, or you will not leave here today.'

'The police are watching this house, you must know that.'

'Let me rephrase what I've just said. You will leave this house as a free man innocent of all crimes, or you will leave as a condemned man, the date of execution not yet determined. Which is it to be?'

'I wish to live, but for how long?'

'I will make you a promise. Do what I want without hesitation, and I will leave you alone. You are not the first to attempt to kill me, and some have died, some have lived. I do not blame you, I only pity your stupidity. Now, admit that you wanted me dead.'

'I did, but purely for my own survival.'

'Then we are honest with each other. Cojocaru, I do not like you or any of your Romanian friends, and you don't like me and what I represent. Openness is the way forward, and I want Becali dead as a token of our agreement here today.'

'And afterwards, when my usefulness has been exhausted, then what?'

'You will be free to do what you want.'

A confused man left the house, a man who knew that he was condemned whichever way he turned, but then he had known that since Ivanov and his Bratva started to make inroads into England. Peskov smiled as Cojocaru walked down the steps to the road. At that moment, Cojocaru wished that Becali was still in the flat that he could see up above him; he wished that the man was there to take a shot at him, and not to miss.

Chapter 25

Wendy attended the funeral of Ralph Ernest Begley, and watched as the young man's mother mounted the steps to the lectern at the front of the church and spoke of her son.

In the front row of the church, Begley's father and Rosy, the fifteen-year-old child who has flirted with danger and promiscuity. The two did not sit close to each other. On the left-hand side of Fred Begley, a police officer sat. To compound Ralphie's death, investigations into Fred and his step-daughter revealed that the man had been guilty of crimes against her, and he was now on remand awaiting trial. Rosy was dressed in black, the nose ring removed, the tattoos covered. Wendy looked over at her; she smiled back. At the conclusion of Ralphie's mother's eulogy, Rosy got up and helped her back to her seat. The young woman then mounted the steps to the lectern and spoke from the heart. The mother had been tearful but her eulogy devoid of any content other than a mother's love for a son and how he had always been a good child, rarely crying, and how his future had looked promising, and that she would miss him. Rosy, her face no longer caked in makeup, spoke of her brother, and how they would talk, sometimes into the night, and to her, he was the most important person in her life. She did not mention the father, nor did she look at him. To Wendy, it was as if she was talking to her, and it brought a warm glow to her; as if the death of Ralphie had not been in vain, and that the young woman had a chance of redemption, the chance her brother had never had.

Outside the church the young woman came over and put her arms around Wendy. 'Thank you for coming. Ralphie would have appreciated it,' she said.

'He wanted to be someone better. You seem better equipped to succeed.'

'I am. I was always top of my class at school, and I've refocussed myself on my studies. Please stay in touch. My father will not be around, not that he ever was, not when it was important, and my mother, well, you know what she is.'

'Call me if you need me,' Wendy said as she walked away and to her car. She had a smile on her face; for once, amongst all the misery and despair, a ray of sunshine, the possibility that she may have made a difference.

As she reached the car, Rosy came running up. 'I remembered the name of the other man. Anton something.'

'Antonescu?'

'That's it. Crisp?'

'Crin?'

'That's what Ralphie said. Do you know him?'

'I know him, but he's dead.'

'Are you sure?'

'As sure as I can be.'

'I hope it helps.'

'It does,' Wendy said as she gave Rosy a hug. 'Look after yourself.'

'I will.'

***

Commissioner Alwyn Davies was angry, and it was Detective Chief Superintendent Richard Goddard who was on the receiving end of the man's invective.

'How do you think this is going to reflect on the London Metropolitan Police?' Davies said. 'Twice they've tried to kill him, and the second time he's in intensive care at St Mary's Hospital, a guard on the door. What did you think, that they'd give up after the first attempt?'

'We provided the best security we could,' Goddard said. 'It was touch and go if the man would live after the first attempt.'

'But he did, and now he's back at his house. Do we have security there?'

'He's employed a private security company, very expensive, professional. They provide security to diplomats in the city, influential visitors.'

'Questions are being asked about Ivanov,' Davies said. His tone was almost conciliatory; before it had been combative. Goddard didn't like the change. He knew Davies to be a political animal, more concerned with his own survival than that of others.

'Enough money and questions go away.'

'What does that mean?' Davies's voice once again combative.

'Not bribery or corruption, but Ivanov entered this country with his pockets full of money and no criminal convictions overseas. He came on a Tier 1(Investor) Visa, two million pounds to invest. After two years, he injected another fifty million, although the minimum requirement was ten. He followed the correct procedures and we can't deport him.'

'If he's a legitimate investor in this country, then why are people trying to kill him?'

'It's in the report.'

'Goddard, don't get smart. Tell me why.'

'Stanislav Ivanov is the head of a criminal organisation that calls itself the Tverskoyskaya Bratva. Mafia, if you like. He'll claim that he isn't the head, and even if he is, there are no convictions against him, and he's done nothing wrong in this country.'

'What about the Romanians?'

'Serious players in the importation of illicit drugs and distribution. The Russians are attempting to muscle in, either use them or kill them.'

'And in your patch?'

'That's where Nicolae Cojocaru, the most significant of the Romanians, is based, but his operations spread out from there.'

'Yes, I've heard this all before, but what are you doing about it? What are you doing about Ivanov? These rogues sneak into our country, flashing their money and we do nothing.'

'We're here to police the wrongdoers, not to say who comes in or not,' Goddard said. 'We need to wrap up the shooting at Briganti's first. Serious and Organised Crime Command have Ivanov in their sights, but unless the man makes an illegal move, they're powerless.'

'He won't.'

'DCI Cook is maintaining the pressure on Nicolae Cojocaru. He's behind the attempted assassinations, not Briganti's though.'

'Can you be sure of that?'

'There's one inconsistency which doesn't make sense.'

'Which is?'

'Sal Maynard, a celebrity-obsessed woman, was in Briganti's, died there. It appears that she was spending time with Cojocaru's two lieutenants.'

'Then that's a clear tie-in, or am I missing something?'

'Cojocaru had no reason for Briganti's, Ivanov did. It's Ivanov for Briganti's, yet Sal Maynard is tied to Cojocaru. Not that she probably knew, not too bright according to reports, and now her friend from where she lived is dead as well. The trail continues to lead back to Cojocaru, yet we know it's not him.'

'Goddard, I've little confidence in your DCI Cook, you know that. I'd prefer my man Caddick in charge, but I've kept him out for the time being, hoping that you'd deal with the investigation.'

'Superintendent Caddick would not be advisable at this time,' Goddard said. He knew that a direct statement that the man was Davies's lackey and incompetent would have met with an immediate rebuke.

'Very well, have it your way. Goddard, for once you make sense. Now go and stir up your team, and leave me to deal with running the Met. You're not the only one who worries me.'

Richard Goddard sensed that for once the man did not mean what he had just said. It was as if there was a begrudging admission from Commissioner Davies that Chief Detective Superintendent Richard Goddard was a good police officer doing a decent job under difficult circumstances.

Goddard could not think the same of his commissioner, a man he still loathed.

***

'I've told you because I don't want to kill you,' Cojocaru said. The two men were in Cojocaru's penthouse; neither was interested in the view.

'If Ivanov knows that you are telling me, he'll have you killed,' Becali said. 'We will not succeed a third time. Have you admitted to our previous attempts?'

'I had no option. If I kill you, then I will survive a little longer.'

'Then do it,' Becali said.

'Why?'

'I don't mean me. Kill someone, make it out to be me, body destroyed beyond recognition.'

'You would do this?'

'For you, Nicolae Cojocaru, I would.'

'But who?'

'Does it matter?'

'Ivanov will want proof of your death.'

'Then Ivanov must die. What about the other Russians?'

'Ivanov's Bratva will do nothing, business is more important to them. As for the other Bratvas, they will not act. The only risk is Gennady Peskov. He is loyal to Ivanov, the same as you are to me. He will forfeit his life if necessary to avenge Ivanov's death.'

'Then he must die as well.'

'But how?'

'You must stay here. This time I need to get close to the man.'

'You will die.'

'If I survive, get me out of the country,' Becali said. 'And I want the truth of what happened to Antonescu.'

'It seems that we will both be growing vegetables back in the old country,' Cojocaru said.

'The truth.'

'I was given an ultimatum in France. Either I shot Crin, or they would shoot both of us there and then.'

'And you shot him in cold blood?'

'They had severely beaten him. I apologised before I pulled the trigger. He forgave me before he died.'

'You had no option, but now, we do.'

***

At Challis Street Police Station, a quandary on how to move forward. Larry met with Claude Bateman, the second time in as many days, a café close to Notting Hill.

'The calm before the storm,' Bateman said. 'It's a wait and see, and none of us wants to be involved. Ivanov's recovery frightens us. We do not believe that Cojocaru will live long, now that it is proven that Becali shot at the Russian twice.'

'Proven?'

'Yes, we know that he did. I did not tell you the full story last time, too dangerous. Becali was seen going into that flat. I have a witness who will come forward when needed.'

'Who? There is only one we know of, a covered woman in one of the flats on the same floor.'

'It was not her.'

'Then her husband.'

'He will not talk without certain assurances.'

'Such as?'

'Protection and the right to stay in this country.'

'You cannot give him that,' Larry said.

'But you can. If he gives you what you want, it is the lever to deal with Cojocaru, the opportunity to free ourselves from his influence.'

'Would you welcome this?'

'What option do we have?'

'You're admitting to criminal activity. I could have you arrested. Our conversation here today could be used as evidence.'

'You will not arrest me or others,' Bateman said. He took out a cigar from his pocket, put it back again.

'Why not?'

'The chance to rid yourself of Cojocaru is more important than arresting me. And besides, if what we plan works out, we can re-establish ourselves. And maybe Ivanov will go, and I will take the Romanian's place.'

Bateman was not a fool, Larry knew that, but the man was indiscreet and naïve. He had seen how Cojocaru had dealt with those he did not trust or want. The West Indians were violent and handy with a knife and a gun, but they still retained the Caribbean sentimentality, and death, even if they were responsible, was met with sorrow by them and the community.

'You are taking a risk, you must know that,' Larry said.

'There will be winners and losers, but to stand on the sidelines will achieve little. You can have Fahad Shaikh once you have satisfied his concerns.'

'We can pull him in anytime. Why does he trust you?'

'Who else can he trust? He has exceeded his visa, and he has been working two jobs, cash in hand. He came to me, not out of fondness, but out of desperation. He knew what would happen if he had come to you directly.'

'We would have secured his visa for as long as necessary.'

'For as long as it took to convict Becali. Shaikh needs more, and now, you have a man you can arrest. How much is this worth to you?'

'Why have you protected him for so long?'

230

'Leverage. He wants a commitment from you, in writing. I want your word that you will remove the malaise of Cojocaru and Ivanov.'

'Guarantees I cannot give. Cojocaru is possible, Ivanov is uncertain. The jobs that Shaikh has been doing. For you?'

'It is better that I do not answer, wouldn't you agree?'

'I would. Where can I find Fahad Shaikh?'

'He is at his flat. No agreement and he will not talk. He has placed his trust in me, not you.'

Larry knew that Bateman was right. Fahad Shaikh would give the team their first arrest and with the man's testimony their first conviction.

****

'Can't be done,' Richard Goddard said. He was sitting in his office on the third floor at Challis Street. On the other side of his desk, Isaac Cook and Larry Hill.

'But the man's a material witness. We need his evidence.'

'Where is he now?'

'Sergeant Gladstone is with him. I've organised two officers from Armed Response to ensure his safety.'

'Okay, put him and his family in a safe house. I'll see what can be done. Becali's trial will stretch out for some time. I'll make a few phone calls on behalf of the man, pull in a few favours. No promises, but it's the best we can do for now.'

Isaac left his chief superintendent's office and travelled out to Shaikh's flat.

'Everyone's curious as to why we're here,' one of the armed officers said.

'We're moving the family,' Isaac said. 'A safe house.'

'Now?'

'Yes. I need to go in.'

Isaac knocked on the door, Wendy answered it. 'I need to talk to Mr Shaikh.'

'He's frightened. They had a rough time back in Pakistan, and neither he nor his wife wants to go back.'

'We can get him a year in the UK, and DCS Goddard's trying for more. Becali's conviction will go in his favour.'

After five minutes, while Fahad Shaikh's wife moved to one of the bedrooms, Isaac entered the previously forbidden flat. He explained the situation, offered no guarantees, only emphasised the British sense of fair play and decency. Shaikh listened intently, finally agreeing with what he had been told. Two hours later, Wendy left with the family and five suitcases, the extent of their worldly goods in England. It wasn't much, Wendy had to admit, but it was probably more than where they had come from. Shaikh's wife grabbed her arm as they left the flat for a small house in the country. Fahad carried one of the children, his wife, another, and Wendy held the hand of a pretty girl of four.

Downstairs, a four-wheel drive waited for them. Wendy followed in her car for the fifty-minute drive. Whatever the future held for the Shaikhs, it was better than the depressing little flat they had left, Wendy thought.

***

An all-points warning had been put out for the arrest of Ion Becali, possibly armed and dangerous. Oscar Braxton was in Isaac's office, as was Richard Goddard, who left soon after to phone Commissioner Alwyn Davies about the breakthrough.

At the same time, a desperate man, unaware of his fate, sat in a café two streets from Ivanov's home. He knew what needed to be done, but not how to do it. He had walked up Ivanov's street fifteen minutes earlier, suitably disguised, and had seen the security, professional and alert, not like the Russians who stood to attention when needed, slouched when no one was looking.

Becali left the café. He was not thinking straight, and his plan, which had seemed plausible at Cojocaru's, now seemed foolish. There he had been willing to sacrifice his life for the man who had saved him from a life of subsistence and had brought him to England, but now he did not want to die, only to live. The future lay with Ivanov. He walked the two streets to Ivanov's house and shouted to the bodyguards on the road.

'I want to see Ivanov,' Becali shouted. 'I'm laying my weapon down.'

'Slow and easy. Which side of the body is the gun, right or left?' one of the men shouted back.

'Left.'

The four men standing outside the house moved behind a Range Rover on the street.

'Remove the weapon using your left hand and put it on the ground.'

Becali complied. He knew that the men ahead of him were English and unarmed, but from one of the windows to the left of them, two pairs of eyes watched. They would be armed, he knew.

'Now lie down spread-eagled, arms and legs stretched out. One of us will come over and check that you're not carrying any other weapons.'

Becali complied with the request; another man came over. He placed one of his boots firmly on the Romanian's back, pinning him to the ground.

'Don't move, not till one of the others has checked you out.'

A second man came over and frisked Becali thoroughly, pulling his wrists together behind his back and securing them with a cable tie.

'You can stand now,' the man said.

'I need to meet with Stanislav Ivanov,' Becali said. The cable tie was unexpected, and he knew it had to be removed.

'The police have issued an all-points for your arrest.'

'I need to see Ivanov first, it's important.'

'We're here to protect the man, not to let scum like you through. A police car will be here soon enough. You can either comply, or I'll flatten you. Your choice.'

'I'll comply.'

Becali realised that his chance to strike a deal with Ivanov was gone, but he was still alive. It wasn't the outcome that he had wanted, but it could have been worse.

Chapter 26

Nicolae Cojocaru realised forty-eight minutes after Ion Becali had left that he had made the wrong decision. A man stood in front of him, a man he had not expected to see.

'Becali has been seen close to Stanislav Ivanov's house. What did you expect? Did you imagine that he would be successful on his third attempt?'

'I killed you in France,' Cojocaru said.

'Ivanov was right. You are a fool, easily duped.'

'We were friends.'

'We never were. To you, I was a man who committed violence when it was needed, nothing more. You were willing to kill me to save your life.'

'I had no option. Neither of us would have left Ivanov's villa if I hadn't.'

'You were told to kill Becali. Stanislav Ivanov is a forgiving man to those who are loyal to him, indifferent to those who aren't.'

'I could not kill Becali. He has always been loyal to me.'

'Ivanov was willing to abide by his agreement, the same as he has with me, but now, your fate is sealed.'

'Can we make a deal? It is not too late to save us, you included. Anyone who knows what Ivanov is in England, the crimes he has committed, will die.'

'I have seen nothing, nor will I. The man has my allegiance, you do not.'

'But I shot you.'

'A subterfuge to test you. You did not check the gun, it contained a blank, and I was wearing a bulletproof vest. Ivanov wanted to know if you were capable of violence and whether you would shoot me in the chest.'

'It makes no sense.'

'Not to us, but we are not smart men, not as smart as Ivanov. I had to decide, the same as you. I chose Ivanov, you chose to die,' Crin Antonescu said.

Cojocaru, not sure what to say or do, sat down on a chair. Antonescu sat too, always ensuring that the gun he held was pointed at his former boss.

Neither man moved, except to maintain their gaze at the other. Cojocaru could see the impassiveness in the other's eyes, but he was not surprised. Crin Antonescu had always been emotionless when violence was involved, whereas Ion Becali had followed orders, and now he was in police custody.

'It would be better if you shot me now,' Cojocaru said.

Antonescu shot Cojocaru once in the head, the man's lifeless body slumping forward. After the man had died, Antonescu reflected on what he had just done, feeling a pang of regret.

He knew that Cojocaru, for all his faults, had supported him, and what he had done in France was only what he would have done if the positions had been reversed. He left the penthouse with a heavy heart and drove back to his hotel. He had re-entered England under a false name, his dark hair dyed blond and cropped short. Life was as uncertain for him as it had been for Cojocaru and for Becali. He knew that he needed to leave the country as soon as possible.

***

Ion Becali sat in the interview room at Challis Street Police Station. In front of him, a cup of tea, to one side, his lawyer, a naturalised British citizen from Romania. Across from the two Romanians, Isaac Cook and Larry Hill.

Isaac followed the procedures required, informed Becali of his rights and that what he said could be used in evidence. He had said it many times in the past, and he knew it verbatim, but it was imperative that Becali, a man with a good level of fluency in English, understood it as well, the Romanian lawyer ensuring that he did.

'Mr Becali, you have been arrested outside Stanislav Ivanov's house. You were armed. Why?'

'My client has nothing to say,' Klaus Ponta, the lawyer, said. The man's English was flawless. He was in his mid-forties, starting to put on weight, his hair beginning to thin. Isaac felt that Becali had chosen his lawyer well.

'Carrying a loaded gun is a crime in this country,' Isaac said. 'There is a minimum five-year prison term for the offence. Mr Becali needs to be made aware of this.'

'I am,' Becali said.

'What was your intent on approaching Mr Ivanov's house?'

'I wanted to talk to him, to reason on behalf of Nicolae Cojocaru.'

'With a gun?'

'I knew that Ivanov would have guns in the house. It was for personal protection.'

'Are you telling us that Ivanov is a criminal?'

'I am not.'

'Then why would Cojocaru want to make a deal with Ivanov? Ivanov is a man without a criminal record, but we all know in this room that Cojocaru is responsible for distributing large quantities of illegal drugs throughout the area and the country.'

'No charges have been laid against Mr Cojocaru,' Ponta said. 'Supposition is not the basis for an interview, neither is putting words into the mouth of my client, who may or may not fully understand the legal implications.'

'Mr Becali, we can prove that you were in the flat where the first assassination attempt was made. We believe that you intended to try a third time, although that would have almost certainly resulted in your death.'

'I am not guilty of murder.'

'As an assassin, you have proved your incompetence. As a prisoner, you may be more effective. The choice is yours. If we release you with no charges, then Ivanov may choose to remove you, or maybe Cojocaru will. And what about Sal Maynard and the shooting at Briganti's? Was it you?'

'I've told you before, I may have been with the Maynard woman, nothing more.'

'We now believe that she was also involved with Crin Antonescu. Did you know this?'

'It's possible.'

'Ryan Buckley, an inspector with the Irish police, was murdered. We know it wasn't you, although it is possible that you know the reason why.'

'Why should I?'

'Buckley was a friend of Seamus Gaffney, a man who kept his nose to the ground. We believe he knew something which he told Buckley. Buckley, we know, killed Gaffney and then attempted to strike a deal with someone, either Cojocaru or Ivanov.'

'It appears that you have nothing against my client, other than carrying a weapon,' Ponta said.

'You can try if you want to dismiss that charge, but the charge of attempted murder still applies.'

'How?' Becali said.

'We have a witness,' Larry said. 'A witness that will testify that you were in the flat where the shot on the first attempt was made. Also, on the second attempt, CCTV footage of a person fleeing the area, as well as a shoe print. We have enough to make a conviction stick. Mr Becali, I would suggest that you start to tell the truth.'

'Why? You intend to convict me of crimes I didn't commit.'

'We have sent a vehicle to pick up Nicolae Cojocaru. He will be offered the chance to make a statement. If he knows you are to be convicted of attempted murder, what do you think he will say?'

***

Isaac had to agree that the evidence against Becali was not tight. The man was guilty, but it was mainly based on incomplete evidence. Even the gun recovered from outside Ivanov's did not have fingerprints, Becali having worn leather gloves on account of the cold morning. And Fahad Shaikh, a recent arrival in the country with his young wife, probably a first cousin as was the tradition, and his involvement on the periphery of crime, would be regarded as a marginal witness. Careful manipulation of the jury by a skilled defence lawyer would ensure prejudice against the Pakistani, and his testimony would be debased as a result.

Even so, it was a win of sorts, and the first arrest in an investigation that had gone on for too long.

Isaac sat on his chair in his office, his hands clenched behind his neck, leaning backwards, the weariness of the long hours starting to tell. He would have remained there for longer except that Brigitte came rushing in.

'Cojocaru,' she said. 'He's dead.'

Isaac left Challis Street soon after, Wendy with him. Larry, who was out of the office, cancelled his meeting with Bateman and headed out to Cojocaru's penthouse.

On the street, the crime scene tape, the barriers being erected. A uniformed police officer let the three of them through, Gordon Windsor did not. 'Get kitted up if you want to go in,' he said.

'Have you seen the man?' Isaac asked.

'One shot to the head. One to two hours ago.'

'Who phoned the police?' Larry asked.

'The man's housekeeper. She's available,' Windsor said.

'Wendy, talk to her and get a preliminary report. I'll go up with Larry,' Isaac said.

Three men, kitted up with coveralls, gloves, and overshoes, entered the penthouse, stepping to one side of a crime scene investigator who was on the floor checking for evidence. At the other end of the hallway, the main living area, a man slumped on a chair.

'Not a pretty sight,' Windsor said.

'Any signs of a weapon?' Larry said.

'Not here. It's a clean kill, and whoever did it was smart enough to black out the CCTV cameras in reception.'

'Fingerprints?'

'Not yet. Don't hold your breath on this one.'

'Becali?' Isaac said.

'If it's one to two hours since the man died, Becali didn't shoot him,' Larry said.

'This may loosen his tongue,' Isaac said.

Chapter 27

Two days passed; two days when the initial flush of success after the arrest of Ion Becali had ground back into a routine.

The team at Challis Street met each morning early, and the days stretched into the nights, no one going home until late; nobody complaining either.

The body of Nicolae Cojocaru had been examined by Pathology, the man's penthouse had been checked by Gordon Windsor and his team, and Forensics had conducted tests on the bullet removed from the body. Nothing new had been found, and frustration at the lack of progress was felt by all.

Commissioner Alwyn Davies had been on the phone to Chief Superintendent Richard Goddard who had been in Homicide attempting to rally the team – it was not needed.

Stanislav Ivanov stayed in his house, apart from a brief excursion out to his football club for a function, his wife accompanying him. The man had made a speech about how pleased he was that they had won the most prestigious footballing competition in the country, the FA Cup, and sorry that he had not been there to cheer them on, but he had been otherwise occupied.

Ivanov made light of the assassination attempt, and Isaac, who had made sure to be in the back of the room at the function, could only imagine what the man really thought.

Annie O'Carroll had been on the phone from Ireland to let Larry know that leads had dried up there, and whoever it was that had shot Ryan Buckley, he wasn't Irish, but that was known already.

Another man sat in his hotel room; a man not used to inactivity and apathy; a man who needed to get out from the four walls and room service.

At four in the afternoon of the third day after Cojocaru had been shot, Crin Antonescu stepped out through the front door of his hotel and walked down the street. He needed a drink first and then a meal. The pub he chose, five miles from where Cojocaru had lived, five miles from the West Indian gangs and Challis Street, seemed safe enough for him.

He ordered a beer and a pub lunch. He then sat down in the corner of the bar. It was not ideal, but it was better than nothing, he realised. He looked up at the television mounted high on one wall and saw the face of Ivanov beaming back; it was a face he had trusted, but now the man was not answering his calls.

Without finishing either his beer or his lunch, he walked down the street, absent-mindedly, not knowing where he was going. He reflected on what had been, the early years in Romania, the setting up in England, on Ion Becali, on the woman who had fallen for him, and even though he had not loved her, there was a warmth in her, a genuine wish to be with a short, stocky ex-wrestler from Romania. But she was dead in that hairdressing salon with the others. He had sent her to her death, and he was sorry, an emotion he did not feel comfortable with. He phoned Stanislav Ivanov one more time – no answer. Gennady Peskov answered on the second ring when he phoned again.

'You were told to wait,' Peskov said. He had hated Antonescu from the first time he had met him in France.

A man who is willing to change sides was not a man to be trusted, and now the man was phoning him.

'I have completed my task. It is for you to protect me, to get me out of the country.'

'Then wait.'

'For how long?'

'For as long as is needed. Ivanov does not forget those who are loyal, and you have done what is required. Your hotel has been paid for, and extra money has been given to you. You have no reason to complain.'

Peskov cut the call; Antonescu kept walking.

It was after nine in the evening when Crin Antonescu walked into the police station at Challis Street. The appearance of the man caused consternation in Homicide and alarm with Ivanov when he heard.

'I will tell you what I know,' Antonescu said in the interview room. He did not have a lawyer with him.

'We have always assumed you to be dead,' Isaac said.

'I am guilty of entering this country under a false name and with a false passport. I wish to return to Romania.' The man spoke slowly and with great thought.

'What other crimes are you guilty of?'

'I have committed no other crimes in this country.'

'Ion Becali has been charged with attempted murder. Nicolae Cojocaru is dead.'

'That I know.'

'How?'

'It is on the news.'

'Why have you come here?'

Isaac realised that his questions were inane, but he wasn't sure what else to ask. Across the table from him and Larry was a savage killer, the man who had probably

244

killed Cojocaru, almost certainly had murdered Ralph Begley, yet there was nothing to tie the man to the crimes. It was as if Antonescu was playing with them, but Isaac knew he was not. Antonescu was not an intellectual, not a strategist, but a man who thought a passport violation would get him transported out of the country.

'There's no reason for me to be here now.'

'You came in illegally. Couldn't you leave the same way?'

'There are others who will not let me leave alive.'

'Why? Because you have murdered for them? And what's the truth with Sal Maynard?'

'She was a decent person and I mistreated her.'

'By making her go into Briganti's?'

The man's behaviour concerned Isaac and Larry. Antonescu had spent his life as a violent criminal, and now he was being circumspect and remorseful. It was an act, and it was convincing, and if the man's history had not been well known, others might have been duped.

Isaac knew that whenever a villain was contrite, it meant something else. The man had said that others would not let him leave alive, but why?

'Before we can help you, we need to know why they want you dead, and why did you return to this country illegally?'

'I needed to make peace with Nicolae Cojocaru.'

'A phone call would have sufficed. What happened at Ivanov's place in France? You went in but never came out.'

'I am out now, and I am willing to tell you what you need to know.'

'The truth?'

'All of it.'

'Then let's start with what happened in France.'

'Cojocaru shot me.'

'Why?'

'Because Stanislav Ivanov wanted proof of his loyalty.'

'An unusual way to test a person.'

'Not with the Bratva. I cannot blame Cojocaru.'

'Would you have done the same?'

'With a gun to my head if I didn't?'

'That's not an answer. I'll repeat the question. Would you have shot Cojocaru if the positions had been reversed?'

'Yes, and so would you.'

Isaac ignored the man's attempt at justification. 'Have you killed a man before?'

'In self-defence.'

'In England?'

'Never. Nicolae Cojocaru was always careful to ensure that we trod lightly with breaking the law.'

'Was the man importing drugs into this country?'

'Yes.'

'Then you are guilty of more than a passport violation.'

'My job was to protect him, not to become involved in his business.'

'Yet you stayed in France and now the man is dead. What do you say about this?'

'I failed in my duty.'

'And France?'

'What could I do? I either sided with Ivanov or I was dead. Cojocaru would have taken the shot, and I would not have been wearing a bulletproof vest.'

'Your story makes no sense,' Larry said.

'Then release me, and I will chance my luck on the street.'

'Ivanov has not committed murder in this country. Why is your life in danger?'

'If you guarantee that I will be protected and you will deport me to Romania, then I will tell you all.'

'Including how you killed Marcus Hearne?'

'I didn't kill him and you can't prove that I did.'

Isaac could see that they were hitting the proverbial brick wall. A conviction for Ion Becali was based on the testimony of an illegal migrant, not on forensic evidence. A smart lawyer would have argued that Ion Becali wanting to see Ivanov was not unreasonable and there was no proof that his intent had been murderous. Men such as Ivanov, men as rich as Midas, received requests all the time from people down on their luck.

'Then who killed Hearne?' Larry asked. 'We can't help you if you don't cooperate.'

'I was wrong to come in here. I want to leave this country; not admit to a murder I did not commit.'

'Tell us about the meeting. What happened?'

'I don't know. I was not there.'

'Let me come back to Becali. Did he kill Marcus Hearne?'

'If I say he did, you will keep me in this country.'

'As a witness.'

'What life is that for me? I will be on the street and Ivanov will have me killed.'

After one hour of questioning, a break in the proceedings. Antonescu asked for a pizza, which was duly delivered to the police station. Isaac and Larry went back to Homicide, and Larry phoned Annie O'Carroll in Ireland.

'What do you have?' Larry said after he had updated her.

'Unreliable witnesses, a possible man on Buckley's street twenty minutes before he was shot.'

'Possible?'

'Someone was taking selfies with an iPhone. There's a man in the background. The time's right, but we can't recognise him.'

'Short, stocky?'

'We've been through this before,' the Irish police officer said.

'Humour me.'

'Very well. The man that we have is short, but we've been through the faces you sent before. Came up with nothing.'

'Okay, try this. Blond, hair cut short, not as stocky as before.'

'It's probable, but it's an image from an iPhone, not in focus either.'

'We've got Brigitte checking through the flights to Ireland and the ferries crossing the Irish Sea. Any chance for you to check with the car rental companies in Dublin?'

'We checked before, went nowhere.'

'That was before. We've got one man for attempted murder, another at Challis Street who's claiming to be innocent. He was thought to be dead, but here he is, and he's altered his appearance. A thug, as bad as they get, and not too bright. If he were in Ireland, he could have made a mistake. Check the clubs, pubs, anywhere a degenerate could get to, and the man's accent is strong, so he would probably stand out.'

'Briganti's?'

'It's possible he's involved. We don't know how long he's been on Ivanov's team, but they've dumped him now. Probably trying to distance Ivanov from Cojocaru's

248

death, but why they left Antonescu on the street, we're not sure. It seems to be an error on their part, and Ivanov doesn't make many errors, but if it wraps up the murder investigations, then we'll pursue it at all costs. Annie, bring in whoever you can and let's get this man.'

'Send me an updated photo.'

'Five minutes and you'll have it. We can't hold the man for long. He's here voluntarily.'

Isaac phoned Gordon Windsor. 'Any updates on Cojocaru?'

'The man's with Pathology, but they'll not be able to tell you much more. We've not found any clear evidence at the murder scene, other than a blond hair.'

'Is it with Forensics?'

'It is. Significant?'

'Test it against Crin Antonescu. You should have a sample of his DNA.'

'Should we? I don't think so, not unless he's on our database.'

'Very well. Send one of your people down to Homicide, and we'll get you a sample.'

***

Crin Antonescu, who in an act of desperation had willingly walked into Challis Street Police Station, now found himself charged with the murder of Nicolae Cojocaru. Not that the proof was certain, Isaac knew that, but they needed Antonescu's DNA to move forward. With an arrest, the man would be forced to comply.

The sample was with Forensics within the hour, a swab from inside the man's mouth, a strand of hair. Antonescu had complained, but legally he had no option.

Back in his cell, the Romanian sat quietly, taking his meals when they came, and asking for coffee every twenty minutes. Isaac and Larry looked at the man on the camera in the cell, unable to make any sense of a villain who came into a police station uninvited. It was behaviour they had not experienced before; the assumption was that he was more frightened of Ivanov than of the police. That was understandable, but why had he returned to England, why not go somewhere else? Ivanov frightened Isaac and Larry. The man was distinguished, and some would say charismatic, and the general view of the populace was that he was a man who had made good in the new Russia.

Oscar Braxton was over from Serious and Organised Crime Command. He was sensing a victory of sorts, but not total. 'We'll never get Ivanov,' he said.

'Any worth in talking to him again?' Isaac said. The three, including Larry, were sitting in Isaac's office.

'He'll not admit to anything, and Becali outside his house is circumstantial. Damning to Becali and to us, but Ivanov will have the best legal minds with him. He'll come out clean, and if he was behind Briganti's and Cojocaru's death, where is the connection?'

'Leave him for now, focus on wrapping up the murders. Any word from Inspector O'Carroll?' Isaac said, directing his glance over to Larry.

'Not yet. She's trying, but there's no forensics to back it up. We may get Antonescu for Cojocaru, but not for Buckley, even if he's guilty.'

A phone call from Gordon Windsor, a look of relief on Isaac's face. 'Bring Antonescu back up. We've made the connection to Cojocaru. He's already been charged, but this time it's up to him to see if he's willing

to admit to the crime and whether he's willing to
implicate others.'

Chapter 28

Annie O'Carroll phoned from Ireland. The indications were that Antonescu had been in Ireland, although the photo, enhanced as best as it could be, was not good enough to be proof positive. It appeared that the murder of Buckley would remain without a convicted murderer, although there was no doubt about who was responsible.

Antonescu sat in the interview room once more. Klaus Ponta, who had represented Becali, sat to his side, the charged man having relented about the need for a lawyer.

'Mr Antonescu, you've been charged with the murder of Nicolae Cojocaru. Is there anything you want to say in your defence?' Isaac said.

'Your evidence is circumstantial,' Ponta said. 'My client has not admitted to the crime.'

Isaac respected Ponta; the man was just doing his job.

'It's not, and with added focus, we'll find more evidence. We're also certain that Antonescu shot Inspector Ryan Buckley in Ireland. Your client, if he is not able to offer an alternative explanation of why he was at Cojocaru's penthouse, and why he was in Ireland, will stand trial.'

'I didn't do it,' Antonescu said. He slammed the table with his fist, almost causing a glass of water that Larry had brought into the room to topple off and onto the floor.

'There are unresolved questions,' Isaac said. 'The first is what did Inspector Buckley find out from Seamus

Gaffney that condemned him? And who did he tell it to? The fact that he wasn't killed by Mr Antonescu indicates that Gaffney either hadn't revealed what he knew or that Buckley killed him first. Antonescu, what do you have to say?'

'Ion Becali killed Buckley. Seamus Gaffney had dirt on Cojocaru, not Ivanov. I wasn't involved,' Antonescu said.

'But you know the story?'

'I'm not saying anything. All I know is that Gaffney was trying to blackmail Cojocaru and that Becali killed Buckley.'

'It wasn't Becali. We can trace his movements at the time of Buckley's death; yours, we can't.'

'My client has no more to say,' Ponta said.

'Let's move on,' Isaac said. He was feeling increasingly comfortable with the situation. Oscar Braxton was listening in from another room, as was Richard Goddard.

'To where?'

'Marcus Hearne.'

'The black man,' Antonescu said sneeringly.

'Do you have an issue with people of colour?'

'Not me. I knew him, didn't like him, although I suppose you did.'

Isaac could tell that the Romanian was racist, not that it impacted the investigation, unless it was a motive.

'Cojocaru attempted to bring the West Indian gangs in, the reason that four of their leaders accepted his hospitality. Claude Bateman, Devon Harris and Jeremy Miller made it to the meeting, Hearne didn't. Why?'

'I'll not answer that question.'

'Because you can't, or you don't want to?'

'My client has been charged with one murder. We will address the falsehood of that, not other purported crimes,' Ponta said.

'Dead in a ditch is not purported,' Larry said.

'To you it's important, but not to my client who is innocent. He is concerned with a false accusation against him. He came to this police station, not to be charged with murder, but for assistance. He is fearful for his life, and now you have jeopardised it further.'

'Why?'

'Nicolae Cojocaru has powerful friends in Romania. They will not take his death lightly.'

'The man had no friends in Romania. He was a social pariah, convicted of crimes in absentia, derided by the villains there. Let's not pretend otherwise. The man's dead and no one is going to miss him.'

'Then someone did you a favour,' Antonescu said.

'They did, but it's still murder, and you did it.'

'Gentlemen, this is going nowhere,' Ponta said. 'Mr Antonescu wants to help, but with a murder charge against him, he is reluctant to say more. If an accommodation could be made, then it may be possible that he can further assist.'

'We can't grant him immunity from prosecution, not for murder,' Isaac said.

'Then he has no more to say.'

***

'What can Antonescu do against us?' Gennady Peskov asked. He was in Ivanov's house, a glass of whisky in his hand, the same as Ivanov.

Ivanov touched the plaster on his head, felt a slight pain as he applied pressure. Apart from that he felt fine, although he realised that his mental acumen was still not up to speed. He had erred with Antonescu, underestimated the stupidity of the man.

'Antonescu can do nothing against me,' Ivanov said. 'You allowed him to be arrested. What do you intend to do?'

'But you commanded me to tell him to kill Cojocaru.'

'And then you were meant to kill Antonescu and to ensure his body was never found. Why didn't you?'

'It was planned. He may have sensed that others were coming for him.'

'He sensed nothing. He is just a mindless thug. The same as you, Gennady Peskov, have proven to be.'

'I gave instructions for him to be killed after he left Cojocaru's.'

'You are not the mastermind, I am. I entrusted you with more responsibility after you stayed by my side in the hospital, but it appears that my weakness in crediting you with brains was a mistake.'

'I will discipline those that have failed us.'

'Failed you. Can your command be tied back to you, to me? Can these men be trusted again?'

'Not in this country.'

'Then they must leave immediately. Where are they now?'

'They are nearby.'

'A plane is waiting for them, make sure they are on it. I want them out of England within two hours, is that clear?'

'And what of me?'

'You will stay. You will protect me at all costs, even your own life. But you are a fool. I will need to keep a watch on you from now on.'

'I will not let you down,' Peskov said.

'If you do, I will not be so generous the next time,' Ivanov said. He knew that he was not generous, only astute. Gennady Peskov, for all his faults, was the one man who would stand between him and a bullet.

In another part of London, a group of police officers discussed the situation.

'Marcus Hearne?'

'Becali or Antonescu, probably both,' Isaac said.

'Ivanov is still free,' Larry said.

'And will remain so,' Oscar Braxton said. 'He's taken on a couple of Queen's Counsels to protect him legally, and a PR company to deflect the negative publicity that's stuck to him. Expect to see more of Ivanov at charitable functions in the next month or so, overly-generous donations as well. We can't beat him, not while money speaks.'

'Briganti's?' Wendy said.

'It still needs to be solved. Marcus Hearne knew something, or Cojocaru couldn't trust him, not after he was speaking to me,' Larry said.

'He's not the first person who's given you information that has died,' Isaac said.

'Not the first, not the last,' Larry agreed, 'but Wendy's right. What about Briganti's?'

Isaac made one more phone call, Gordon Windsor answered.

'Antonescu was at Cojocaru's penthouse; we can prove that from a strand of hair on a chair that he sat in,' Windsor said. 'It's recent, the chair had been cleaned in the last couple of weeks. We've also checked Antonescu against Briganti's. No shortage of hair there, a hairdressing salon, but we found proof that he had been in there as well. Not blond and dyed, dark and natural.

256

How the man pulled it off and managed to walk out of there unseen, we don't know. But he's your man. He killed those people at Briganti's.'

Isaac relayed Windsor's findings to the team. 'He must have been working for Ivanov for a long time,' he said.

'Poor Sal,' Wendy said. 'She thought it was love and then the man killed her.'

'The others didn't deserve to die either. What about Ralphie, who killed him?' Isaac said.

'Antonescu. Sal used to speak to Ralphie. He phoned the man, probably trying to get money out of him and was killed for it.'

Isaac picked up his phone and made one more call. The phone at the other end was answered.

'Detective Chief Superintendent Goddard,' the voice said.

'Antonescu killed the people at Briganti's, Cojocaru as well. The other murders are either him or Becali; both are in custody. You can phone Commissioner Alwyn Davies.'

'And Ivanov?'

'Expect to see him on the television and gracing the social pages of the newspapers. He's on a charm offensive now, and there's nothing we can do about it.'

'The biggest villain walks free, is that it?'

'It is,' Isaac said.

The end of a long-running murder investigation should have been a time for satisfaction at a job well-done. No one in Homicide felt in the mood for a pat on the back or a celebratory drink at the pub.

The End.

ALSO BY THE AUTHOR

Death by a Dead Man's Hand – A DI Tremayne Thriller

A flawed heist of forty gold bars from a security van late at night. One of the perpetrators is killed by his brother as they argue over what they have stolen.

Eighteen years later, the murderer, released after serving his sentence for his brother's murder, waits in a church for a man purporting to be the brother he killed. And then he too is killed.

The threads stretch back a long way, and now more people are dying in the search for the missing gold bars.

Detective Inspector Tremayne, his health causing him concern, and Sergeant Clare Yarwood, still seeking romance, are pushed to the limit solving the murder, attempting to prevent any more.

Death at Coombe Farm – A DI Tremayne Thriller

A warring family. A disputed inheritance. A recipe for death.

If it hadn't been for the circumstances, Detective Inspector Keith Tremayne would have said the view was outstanding. Up high, overlooking the farmhouse in the valley below, the panoramic vista of Salisbury Plain stretching out beyond. The only problem was that near where he stood with his sergeant, Clare Yarwood, there was a body, and it wasn't a pleasant sight.

Death and the Lucky Man – A DI Tremayne Thriller

Sixty-eight million pounds and dead. Hardly the outcome expected for the luckiest man in England the day his lottery ticket was drawn out of the barrel. But then, Alan Winters' rags-to-riches story had never been conventional, and there were those who had benefited, but others who hadn't.

Death and the Assassin's Blade – A DI Tremayne Thriller

It was meant to be high drama, not murder, but someone's switched the daggers. The man's death took place in plain view of two serving police officers.

He was not meant to die; the daggers were only theatrical props, plastic and harmless. A summer's night, a production of Julius Caesar amongst the ruins of an Anglo-Saxon fort. Detective Inspector Tremayne is there with his sergeant, Clare Yarwood. In the assassination scene, Caesar collapses to the ground. Brutus defends his actions; Mark Antony rebukes him.

They're a disparate group, the amateur actors. One's an estate agent, another an accountant. And then there is the teenage school student, the gay man, the funeral director. And what about the women? They could be involved.

They've each got a secret, but which of those on the stage wanted Gordon Mason, the actor who had portrayed Caesar, dead?

Death Unholy – A DI Tremayne Thriller

All that remained were the man's two legs and a chair full of greasy and fetid ash. Little did DI Keith Tremayne know that it was the beginning of a journey into the murky world of paganism and its ancient rituals. And it was going to get very dangerous.

'Do you believe in spontaneous human combustion?' Detective Inspector Keith Tremayne asked.

'Not me. I've read about it. Who hasn't?' Sergeant Clare Yarwood answered.

'I haven't,' Tremayne replied, which did not surprise his young sergeant. In the months they had been working together, she had come to realise that he was a man who had little interest in the world. When he had a cigarette in his mouth, a beer in his hand, and a murder to solve he was about the happiest she ever saw him, but even then he could hardly be regarded as one of life's most sociable people. And as for reading? The most he managed was an occasional police report, an early morning newspaper, turning first to the back pages for the racing results.

Murder has no Guilt – A DCI Cook Thriller

No one knows who was the target or why, but there are eight dead. The men seem the most likely, or could have it been one of the two women, the attractive Gillian Dickenson, or even the celebrity-obsessed Sal Maynard?

There's a gang war brewing, and if there are deaths, it doesn't matter to them as long as it's not them. But to Detective Chief Inspector Isaac Cook, it's his area of London, and it does.

It's dirty and unpredictable, and initially, it had been the West Indian gangs. But then a more vicious Romanian gangster had usurped them. And now he's being marginalised by the Russians. And the leader of the most vicious Russian mafia organisation is in London, and he's got money and influence, the ear of those in power.

Murder of a Silent Man – A DCI Cook Thriller

No one gave much credence to the man when he was alive. In fact, most people never knew who he was, although those who had lived in the area for many years recognised the tired-looking and shabbily dressed man as he shuffled along, regular as clockwork on a Thursday afternoon at seven in the evening to the local off-licence. It was always the same: a bottle of whisky, premium brand, and a packet of cigarettes. He paid his money over the counter, took hold of his plastic bag containing his purchases, and then walked back down the road with the same rhythmic shuffle. He said not one word to anyone on the street or in the shop.

Murder in Room 346 – A DCI Cook Thriller

'Coitus interruptus, that's what it is,' Detective Chief Inspector Isaac Cook said. On the bed, in a downmarket hotel in Bayswater, lay the naked bodies of a man and a woman.

'Bullet in the head's not the way to go,' Larry Hill, Isaac Cook's detective inspector, said. He had not expected such a flippant comment from his senior, not when they were standing near to two people who had, apparently in the final throes of passion, succumbed to what appeared to be a professional assassination.

'You know this will be all over the media within the hour,' Isaac said.

'James Holden, moral crusader, a proponent of the sanctity of the marital bed, man and wife. It's bound to be.'

Murder in Notting Hill – A DCI Cook Thriller

One murderer, two bodies, two locations, and the murders have been committed within an hour of each other.

They're separated by a couple of miles, and neither woman has anything in common with the other. One is young and wealthy, the daughter of a famous man; the other is poor, hardworking and unknown.

Isaac Cook and his team at Challis Street Police Station are baffled about why they've been killed. There must be a connection, but what is it?

Murder is the Only Option – A DCI Cook Thriller

A man, thought to be long dead, returns to exact revenge against those who had blighted his life. His only concern is to protect his wife and daughter. He will stop at nothing to achieve his aim.

'Big Greg, I never expected to see you around here at this time of night.'

'I've told you enough times.'

'I've no idea what you're talking about,' Robertson replied. He looked up at the man, only to see a metal pole coming down at him. Robertson fell down, cracking his head against a concrete kerb.

Two vagrants, no more than twenty feet away, did not stir and did not even look in the direction of the noise. If they had, they would have seen a dead body, another man walking away.

Murder in Little Venice – A DCI Cook Thriller

A dismembered corpse floats in the canal in Little Venice, an upmarket tourist haven in London. Its identity is unknown, but what is its significance?

DCI Isaac Cook is baffled about why it's there. Is it gang-related, or is it something more?

Whatever the reason, it's clearly a warning, and Isaac and his team are sure it's not the last body that they'll have to deal with.

Murder is Only a Number – A DCI Cook Thriller

Before she left she carved a number in blood on his chest. But why the number 2, if this was her first murder?

The woman prowls the streets of London. Her targets are men who have wronged her. Or have they? And why is she keeping count?

DCI Cook and his team finally know who she is, but not before she's murdered four men. The whole team are looking for her, but the woman keeps disappearing in plain sight. The pressure's on to stop her, but she's always one step ahead.

And this time, DCS Goddard can't protect his protégé, Isaac Cook, from the wrath of the new commissioner at the Met.

Murder House – A DCI Cook Thriller

A corpse in the fireplace of an old house. It's been there for thirty years, but who is it?

It's murder, but who is the victim and what connection does the body have to the previous owners of the house. What is the motive? And why is the body in a fireplace? It was bound to be discovered eventually but was that what the murderer wanted? The main suspects are all old and dying, or already dead.

Isaac Cook and his team have their work cut out trying to put the pieces together. Those who know are not talking because of an old-fashioned belief that a family's dirty laundry should not be aired in public, and never to a policeman – even if that means the murderer is never brought to justice!

Murder is a Tricky Business – A DCI Cook Thriller

A television actress is missing, and DCI Isaac Cook, the Senior Investigation Officer of the Murder Investigation Team at Challis Street Police Station in London, is searching for her.

Why has he been taken away from more important crimes to search for the woman? It's not the first time she's gone missing, so why does everyone assume she's been murdered?

There's a secret, that much is certain, but who knows it? The missing woman? The executive producer? His eavesdropping assistant? Or the actor who portrayed her fictional brother in the TV soap opera?

Murder Without Reason – A DCI Cook Thriller

DCI Cook faces his greatest challenge. The Islamic State is waging war in England, and they are winning.

Not only does Isaac Cook have to contend with finding the perpetrators, but he is also being forced to commit actions contrary to his mandate as a police officer.

And then there is Anne Argento, the prime minister's deputy. The prime minister has shown himself to be a pacifist and is not up to the task. She needs to take his job if the country is to fight back against the Islamists.

Vane and Martin have provided the solution. Will DCI Cook and Anne Argento be willing to follow it through? Are they able to act for the good of England, knowing that a criminal and murderous action is about to take place? Do they have an option?

The Haberman Virus

A remote and isolated village in the Hindu Kush mountain range in North Eastern Afghanistan is wiped out by a virus unlike any seen before.

A mysterious visitor clad in a space suit checks his handiwork, a female American doctor succumbs to the disease, and the woman sent to trap the person responsible falls in love with him – the man who would cause the deaths of millions.

Hostage of Islam

Three are to die at the Mission in Nigeria: the pastor and his wife in a blazing chapel; another gunned down while trying to defend them from the Islamist fighters.

Kate McDonald, an American, grieving over her boyfriend's death and Helen Campbell, whose life had been troubled by drugs and prostitution, are taken by the attackers.

Kate is sold to a slave trader who intends to sell her virginity to an Arab Prince. Helen, to ensure their survival, gives herself to the murderer of her friends.

Malika's Revenge

Malika, a drug-addicted prostitute, waits in a smugglers' village for the next Afghan tribesman or Tajik gangster to pay her price, a few scraps of heroin.

Yusup Baroyev, a drug lord, enjoys a lifestyle many would envy. An Afghan warlord sees the resurgence of the Taliban. A Russian white-collar criminal portrays himself as a good and honest citizen in Moscow.

All of them are linked to an audacious plan to increase the quantity of heroin shipped out of Afghanistan and into Russia and ultimately the West.

Some will succeed, some will die, some will be rescued from their plight and others will rue the day they became involved.

ABOUT THE AUTHOR

Phillip Strang was born in England in the late forties. He was an avid reader of science fiction in his teenage years: Isaac Asimov, Frank Herbert, the masters of the genre. Still an avid reader, the author now mainly reads thrillers.

In his early twenties, the author, with a degree in electronics engineering and a desire to see the world, left England for Sydney, Australia. Now, forty years later, he still resides in Australia, although many intervening years were spent in a myriad of countries, some calm and safe, others no more than war zones.